The Stars Have Fallen

OrangeBooks Publication

1st Floor, Rajhans Arcade, Mall Road, Kohka, Bhilai, Chhattisgarh 490020

Website: **www.orangebooks.in**

First Edition, 2025

ISBN: 978-93-6554-178-6

Price: Rs. 399.00

Printed in India

The Stars Have Fallen

Bollywood

Varun Singh

OrangeBooks Publication
www.orangebooks.in

Disclaimer

This is a work of fiction. Names, characters, places, and incidents are either the product of the author's imagination or used in a fictitious manner. Any resemblance to actual persons, living or dead, or actual events is purely coincidental.

While the story is set against the backdrop of the Indian film industry (commonly known as Bollywood), it does not depict any specific individuals or real-life events. The novel does not intend to defame, malign, or harm the reputation of any individual, company, or institution.

The views and opinions expressed by the characters do not reflect those of the author or publisher. Reader discretion is advised.

Foreword

The word Bollywood often conjures up images of dazzling lights, red carpets, glamorous stars, and blockbuster dreams. To the outside world, it is a world of magic — where anyone with a spark can rise to fame, fortune, and eternal stardom.

But beneath that glitter lies another reality — one rarely seen, often silenced, and seldom told. It is a world where ambition collides with manipulation, where innocence meets exploitation, and where the price of success can often be more than what a dreamer bargained for.

This novel is born out of that unseen side — the backstage shadows behind the spotlight. It is a tribute to the countless newcomers who arrive in Mumbai every day with stars in their eyes and fire in their hearts. Some break through. Many break down. But all carry stories worth telling.

The characters in this book are fictional, yet their emotions are real. Their struggles mirror the journeys of many who dared to dream. Through their paths — winding, painful, and at times triumphant — I hope to capture a slice of truth about an industry that is as seductive as it is brutal.

To every aspiring artist who has ever waited outside a studio gate, rehearsed in a cramped room, or fought to hold onto their dignity in a world of illusions — this story is for you.

I was one such newcomer to the world of Bollywood, who also dreamt of going down the golden path of tinsel town, by producing an independent film, and was torn down by the brutal reality of the glamorous film world

Acknowledgment

In every story, there are those who work quietly in the wings, shaping the final scene before the curtain falls.

I extend my heartfelt gratitude to my dear friend and acclaimed film director Rajiv Ruia for his invaluable insight into the world of cinema. My thanks also to my friend and talented actor Raj Kumar Kanojia, as well as Hemant Pandey, whose presence and encouragement meant a great deal. I am deeply appreciative of my friend and Hollywood actor John Delong for his thoughtful advice, and to music director Vivek Kar for sharing numerous industry anecdotes that greatly enriched the writing of this book.

Above all, my deepest thanks go to my family—Meenu, Abhay, and Neha—for their unwavering love, patience, and support throughout this journey.

Book – 1

Humble Beginings

CHAPTER - 1

KANGNA - Early Days (1988)

Palak pedaled her bicycle, Kangna perched precariously on the back. Their lunchboxes and water bottles rattled in the front basket, school bags digging into their shoulders. The army school was a good three kilometers from their farm, a government-owned plantation near Babugarh, a small town about a hundred kilometers outside of Delhi. Their father, an accountant with the Uttar Pradesh irrigation department, had managed to get them admitted, since the school was on the adjacent army campus.

"Kangna, seriously?" Palak huffed, her eleven-year-old legs straining under the combined weight, "If you're late one more time, I'm leaving without you."

Eight-year-old Kangna, who idolized her elder sister, was contrite. "I'm sorry, Didi. I promise I won't be late tomorrow." Palak, despite her grumbling, softened. She adored her little sister, even though Kangna was a constant source of mischief. Kangna's pranks frequently landed her in hot water, not just at school, but at home too, especially with their father.

Their father was a stickler for discipline, a man of few words and even fewer compromises. Their mother, quiet and unassuming, rarely voiced an opinion in his presence. Palak, as the eldest, had learned to navigate their father's strict regime. But Kangna, born three years later, was a different story. Mischief seemed to be in her DNA, and she chafed under the rigid rules. Initially, their father had found her antics amusing, but as she grew older, the laughter faded, replaced by exasperation and punishment. Their mother retreated into the background, a silent observer. Palak, feeling helpless against their father's authority, became Kangna's protector, a source of unwavering love and support. Kangna, in turn, clung to Palak, her big sister, her confidante.

Today at school, math was a disaster, as usual. Kangna's brain seemed to short-circuit the moment she faced numbers. Mrs. Rao, the math teacher, handed out a surprise test on complex multiplication. The numbers swam before Kangna's eyes, blurring into an incomprehensible mess. The result? A big, fat zero.

Mrs. Rao, who seemed to have a special dislike for Kangna, seized the opportunity. "Kangna, another zero? I am impressed! Keep up the fantastic work," she sneered.

"Sorry, Ma'am," Kangna mumbled, "I was absent when you taught this." A few kids snickered.

"Silence, class! And you," Mrs. Rao said, turning back to Kangna, "Diary, please. I'll write a little note for your father. Let's see what Mr. Sharma has to say about his brilliant daughter's performance."

Babugarh was a small town. Everyone knew everyone, and Mr. Sharma was acutely aware of his social standing. That evening, after dinner, Kangna reluctantly presented the diary to her father. His face flushed crimson as he read Mrs. Rao's comments. He saw Kangna's poor grades as a personal affront, a stain on his family's reputation.

"I'm going to teach you math tonight," he declared, his voice tight with anger, "even if it takes all night." He began to drill her, his voice rising with each failed attempt.

The louder he shouted, the more Kangna's mind went blank. She stared back at him, silent and uncomprehending; no tears, no expression, just a wall of resistance.

Mr. Sharma's rage boiled over. "Look at this shameless girl!" he yelled. "She just stares at me! First, she refuses to learn, and now she has the audacity to disrespect her elders!" He grabbed her math book and ripped it apart, throwing the pieces at her.

Kangna remained silent, her gaze fixed on her father. Her mother, as usual, busied herself with chores, pretending not to notice the escalating situation.

"What a useless child you've given me!" he continued, his voice laced with bitterness. "She'll only bring us shame and misery..."

Finally, exhausted and frustrated, Mr. Sharma switched off the light and stormed off to his bedroom. Her mother followed silently behind.

Once they were gone, Palak pulled Kangna into a tight hug. In the warmth of her sister's embrace, Kangna's defiance melted. Silent sobs shook her body as she buried her face in Palak's shoulder, her tears soaking through the fabric of her top.

CHAPTER - 2
KANGNA - Troubled Teens (1994)

Kangna had turned fourteen the previous winter and was now anxiously awaiting her board exam results. School had been a drag this past year, ever since Palak left for college in Chandigarh. The daily commute felt endless and lonely without her sister's companionship. Studies were the least of Kangna's concerns; school was bearable only because Palak was there. Now, with Palak gone, Kangna felt adrift. Visits from her sister were infrequent, a few days every couple of months, leaving Kangna feeling more isolated than ever.

Loneliness gnawed at her, but she had no one to confide in. Her father had become even more self-absorbed, obsessed with appearances and his own fragile ego. Her mother remained a ghost, a silent, subservient figure in their father's shadow. Kangna had few close friends at school, so she navigated this year in a haze, going through the motions, but not truly living.

The post-exam vacation only amplified her isolation. She spent most of her time at home, trapped in the stifling atmosphere.

Finally, the results arrived. Kangna had managed 64 percent, a respectable average but miles away from the 90-plus scores many of her classmates achieved. Math and science, her academic Achilles' heel, had dragged her down. She'd done well in the subjects that actually interested her: commerce and social studies. Now, she had to choose her senior secondary electives. She planned to take humanities and dramatics, subjects that resonated with her. She'd filled out the form and just needed her father's signature before submitting it.

Mr. Sharma, now noticeably older and frailer, had suffered a heart attack the previous year. When he returned from work and finished his dinner, Kangna hesitantly showed him the form.

He scanned it, his face hardening. "What is this nonsense? Have you lost your mind? After those dismal grades, you want to take humanities and dramatics? Are you planning to become a street performer? How will you get a job? Do you want to end up begging at traffic signals?"

Kangna met his gaze. "The reason I didn't do well is because I hate math and science. My passion is humanities and dramatics. If I study what I love, I'll do much better."

"Those aren't subjects," he scoffed. "They're excuses for lazy students who don't want to work hard. And those people end up as failures. Is that what you want to be?"

"Why can't you understand?" Kangna pleaded, her voice rising. "I can't do those other subjects. Times are changing. You don't have to be a doctor or engineer to be successful. If I can excel in what I'm good at, I'll have better career prospects."

Her father's face flushed crimson. "Do whatever you want!" he roared. "Why do you even bother asking for my approval if you're going to ignore me anyway? I refuse to pay your school fees for this ridiculous pursuit. If you want me to fund your education, you'll do as I say."

"If you don't pay for the subjects I choose," Kangna retorted, her voice trembling but firm, "I won't go to school at all. See how you like that."

He exploded, tearing the form in two. "This girl is a curse!" he raged. "So disrespectful, arguing with me like I'm her enemy. She has no regard for our feelings. Look at her, staring at me like that! I'll have another heart attack because of her!" He clutched his chest, gasping for breath, and stormed out of the room, muttering under his breath.

Her mother, ever the peacemaker, intervened. "Kangna, your father is only advising you for your own good. He has more experience than you. Why can't you just listen? Do you want him to die? The doctor said he shouldn't be stressed."

"Did I ask him to get stressed?" Kangna shot back, her voice laced with bitterness. "My life means nothing to him. All he wants is people to fawn over him and inflate his ego."

"Kangna, how can you say that?" her mother pleaded. "Look at your sister, Palak. She never gave us any trouble. You, on the other hand, are nothing but a constant source of worry. I beg you, just let us have some peace." She trailed after her husband, her shoulders slumped.

CHAPTER - 3

KANGNA - Finding Friends (1995)

Kangna had become a permanent fixture in the back row. Her quarterly and half-yearly exams were a disaster, and it was painfully obvious to everyone, herself included, that she was heading for a spectacular fail in the finals. Not that she cared anymore.

Her hormones were raging though, and she was blossoming into a striking young woman.

Communication with her parents had dwindled to almost nothing. She seethed with resentment towards her father, his hypocrisy and the emotional tyranny he inflicted on the family. Her mother, a silent, passive witness to Kangna's suffering, earned even more of Kangna's scorn. She often wondered why some people even had children if they were completely clueless about raising them. Weren't parents supposed to nurture and guide their kids into becoming healthy, well-adjusted adults?

She finally understood what Palak must have gone through. Her sister was probably exploring her own identity, finally free from their father’s stifling control, embracing a world beyond their dysfunctional family.

Kangna felt orphaned, utterly alone. This kind of isolation could break a person, forcing them into submission, mirroring their mother's quiet resignation. Or, it could ignite a rebellion, a fierce determination to forge their own path.

Kangna chose rebellion. She became a rebel without a cause, challenging authority in any form. She ditched classes more often than she attended. She’d sneak off to the secluded areas of the school grounds, to smoke. She picked fights with girls from other classes over trivial things. She even had the audacity to brazenly read porn magazines during math class. She cultivated a disruptive persona, a walking challenge to anything conventional. She refused to do assignments, openly defiant. She practically dared teachers to engage her in arguments, to the point where they simply gave up, not wanting to deal with "Kangna's drama."

Inevitably, she became a leader. Students were drawn to her – bold, beautiful, and unapologetically rebellious.

But beneath the tough exterior, Kangna was hurting. She envied the girls in the humanities and dramatics streams, feeling a kinship with them that she never felt with the science nerds in her own class. Since she was skipping so many classes, she gravitated towards other like-minded rebels, forming a notorious clique. Two girls, in particular, became her closest confidantes: Mamta, who hailed from Kolkata, and Samira, from Kashmir. Both were hostel residents. The three of them would regularly ditch classes, holing up in the dorms. Since students weren't allowed in the dorms during school hours, they'd found a workaround: sneaking into the rarely-used amenities room through a window. Locked from the outside, it was their secret hideaway. They'd smoke, play cards, and sometimes even manage to score some weed. Life went on.

One day, they were chilling in their usual spot, smoking up and doing impressions of their teachers.

Kangna was a gifted mimic, when she put her mind to it. And Mrs. Rao, the math teacher, was a frequent target of her impersonations. Kangna wasn't sure if she hated math because she hated Mrs. Rao, or vice versa. As Kangna launched into a particularly scathing impression of Mrs. Rao, Samira cracked up. Mamta, however, was unusually quiet.

Kangna and Samira exchanged a look.

"Mams, what's up, babe? Something on your mind?" Kangna asked.

"You know I'm the prefect of the dramatics club," Mamta sighed. "We're putting on a fashion show in three days, and I'm swamped. I had twelve girls lined up, but Shivani and I had a major blowup. I threatened to kick her out if she kept acting up, and now the little bitch has stormed off with three of her cronies."

"Yeah, I heard about the fight," Samira chimed in, "but I didn't realize it was that serious."

"Why don't you just postpone the show?" Kangna suggested. "Let things cool down, and you can do it later."

"No way," Mamta groaned. "The principal has invited some bigwig international guests, and they'll be accompanied by a celebrity from the National School of Drama. The dramatics club has to put on a killer show to impress them."

"So, what now?" Samira asked.

"I'm not going to beg Shivani," Mamta declared. "I need four replacements, and fast. The problem is, there's no time for rehearsals. These new girls won't be in sync with the rest of the models. I wanted this show to be perfect."

"I have an idea!" Kangna exclaimed.

"You've got eight models left," she continued. "Why don't you throw in four nerds, complete with their nerdy outfits, glasses, and a deliberately clumsy walk?"

Mamta looked horrified. "You want me to get kicked out of the dramatics club?"

But Samira was intrigued. "Hey, that's not a bad idea," she mused. "Imagine the contrast!"

Kangna chimed in, "And you won't have to train them to be in sync!"

"Kangna," Mamta said, a slow smile spreading across her face, "let me think about this. It might actually work. At least I won't have to waste time training anyone."

The three girls erupted in cheers, hugging each other in excitement.

CHAPTER - 4

KANGNA - The Eureka Moment (1996)

The show was a massive success. Kangna, Samira, and two other girls had played the nerds, flipping the script on everyone's expectations. The audience was spellbound. When the final scene ended, the auditorium erupted in applause, the kind that made your skin tingle. Even the guests from NSD (National School of Drama) hadn't expected such a twist.

After the performance, the girls were introduced to Mr. Mukherjee, a visiting director from NSD. He smiled warmly as he shook their hands.

"You girls were phenomenal," he said. "You have something special, don't let it go to waste." Then, looking directly at Kangna, he added, "Sitting safely in a tree, the hills look inviting but distant. But unless you take off, unless you leave the nest, you will never reach them. Every great achievement begins with an adventure."

His words lingered in Kangna's mind, long after the applause had faded.

That night, lying on her bed, staring at the ceiling, she couldn't shake the feeling that something inside her had shifted. She had loved every second of preparing for the show, the brainstorming, the rehearsals, the camaraderie. It had been exhausting, but it never felt like work. If she had taken dramatics seriously, if she had actually pursued it, maybe she could have been one of those students the school admired, rather than the one every teacher rolled their eyes at.

Instead, what was she? A rebel without a cause. A troublemaker. A name on every professor's list of 'students to look out for,' and not in a good way.

Why had she let herself drift so far off course?

Was it because of her parents? No, because of her father. The thought of him made her fists clench. She could never understand him. Why did he insist on controlling every aspect of her life? Were all fathers like this, or was it just him? Maybe all parents tried to mold their kids into versions of themselves, but Kangna wasn't willing to fit into his expectations. She wasn't someone who backed down. She fought. She confronted.

And look where it had gotten her.

Palak had a different approach. She managed to do what she wanted without open rebellion. She played the game, kept the peace, and escaped her father's grip at the right time. Maybe that was the smarter way to do things. Water always takes the path of least resistance, doesn't it? Maybe that's what nature teaches you; to adapt, to flow, to survive.

But why couldn't she do that? Why did she have to fight? Why did she have to be the one who got burned?

The final exams were around the corner. The entire college was drowning in books. Even the so-called carefree girls like Samira, Mamta, the ones who usually bunked classes were making a show of studying.

Kangna couldn't bring herself to care. She wasn't scared of failing. She just couldn't see the point. She spent her time under her favorite banyan tree, cigarette in hand, lost in thoughts that refused to settle.

One afternoon, she noticed a squirrel foraging with her two tiny pups. They were adorable; tiny paws gripping seeds, nibbling away. Kangna watched them absentmindedly until, out of nowhere, the mother squirrel let out a sharp cry and bolted up the tree. One of the pups followed. The other didn't move. It just sat there, frozen.

A second later, a vulture swooped down, talons outstretched, and in a blink, the pup was gone.Kangna's breath caught in her throat. One moment, they were just eating, playing, living. The next, one of them had been wiped out of existence. Just like that.

She stared at the sky long after the vulture had disappeared.Why would life be this cruel? How could something so innocent, so small, be so easily destroyed? If God existed, what was He even doing? Watching? Allowing it? The squirrel had done nothing to deserve this. And yet, it was gone.

Her mind raced, spiraling. Wasn't her life just like that little pup's?

A realization hit her like a punch to the gut.

Life doesn't care.

No one is going to save you.

It's your life. No one else's. Not your father's. Not your mother's. Not society's. It's yours.

She took a long drag from her cigarette, exhaled, and let the thought sink in.

She had spent so much time fighting, proving a point, battling expectations. But why? For whom?

She wasn't responsible for making her parents happy. She didn't owe anyone an explanation for who she wanted to be.

She thought back to Mr. Mukherjee's words. If she wanted to see the world, she had to leave the nest. If she wanted to live, really live, she had to take flight.

And just like that, something inside her shifted.

Kangna wasn't just a rebel anymore. She wasn't just angry.

She had a purpose.

A new Kangna was born; bolder, stronger, unshackled. Still a rebel, yes. But now, a rebel with conviction.

CHAPTER - 5
KANGNA - Reality hits (1997)

Kangna had been in Delhi for almost nine months now. As she woke up, the sun was already up in the sky. She looked around and saw that her phone was switched off.

Not that it mattered- she was not expecting any calls and had nowhere to go, as of now.

She continued to lie in bed as she recollected how life had dealt with her in the past one year.

She thought whimsically. *Does life deal with us, or do we deal with life?* She laughed to herself. She was still light-headed with all the beer in her system, from last night.

She remembered that day under the banyan tree, while she sat all alone.

Suddenly, her mind was enveloped with a dark grey cloud of foreboding. Did she do the right thing? Or, was her father, her family, the society at large, right? Was she a fool to think these thoughts that she could carve her destiny?

There was no way that she could go back now? What was the way out? Should she just take the easy way out? The rope? She looked at the fan above. Would it hold her weight? Or would she fail in that too?

She recollected that day, almost a year earlier, when she had her eureka moment. The exams were only a week away. She had continued not to study. Since her friends were busy in their preparation, she did not want to disturb them.

She had looked up the phone number of NSD and called their office. "Can I speak with Mr. Mukherjee?"

"He is not in the office. Please call tomorrow morning."

She called the next day again. "He is taking a lecture. You can call again in an hour."

Finally, on the sixth try, she got him on call.

"Mukherjee Sir, this is Kangna from Babugarh army school!"

"Kangna…who?"

"Sir, I am that girl who did the fashion show when you came with the overseas visitors to our school in Babugarh. You liked our fashion show very much."

"I still don't remember."

"Sir, we had organized the fashion show, with regular models and nerds, and you liked the concept very much."

"Sorry, I cannot recollect."

"Sir, you gave that wonderful speech, and you said the bird could not experience the mountains till it flies out of the tree."

"Oh, yes, now I remember, please tell me."

"Sir, I am about to fly from the nest."

"Huh, what do you mean?"

"Sir, I am planning to come to NSD. Can I meet you for some modeling work?"

"Oh no, no, you are still very young. Finish your college, and then meet me."

"I am not young, Sir, I am 18 years old", she lied, "and I have already decided, so I will meet you next week, Sir."

"Okay, if that is the case, I will meet you, but I can't promise anything."

"Thank you, Sir."

Now that Kangna had decided to run away from home, she needed to plan the details. How would she get to Delhi? She had never left this small town on her own. What would she do for money? Where would she stay in Delhi, and so on? Of course, she could not tell many people - if the news leaked out, her parents would come to know of it, and her plans would be nipped in the bud. Even so, she did not plan to leave just like that. She wanted to give a strong message to her dad and the whole world.

The next day, she called Samira and Mamta to their little hideout in the amenities room and narrated her plan. They nearly jumped out of their skin.

Mamta was the first to go, "Have you gone mad, Kangna? What will happen to your parents? What will you do? You will ruin your life."

Samira pitched in, "It's difficult to survive alone in our country. People are such hypocrites, they will show false sympathy, but no one will help you out. What if you have to come back?"

Kangna listened to them calmly. After all, what they were saying was not far from the truth. And this was her think tank. "Listen, Mamta, Samira. I have thought things over, and this is not an impulsive decision. Hear me out, and then I need your help to make this plan work."

She continued, as both the girls listened attentively, "See, I want to leave my house, not just to run away from home, as I realise that my parents do not understand me, and they will never support me in my life, the way I want to live it. If I tell them I want to live independently, they will not agree to that. And it is always about their reputation, and what people will say, etc. Their whole life revolves around that, and I do not want to be a part of this meaningless circus. So, I have to move out. And thanks to you, I have found my passion, which is dramatics and modeling. So that's a career I will pursue. And for that, there is no need for me to study math and science, so I need to move on and build my life."

Samira said, "But how will you survive? What will you do for money?"

"Yeah, I have thought of that too. If my parents were to put me in college, they would invest a few lakh rupees in my fees, so I have decided I will take some cash from home, about 50,000 rupees - I know where my father keeps his cash, and I will take some of my mother's jewellery, as a safety reserve. Moreover, I intend to take this as a loan, which I will repay once I start earning."

Mamta laughed. "Look at her, all planned out. Since, when have you been planning all this?"

"You know Mamta, since I made this decision, I don't know from where I got the strength for all this. Everything is just sort of falling into place."

Mamta nodded. "Why don't you contact Mr. Mukherjee at NSD? He can help you."

"Yes, I already called him, and he asked me to come and see him."

Samira said, "I have relatives in Lajpat Nagar in Delhi. If you want, I can talk to them. You can go and stay with them for a few days, and they can help you find a place to stay."

"Oh, that will be wonderful. That was my main worry," Kangna jumped up and hugged both of them.

They decided to celebrate, as this would perhaps be their last party together. So, as usual, Mamta pulled out the joints, they smoked up, and chatted all afternoon, until Kangna had to leave for her home.

Kangna decided to write all her exams. In every paper, all she wrote was, "You need to call my father to write this exam. This subject was his choice and not mine."

She knew that, when the dam burst, her father would be called to the school, and he would get the message of his wrongdoings. So would the school. She was very clear that the truth needed to be told.

Before her exams, she had bought a bag pack and kept it with Samira at the hostel. She slowly smuggled her clothes, some other belongings, the Cash and jewellery, and was all packed to leave.

She had planned to leave on the morning of the last exam, as everyone would be busy at school, and she could sneak out of the town, undetected. She planned not to attend the final exam. Anyway, it did not matter.

The night before she was to leave, she was gripped with endless thoughts. This was the town where she had been born and spent all 16 years of her life. All her memories, right from childhood, came flooding back. The games she and Palak would play in their house. How they would float paper boats when it rained heavily and the water would fill up in the backyard. Her little fights with Palak. How Palak would embrace her and make her feel so loved. If only Palak had been here, things would not have come to this. Palak would have found a way out of this situation. Many a time in the last few weeks she had thought of calling Palak to seek her help. However, she realised that Palak was facing her final exams and on hearing of her predicament she would rush back here and her entire year of study would be wasted.

Even though she had a bad relationship with her parents now, there were some sweet, nostalgic memories. Her dad, throwing her up in the air, and the emptiness in the pit of her stomach as she came down shrieking with a mixture of fear and joy until he caught her in his safe arms. Her mother, baking those tasty cookies- which she loved so much. Her mind was playing tricks with her. Did she want to leave all this and go away forever? She realised life would never be the same again, once she stepped out. Also, would her father be able to survive? What if he had another heart attack? After all, she did love her father. He had always worked so hard in his life. Maybe he was just concerned about her future, which was why he pushed her to do things she did not want to. And her poor mother, always suffering and silent. What did she do in her life for herself? Nothing! Was she right in giving her parents more torment? And what would come upon them when they found their cash and jewellery missing? A part of her wanted to drop the whole plan and just hug her parents and carry on with her everyday life.

Then, the little squirrel came to her rescue. She remembered what had happened to that squirrel and realised that there was no turning back now. She went into the backyard and lit a cigarette, and took a few deep drags. The acrid smoke in her lungs helped clear her thoughts. The sweet memories for her parents would turn into blame and bitterness if she continued to live this life of compromise. She went inside and took out a sheet of paper and wrote on it very carefully, with a black pen.

"Dear Papa, Mummy, and Palak

When you find this letter, I will not be here- I am going to Bombay.

I am not running away from home, but I am going to have the career that I always wanted for myself- dramatics and humanities.

Papa, we both have been at loggerheads for many years now. I know you are pushing us to do what you think is in our best interest. But please understand, each life that comes into being, brings its destiny, and although parents may think that they know what is best for their children, that may not be the case, as their vision is limited by their own experience. So, things could have been different, if only you had given us all, space and let us be, and just supported us when we needed it the most.

I will be staying with a friend. Please do not try to contact me. I will call once I achieve what I need to.

I have taken 50,000 rupees Papa, and Mummy, I have taken four of your gold bangles. I will return this when I am capabale,

Love you always,

Kangna"

CHAPTER - 6

KANGNA - Down in the Dumps (1997)

A few months later, things were still not much better off. Kangna lay in bed, staring at the ceiling, unwilling to move. A dull headache throbbed at her temples; last night's cheap beer still lingering in her system. She closed her eyes and let her mind drift, replaying the past year like a movie.

It was strange, how when you looked at life from a distance, the little details, the daily struggle to find a place to stay, scrambling to pay rent on time, taking overcrowded buses from Lajpat Nagar to Mandi House, eating roadside omelets, or skipping meals when she ran out of money; faded into the background. These things had consumed eighty percent of her time, yet now, they felt insignificant.

What mattered?

How many modeling gigs had she landed? Any roles in plays or ads? Anything that would actually move her career forward?

The answer was disappointing.

At first, things had looked promising. Mr. Mukherjee had kept his word. Though he had seemed skeptical about her plans, he had introduced her to Ramesh Chibber, an event manager organizing fashion shows. She'd walked the ramp for two big events; one for a luxury car launch and another for a fashion retail brand's store opening. Those gigs had given her confidence and a decent paycheck; rupees 12,000 from one, and rupees 10,000 from the other.

But then reality hit. Rent took rupees 10,000. Food, another rupees 20,000, give or take. Transport and daily expenses drained another rupees 20,000. To survive in Delhi, she needed at least rupees 50,000 a month, which meant five gigs a month. She had naively thought that if she bagged two assignments in the first week, the rest would follow.

They didn't.

Meanwhile, Mr. Mukherjee had also introduced her to Mr. Kelkar, a respected theatre director at NSD. She had started volunteering backstage, handling costumes, wigs, mustaches; whatever was needed for the production. It didn't pay much, but it covered food and transport. More importantly, it let her watch actors up close, see how they transformed on stage. It was mesmerizing; how someone could shed their real self and become a completely different person when the curtains rose.

Kelkar had seen her interest and suggested she enroll in NSD's two-year acting diploma. She had been excited, until she found out the fee was nearly rupees two lakh. There was no way she could afford it. And even if she could, she didn't have time for a full-time course.

So, she kept volunteering, absorbing whatever she could. She started noticing something: some actors were brilliant, while others were painfully mediocre. Why? They all had the same script, the same training, yet some performances felt alive while others fell flat. She couldn't figure out what made the difference.

Then came the play that changed everything.

A historical drama based on the Bhagavad Gita was set to be staged at NSD. The lead role of Arjun was being played by Wasim Bhai, a celebrated Bollywood actor known for his powerhouse performances. The moment Kangna heard about this, she made sure she wouldn't miss a single rehearsal.

The buzz around the play was electric. The theatre was fully booked. VIPs were in the audience. Even Kelkar, usually calm, was on edge, wanting everything to be perfect.

On opening night, Kangna sat in the front row, eyes locked on Wasim Bhai. From the moment he stepped on stage, he was Arjun. His voice, his expressions, the way his body moved; it was as if he had time-traveled straight from the Mahabharata. She didn't blink. She didn't even breathe properly. It wasn't acting. It was something else entirely.

The thunderous applause at the end barely registered in her mind. She was still under his spell.

The next day, she watched the play again, just as transfixed.

When the final curtain fell, she rushed backstage, heart pounding. She needed to talk to him. She needed to understand.

She found him in the green room, still in costume, wiping off his makeup. Without thinking, she blurted out, "Sir, this was the most incredible performance I've ever seen. Please teach me how to act."

Wasim Bhai looked at her, amused. Then he smiled and said, "I don't act. I become the character. For the last two hours, I was Arjun."

Something clicked in her mind.

That was it. The difference between great actors and average ones. The great ones didn't pretend to be someone else; they became them.

It was her second eureka moment.

Maybe she didn't need an acting diploma after all. Maybe she had just learned the most important lesson of her career in that one conversation.

The next couple of months flew by. She started getting small roles in Kelkar's plays, eager to practice what she had learned. One night, she played a frail old woman, bent over, moving with a cane. When the play ended, Kelkar himself pulled her aside, "That was brilliant," he said. "You have something special."

But praise didn't pay the bills.

Theatre was beautiful, but it wasn't lucrative. Even seasoned NSD actors struggled to survive. Kangna still handled costumes as a volunteer, earning just enough for food and bus fare. For her acting roles, she was paid a token amount; sometimes as little as rupees 1,000 per performance.

She called Chibber constantly, desperate for more gigs. After her initial success, she had managed two or three assignments a month for a while. But for the last three months? Nothing.

Her savings ran out.

She had already sold her mother's gold bangles for rupees 50,000; knowing full well they were worth at least twice that. But now, even that money was gone.

Her rent was overdue by two months. The grocery vendor had stopped giving her credit. She could no longer afford auto-rickshaws and had to squeeze into buses every morning to get to NSD.

She started relying on the free meals at the NSD canteen, given to volunteers. She skipped breakfast, waiting for lunchtime. She stayed late, just to get a free dinner before heading home.

This wasn't how she had imagined her dream in Delhi.

But she wasn't ready to give up. Not yet.

CHAPTER - 7

KANGNA - No Way Out (1997)

Kangna finally dragged herself out of bed. She couldn’t afford to sulk any longer. It had been eleven months in Delhi, and things weren’t going as planned. She needed work, urgently. Her landlord, Mr. Sharma, had been after her for weeks about the pending rent. She had run out of excuses, and today, she had to do something about it.

Mr. Sharma managed his small property dealing consultancy from his home. He had earmarked one room as his office. Although it was part of the house, it also had an independent entrance from the front, which enabled his clients with direct access to his office. His wife was a school teacher. Since the schools were closed for two weeks for a festival break, she had gone along with her two school-going children, one of whom was almost as old as Kangna, to her mother's house, in Chandigarh.

Kangna knew that Mr. Sharma would be watching from the window, and if she opened the gate, he would come out and ask for the rent, as he did every day. She did not want to meet him today until she had a concrete reply. Instead of heading to NSD, she called Mr. Kelkar, her mentor in the theatre group, and explained her situation. “Take care of your issues first,” he said kindly. “I will manage here.” At least one person in this city had a heart.

It was already 9.30 AM. Kangna called Chibber, letting the bell ring five times before disconnecting. Maybe, he was busy, in a meeting or something, she thought, perhaps he would call back. After an hour, when he had not called back, she called again. This time she allowed the phone to ring till the recorded message came on "The subscriber you are calling is not answering. Please try again later." She called again. No response. And again. Finally, after the sixth time, he answered, "Yes, Kangna, what is it? You know, I am busy in a meeting."

The hell he was. She knew that he was putting her off. But she wouldn't let go that easily, "Why Mr. Chibber? You have no assignments for me?"

"Sorry, Kangna, you know the market is very dull. There is not much work coming around."

"But Mr. Chibber, there must be something. I need the work... badly." She tried a bit of flattery, "Mr. Chibber, if anyone can get me work in this market, it is you. Mr. Mukherjee and I were talking about you the other day, and he said you are the best in the business."

Chibber was a man of the market. He knew the score. These silly tactics made no dent on him. "Kangna, the market is really bad. I am sorry, I have nothing for you. If there is anything, I will call you."

"Mr. Chibber, can we meet, please? We can discuss it. Give me ten minutes of your time. I will come wherever you say."

She sensed his hesitation. She pushed harder, "Mr. Chibber, please, I have not paid my rent for the last two months. I will be out on the street."

"Okay, 12.30 PM at United Coffee House, Connaught Place."

"Thank you, Sir..." But the line was already disconnected.

She wanted to dress up impeccably for the meeting. She applied her makeup, wore her best dress, and was ready well before time. Now the tricky part was to get out of the house without Mr. Sharma intercepting her on the way out. She would face him in the evening. Today, she would get something out of Chibber, come what may, and then she could throw the rent money on Mr. Sharma's face in the evening. She had her last rupees 1000 note in her purse.

So, she waited in her room, ready to move out. The moment she heard the bathroom door close on the floor below, she took her heels in her hand, tiptoed down the stairs. She got out of the gate very quietly, wore her heels and walked to the bus stand. She grinned as she managed to slip out silently and patted herself on the shoulder.

As Kangna entered the United Coffee House, she spotted Chibber sitting on level one, overlooking the entrance. As he spotted her, he waved. She went up the wooden staircase at the rear and saw him nursing a beer. It had been some time since she had enjoyed the luxury of a chilled beer in a classy restaurant. They shook hands, and Chibber apologised, "I had another meeting nearby and was here 15 minutes back, so I ordered a beer for myself. Would you like one? Or would you have coffee or anything else?"

"Beer is fine."

Chibber waved his hand. The waiter quickly came to their table, and Chibber ordered a beer. Within minutes, a draught Budweiser beer was served. They clinked their glasses "Cheers," and Kangna took a large sip. She was thirsty after the exhausting morning.

Kangna continued from where she had left off, on the phone, "Mr. Chibber, you know you got me my first few assignments in Delhi, and I have so much respect and regard for you. If you try, you can get me some fashion show assignments or some ad campaign."

"Kangna, seriously, the market is really bad. Try and understand. Wait for a month or two. Things will improve. I will keep you in mind."

"Mr. Chibber, I cannot wait even for two days. I need the money urgently. If I don't pay the rent today, the owner will evict me from the house. I will be out in the streets."

Chibber continued to stare at his beer as if some solution would pop out of there.

Kangna became even more desperate. The beer helped her in opening up, "Mr. Chibber, was my work bad in the past assignments? Do I not look attractive enough? Did I not behave properly? What is it, Mr. Chibber? Why am I not getting any assignments?"

This was the opening Chibber had been looking for. He knew that Kangna had her back to the wall. The beer had given him courage too. "Kangna, you know the fashion show assignments that I gave you were a special favor to Mr. Mukherjee. Do you know we needed 16 girls in that project, and we had a list of about 400 to choose from? You wanted to know what was wrong with you. Looks or presentability? Well, out of these 400 girls, all of them were presentable. And if they were not, makeup took care of that. So, how do we choose the girls? The girls who have something extra to offer are the ones who get the assignment."

The waiter offered to refill their beers as their glasses were empty. He brought in a pitcher, and filled their glasses, and left the rest on the table.

"And what about the modeling work? Like advertisements, etc.?"

"Kangna, what have you got on your CV for them to offer you an advertisement? Every company is looking for a known face, either an actress or a sports personality or an accomplished person in some other field. Or at least a known model who has done a minimum of 10 to 15 campaigns and are recognised by the public. So, what have you got, Kangna? Have you got any of these?"

"I have confidence and good looks on my side."

Chibber laughed aloud.

"Don't ridicule me, Chibber. One day, I will be a top celebrity, and you will see that…" Kangna felt tipsy by now.

Chibber looked around consciously and wanted to get out of this situation. "Okay, Miss Kangna, we will wait till you get there."

Again, realising her predicament, she continued, "But Mr. Chibber, how does one get the first ten to fifteen campaigns? To get ten assignments, you need to be known. And to be known, you need to have ten assignments? So how does it work, Chibber, tell me."

"I told you, Kangna, those who get the breaks are the ones who are really lucky or have something extra to offer."

Something about the way he said 'extra' made her stomach tighten.

She leaned in. "What do you mean by extra?"

Chibber took another sip, avoiding her gaze. "You know how this works. We had 400 girls apply for the last show. All of them were pretty. All of them were talented. But only 16 got selected."

"And how did they get picked?"

He didn't answer.

She exhaled sharply. "Are you saying I need to sleep with someone to get work?"

Chibber looked around nervously. "No, I am just saying be nice to the right people. Build relationships."

"Bullshit," she snapped. "Being nice won't get me a job. You mean I need to play along, let some sleazebag paw at me, right?"

People at nearby tables were staring now. Chibber waved for the bill, clearly desperate to escape.

Kangna's speech slurred at this point. "So Chibber, you are telling me that, if I need work, I need to become famous. And to become famous, I need projects. And to get assignments and become famous, I need to offer 'something extra,' and that something extra is my pussy. Is that right?"

"No, I don't mean that."

"Tell me, Chibber, what do you mean?" She refilled her glass. She wanted to get drunk today and vent it all out. A lot of tension had built up inside her.

"You know what, Chibber. You are not an agent. You are just a pimp who eats in 5-star hotels and drives luxury cars. You are a glorified fucking pimp."

Kangna pulled out her last 1000 rupees note and slapped it on the table. "I pay my own damn bills." Then, without another word, she walked out, leaving a bewildered Chibber and other interested onlookers, who by now were staring at her.

She wandered through Connaught Place, mindlessly stopping at stalls, flipping through books she had no intention of buying. She had no plan, no direction.

When she finally decided to head home, she realized she didn't even have money for the bus.

Screw it. She started walking. Lajpat Nagar was at least ten kilometers away, but what choice did she have?

A rickshaw slowed down beside her. "Madam, need a ride?"

She shook her head. "I don't have money."

The driver grinned. "Come on, Madam. I'll drop you. You can pay me with your watch."

Too exhausted to argue, she climbed in.

When they reached Lajpat Nagar, she unfastened her watch and held it out.

The driver looked startled. "Madam, I was joking. Do you really have no money?"

She nodded.

He shook his head. "Keep your watch. You're like my daughter. Just take care of yourself."

And with that, he drove away.

Kangna stood there, stunned.

A complete stranger, a man who probably barely made ends meet, had shown her more kindness than anyone she had met in this city.

Tears welled up in her eyes. She bit her lip, trying to keep them in, but they spilled over anyway.

After months of struggling, months of rejection, months of men like Chibber looking at her like she was nothing more than an object, this one moment of kindness broke her.

She wiped her face, took a deep breath, and squared her shoulders.

She still had no idea how she was going to pay rent. But she wasn't giving up.

Not now. Not ever.

And if this city wanted a fight?

She was ready for it.

CHAPTER - 8
KANGNA – Living Nightmare (1997)

It was about 3.30 in the afternoon, and the streets were a little lazy. As she opened the metal gate, as expected, Sharma was out in an instant, through the wooden door, which led to the residential portion of his house. "Hello, Kangna dear, how are you? You are back early? I did not see you going out today."

Kangna was still in a bad mood and she came straight to the point, "I want to inform you, Sir, I was trying to arrange the rent money, but I have not been able to do so, unfortunately. In fact, today, I went for a meeting for the same purpose, but it did not go as I was expecting it to."

"Oh, oh, so sad. I know you are trying very hard. You work so hard. But unfortunately, only results count," Sharma was sarcastic.

"Yes, Sir, I know, but I will need another month before I can pay off."

"What will change after a month? Will you win a lottery?" Sharma scoffed.

Kangna was losing her patience. She did not like these cat and mouse games such people played. She had had enough for the day, and she was still a little tipsy, and that made her reckless, "that's none of your business, Sir. If I say I will pay you, I will do so, irrespective of where the money comes from."

"Oh, oh! Are you Ambani's daughter that I have to believe in your credit rating? You have been telling the same story for the last two months. Now the third month's rent is also going to be due. I do not run an orphanage here. You have to pay me by 8 pm tonight, or I will have your stuff thrown out on the road and lock you out," and with that he banged the door in her face.

Kangna wanted to cry as she walked up the stairs. How did she allow for such a state of affairs, she could not understand. Her mind was not working. She could not speak to her family. She had not even spoken to Palak since she left home. She did not want to disturb and upset her now. If she spoke to Palak about her condition, she would definitely speak to her parents, and they would come to her rescue. But that would defeat the very purpose of leaving home in the first place. She had tried speaking to Samira once, but she had left for Kashmir, and her phone number was not reachable. Mamta could not do much for her now, as she had her own troubles. With all these nightmares, she did not realise when she had dozed off. Suddenly there was a banging on the door. She looked at her watch. It was 8.30 pm. She knew it was Mr. Sharma. She lay quietly, pretending to be asleep. He banged more loudly. "Kangna, I know you are there. Open the door. Otherwise, I will come in anyway. I have a duplicate key."

There was no way out. She opened the door. She was still wearing the dress she had worn for the meeting in the morning. Her hair was disheveled.

Sharma stared at her, "Where is my money?"

"Please, sir, I request you, I will have all your dues by next month" The beer had lost its effect.

"What happened to your tone? Look, Ms. High and Mighty is requesting me, begging me, in fact."

"Sir, I really mean it. Give me at least ten days of grace. I will clear all your dues."

"I really like this tone of yours. It's so nice. Just like how a woman should behave." He stared at her boobs, and his eyes moved downwards towards her thighs, which were not covered by the short dress. He came closer, "Ms. Kangna, things can be sorted out with a little give and take, don't be so hard on yourself and on others. Life is about give and take, dear."

She smelt the alcohol on his breath. She understood the meaning of 'give and take' after today morning's lesson. She knew she was cornered. She had no other option. She looked at him from top to bottom. He was as old as her father. He had a huge potbelly. In her wildest dreams, she never had imagined she would lose her virginity in this manner and to such a guy, not for love, but for a 'give and take' arrangement.

She held his hand and took him inside. Even Sharma was not expecting such an outcome of his mis-adventure. She removed her top. He needed no further invitation. He unzipped his trousers and took off his polyester shirt and vest.

She pushed him naked on the bed and started to kiss him all over. He was excited. He was pulling her on top of him. She kissed his cheek and said, "Wait, let me bring a condom," and she got up and went into the washroom. After a while, she came out, but she was fully clothed. He pulled her to him, but she kneed him across his chest and slapped him hard. He was in shock and slowly got up from the bed. She threw his clothes at him. "Wear your clothes, Sharma, or I will throw you out of my room, naked, and I will call the police and your wife, and that's how they will find you, naked."

"What will happen to the so-called respectability that you live for? Out of the window, it will go. Do you want me to do that?"

"No, Ms. Kangna, I am leaving right now."

"And I have taken pictures of your ugly naked body, which is so despicable that people will throw up if they see it. So, in case you don't behave in the future, I will make these pictures viral. Do you understand?"

"Yes, Madam."

"Get out now, and I will pay the rent after one month."

That night was as close to hell as she could have imagined. She had dealt with two monsters in one day. They came in different forms, but they both wanted to exploit her.

She lay in her bed. She was beaten and she knew it. She had summoned the courage to face the devils outside, but, was now too weak to face the demonic thoughts eating her.

She had not bothered to charge her phone, and the battery was dead. She had lost complete sense of date and time. She did not get up from her bed for anything, for what must have been two days. Her mind floated in and out of sleep and wakefulness, dream and reality, so much so that in some time, she could not distinguish between reality and her dreams. She had gone into a trance-like state. She laughed to herself, the pointlessness of it all dawning on her. What would she achieve after all? Why did she leave her home? Why did she trouble her family and herself? It was all in vain. Finally, she made a decision.

Kangna wobbled into the washroom. She was very weak as she had not eaten for the last two days. She washed her face and changed her clothes. She collected the coins lying around in the drawers, some in the kitchen, put on her watch as a reserve in case she was short of cash, and walked to the nearby supermarket. She picked up a can of insect spray. Sometimes people used it as a tool to take their own lives. She went to the counter to get it billed. The young cashier, who was normally there, was absent today. The owner's wife, Mrs. Kapoor, was at the billing counter.

She was one hell of a talkative lady. Whenever Kangna visited the store, she would start talking, unilaterally, on her own, until it became a two-way conversation. Mrs. Kapoor did that with all her customers. Everyone knew Mrs. Kapoor and Mrs. Kapoor knew everything about everyone. So, during her many interactions with Kangna, she had extracted all the information from her- where she came from, what she did for a living, so on, and so forth. And even though Kangna was least interested in Mrs. Kapoor's family details, she knew that Mrs. Kapoor was married for 38 years, she had two sons and two daughters, she did not get along with the elder daughter-in-law, the younger daughter-in-law had been trying to get pregnant for the last six years, but without much success so far, etc., etc. She also knew that Kangna had not cleared her account for the last three months.

Kangna was looking around for the young cashier who was usually there, but Mrs. Kapoor would not let an opportunity for small-talk pass.

"Hello Kangna!"

"Morning Aunty."

"Hmm, you have not gone to your drama today?" (Mrs. Kapoor insisted on calling theatre as 'drama')

"Yeah, I was just feeling a little unwell."

"Yes, yes, you look rather unwell. You know, even Meera, my cashier, has not turned up today, and she did not even call and inform, I had no idea that I have to be here. I was casually tending to the garden, suddenly Mr. Kapoor informs me that Meera is not there, then I call her, and she says, I have got another job, and I cannot come any more, tell me, is this the way to work?"

"Oh, that's bad."

"That is not bad, that is really bad. By the way, you don't seem to have eaten for many days, you are looking so sick. Raju, hey Raju, go and get a cup of tea for Kangna from the house."

Kangna wanted to get out of there. "Aunty, please, I need to go. Please bill this for me."

"Oh, you want this insect spray! Too many mosquitoes these days. Yes, yes, you should kill them. They cause so much sickness, but first, you need to eat something."

Raju brought the tea in a white porcelain cup in the meanwhile, and handed it to Kangna.

"Raju, bring some toast from the kitchen too. Tea on an empty stomach causes acidity."

Raju ran off again.

As Kangna sipped her tea, she felt the warmth spreading through her body. She was feeling alive once again.

Mrs. Kapoor continued her rant, "You know my elder daughter-in-law, Priti, she had a nice job in a bank. And she left it, just like that without consulting us. Now that she is not working anymore, I asked her to come down and help me in the store, but she thinks this job is below her dignity. What an attitude she has!"

Meanwhile, Raju came running in with two slices of toasted bread with butter, and handed it to Kangna.

As Kangna took a bite, the old woman continued, "Kangna, you don't be like Priti and Meera. Be very faithful to your job. See, I am so old, but I still like to come down here and work. And I know what you are thinking, 'this old woman talks so much,' but Kangna, you know, that's what keeps me going. I rant about Priti, about Meera and blow away all my troubles." She looked Kangna in the eye and winked at her," and I am not as foolish as I might appear," she took the insect spray bottle and put it back on the shelf.

Kangna looked into her eyes and saw the warmth in them. No words were needed, but both of them clearly understood what was left unsaid, and a tear rolled out of the corner of Kangna's eye. After the tea and toast Kangna felt human once again, and said, "Aunty, can I ask you for a favor. If Meera is not coming back to work, can I work for you as a cashier?"

"Sure, dear, you can start right now if you like. And I will pay the same salary that I paid to Meera, which is Rs. 20,000 a month."

Kangna immediately took on the new role. She could make that much money in two assignments, which she would earn here in a month. But here, she would not have to fight for her self respect and dignity every moment. Besides, the old lady had just saved her life.

The next three months went by uneventfully. She had paid off her rental dues with most of the salary from the store. The old lady was really a kind woman and almost felt like a foster mother. She understood Kangna's plight and would offer her free meals with the family, which Kangna accepted. She spent hardly any money on conveyance, except on the day of her weekly off, which was Monday. She would go to NSD and hang around Mr. Kelkar's theatre group, doing whatever voluntary work was asked of her. Life moved on. She had come back from the brink.

This last year had taught Kangna so much. She understood that there were no free lunches. Life was about 'give and take’. This was the real world. Kangna had grown up. The Sharmas and Chibbers of the world had taught her so much in a year that she would have not learned in a lifetime, living in the safe haven of her home, with her family.

She now knew the score. She still had to learn as to how the game was played though. She had to play a big hand to win. For that, she needed to move to Bombay, where the real action was. At NSD, she would struggle for the rest of her life and still amount to nothing. She had not run away from home to serve customers in a grocery store for the rest of her life. She would have to take the leap of faith and move to Bombay. But she needed some money before she could do that, as she was not prepared to peddle her pussy for work.

It was about two weeks later. She had gone to see Mr. Kelkar on her day off. As usual, he was swamped, preparing for the play, which was scheduled for the next day. She immediately got busy with the costume preparation. As usual, time flew by, and it was about 3 pm when they broke for lunch. They sat down with their plates of Basmati rice and delicious chicken curry and were enjoying their meal, when Mr. Kelkar suddenly recalled, "Hey Kangna, Wasim Bhai called the other day, and he was asking about you."

Kangna almost jumped from her seat, "Really, Sir?"

"He wanted to know if you are busy. He has been offered a movie, and they are looking for a new face in it, someone who is young and attractive and can act, so there is a chance he can recommend you, that is, if you are interested."

"Oh, that's so exciting, Sir! Are there any other conditions to the role?" she asked, thinking about the 'give and take,' which had become part of her world recently.

"What do you mean by other conditions?"

"Oh! Never mind, Sir, how can I contact him? I don't have his number."

"Wait, I'll call him right now. It's after 3, so he should be up and about now. You know it's a sin to call anyone in Bombay before noon," he laughed.

He dialed a number on his phone, "Haan, Wasim Bhai, how are you doing? Hope I didn't disturb you," and then, "you wanted to talk to Kangna about a movie; well, she is here with me."

He handed over the phone to Kangna, "Hello, Sir!"

"Hello, Kangna, let me come straight to the point. I am doing a movie with the Khosla camp. They are looking for a new face and someone who can act well. Kelkar has been all praise for your acting skills. If you are interested, I can recommend you for the role."

"Really, Sir? That will be wonderful. What will I have to do to get the role?"

"Dear, to get the role, you have to come to Bombay for a screen test. Mr. Umesh Khosla is a personal friend of mine, but he is a thorough professional. He will only take you on if you suit the character to be portrayed and deliver on the acting front. My recommendation can only get you a screen test."

"Oh, thanks, Sir, thank you so much. I have been waiting for this opportunity. I really appreciate you for remembering me."

"You are welcome, dear. Just don't let me down, and wish you all the best. Someone from their office will contact you and give you the details. Just ask Mr. Kelkar to message me your number," and he disconnected the line before she could say bye.

Kangna could not believe her ears. She could not believe this was really happening to her. She made Mr. Kelkar message her number to Wasim Bhai right away, in her presence, lest he forget.

Although she was on cloud nine for the rest of the evening and the next morning, she decided to go to work, as usual.

As she reached the store, Mrs. Kapoor, along with Raju, was just opening the doors. Then Raju would mop the floors, wipe the window glasses, dust the shelves and arrange the new deliveries into the respective shelves. Kangna, in the meanwhile, got busy counting the cash. The notes had been stacked on the cash counter denomination wise. She counted the notes of each denomination and wrote the number in her cash register. After counting all the notes, she multiplied the number of notes with the note stack's denomination. Then she totalled all the products that she had written down, and the sum tallied with her computer’s figure from last evening. She handed over the cash from the till to Mrs. Kapoor, leaving behind the float for the loose change. Mrs. Kapoor would then hand over the cash to Mr. Kapoor, who would come in a little later, and then just walk down to the ATM nearby and deposit the cash.

After the morning routine, Mrs. Kapoor asked Raju to bring in toast and tea for both of them, but Kangna declined it, as she was not feeling hungry today. There was a regular customer flow, till about 1 pm, and time just flew by. After that, there was a lull, and Mrs. Kapoor wanted to break for lunch by about 2 pm. She invited Kangna too, who tagged along, and in their absence, Raju would handle any customers that would enter, although, from 2 pm to 4 pm, the customer flow was minimal. It would start picking up again towards the evening.

As Kangna ate the chicken biryani with Mrs. Kapoor, the latter made small talk, as usual. She gossipped about her family, about some of their regular customers in the neighborhood, about what the government was doing wrong in running the country, and so on. Although Kangna had started enjoying the ritual of lunch and gossip with Mrs. Kapoor, today, she was not in the mood to listen to her banter at all. All she did was, check and recheck her phone to make sure if it was still on and the ringer was on loud. As soon as she finished her lunch, Kangna excused herself and came back to the store. She sat at the counter and just kept worrying about why she had not received a call from the Khosla office. After a while, the customers started coming, and thankfully she got busy with them, and before she knew, it was time to close shop.

She came back and lay in her bed and tossed and turned, with no sleep in her eyes, just wondering why they had not called her. Did Wasim Bhai forget to inform the director's office? Were they not interested anymore? She did not have Wasim Bhai's number, or she could have called him. She wondered if she should call Mr. Kelkar but decided against it. She had already ensured that he messaged her number to Wasim Bhai. So, he had no further role to play in the deal. Finally, she fell asleep.

The whole week went by in a similar pattern. At the end of it, she had lost hope. She thought, maybe Wasim Bhai did not even bother to recommend her. After all, why would he, what was he getting out of it?

One busy evening, while she was attending to a customer, her phone rang. It was from a number which she did not recognise. She continued scanning the items, and then suddenly, she remebered it could be a call from Bombay. She gestured for the customer to wait and answered the call.

"Hello?"

"Hello, am I speaking to Ms. Kangna?"

"Yes, Kangna here. May I know who is on the line?"

"I am Raj speaking from Mr. Umesh Khosla's office. We have shortlisted you for a screen test for our upcoming movie project. When can you come to Mumbai?"

"Oh, okay, when do you need me to come in?"

"Can you make it the day after tomorrow, that is Friday?"

"Friday is too soon, I need to book the tickets, and it will take at least one day to travel by train, so is sometime next week possible?"

"You don't have to worry about the tickets. We will make a booking. If it's convenient, I will book you for tomorrow evening's flight. And our chauffer will pick you from the airport and will put you up in the Novotel hotel in Juhu."

Kangna was shocked into silence.

"Mam, is that alright? Can I go ahead with the booking?"

"Yes…yes please," was all she could manage.

"And if you have any issues, please contact me on this number. I will message you the reservation details. Please send me your full name for booking the tickets."

"Thank you."

"Thanks, have a good day," and the phone was clicked off.

The customer in front of Kangna was staring at her angrily. Kangna was oblivious to her surroundings. She could not believe what just happened. Mrs. Kapoor came to her recuse and handled the customers. Finally, when they were winding up for the night, Mrs. Kapoor came to her, "So you got a break in Bombay!"

Kangna filled her in with all the details. Mrs. Kapoor gave her a warm hug. "Go dear, go for it. But you see, you have again left me without a cashier for tomorrow morning."

As Kangna stared speechlessly, Mrs. Kapoor hugged her, "Don't worry, dear, I am just joking." Kangna looked at her. Mrs. Kapoor had tears in her eyes. She continued, "That day when you came to me, I had understood that you were in serious trouble and you seemed so alone, so despondent. I have been through difficult times in my life. I know how difficult life can become sometimes, so I wanted to take care of you, and I am pleased today." Kangna hugged her again for a long time, sobbing tears of joy.

CHAPTER - 9

KAMAL - Growing Up (1981)

Kamal woke up to the sound of the alarm. It was 6 in the morning, and he was in the sixth standard. It was his second year at the Doon School in Dehradun, and he hated every bit of it. He was just back from the annual vacation.

The last year at school had been hell. He hated everything about it, right from waking up at 6 in the morning to the compulsory exercise routine. He hated bathing in the shower with the boys- he was the butt of every joke in his dorm in the south wing. He was obese and very awkward, with thick-lensed glasses perched on his fat nose and a loud squeaky voice; he was a complete disaster. He disliked most of the subject classeses. He even hated the games period, which usually everyone enjoyed.

There were only two things that kept him going. One was English, and the other one was the library period. He enjoyed reading and was a complete bookworm.

Another thing that he enjoyed at the Doon were the meal breaks.

The thought of the delicious omelette and toast and juicy pineapple cake got him quickly out of bed.

It was the fifth period, and the math teacher introduced the concept of integers. Things were going over Kamal's head. He had stopped making a pretense of understanding the concepts anymore. The only exciting thing about this class was that it was the period just before lunch, and the thought of lunch kept him going. It was Wednesday, and the lunch buffet would have chicken curry and peas pulao, which he loved. And Wednesdays, they also served Gulab jamuns for dessert, two per student. Kamal tried to remember who did not like sweets- it was Rohan. Perfect, he thought, let me stand next to Rohan, so I can have his share of gulab jamuns too. His mouth watered.

Suddenly memories of home rushed to his mind. Food was a passion for his family. At dinner, the family would discuss in great detail the menu for the next day's breakfast, lunch, and dinner, right from the soups, to the desserts. His mom ensured that she set the best table in the film clan and the desserts that she made were out of the world. Everyone in his family loved good food. As the saying went in their house, "What did one work so hard for if they did not even enjoy great food?"

Kamal was angry at his father. He wanted his son to be fit and athletic like the other boys of his age. What his father did not realise was that one could not just preach to the children. Instead, the children learned from what they saw. He remembered the conversation more than a year ago at the dinner table before they decided to send him to boarding school.

Kamal had finished a plateful of the delicious mutton biryani. He had a second helping of the irresistible Rasmalai. Now, he wanted a third, "Papa, can you pass me the Rasmalai?"

"Kamal, how many have you already eaten? Food is poison after a limit."

"Papa, but you always say that what is life without good food," Kamal tried to cajole his father.

"There is a limit, Kamal. Yesterday, the doctor said you are overweight by 20 kilos. You eat so much, and you don't exercise. You have to start cutting down, especially the sweets."

Kamal resented being told off like that but dared not antagonise his father. "But the doctor told him also that he is overweight by 30 kilos, so why does he not reduce his diet." Kamal thought to himself.

Although Kamal had not said a word, his thoughts came across through his eyes and were read instantly by his father. After all, he had known his son for over nine years. "Kamal, don't compare yourself with us. We have worked hard all our life. And anyway, you need not make the same mistakes we have made. Look at the other kids your age. See Rinkie, she is so active and smart. She plays all the games and is already very diet conscious. She will surely become a star one day. From tomorrow, I want you to join swimming classes and start going for a morning jog."

"But Dad, Rinkie's mom and dad are film actors, and they are so slim and smart themselves."

“Enough,” he glared at Kamal's mom, "Amrit, you have also played a big role in spoiling him. Cuddling and pampering him like a baby. He needs to be sent away to a boarding school, where he will learn some discipline and make something out of his life."

And sure enough, in the next three months, he was packed away to boarding School, despite all the excuses from Kamal and the promises made by his mother. He hated his father from that day on.

CHAPTER - 10

KAMAL - Hostel Life (1986)

It was Kamal's sixth year at Doon School, and he had barely scraped through each class. While others excelled in sports or sciences, Kamal found his escape in food and books. When he first arrived, chubby and awkward, his suitcase was packed with homemade snacks—his only comfort in an environment that often felt cold and competitive. But over time, it was the fictional worlds he discovered that became his real refuge.

He started with mysteries—The Secret Seven and The Famous Five. The characters—Julian, George, Dick, Anne, and their loyal dog, Timmy—weren't just names on a page; they were friends. As Kamal devoured the Enid Blyton stories late at night under his blanket, he felt like he was right there with them, solving mysteries, tasting the homemade cakes, and feeling the warmth of a family that wasn't his own. When those books no longer quenched his thirst for adventure, he moved on to more intense tales—Biggles, the fearless fighter pilot flying for the Allies during World War 2, and the brilliant, ever-composed Hercule Poirot, who could solve the most baffling crimes.

By the time he reached tenth grade, Kamal was hooked on Alistair MacLean's high-stakes thrillers and James Hadley Chase's edgy crime worlds. But it was Harold Robbins who changed everything. A Stone for Danny Fisher and 79 Park Avenue cracked open a door to a world he had never known; one filled with ambition, desire, and a raw, adult reality. With every turn of the page, Kamal's world shifted. He became aware of feelings; urges—he didn't quite understand but couldn't ignore. His body, once just a burden he carried, became something unfamiliar. He started noticing girls; not just as classmates but as something more. Yet, for all his new discoveries, there was a cruel truth he couldn't escape: his heavy frame and thick glasses made him invisible to the opposite sex.

In a school where athleticism was king, Kamal had always been an outsider. He despised cricket and couldn't care less about football. Science and math bored him to tears. But when the time came to choose his subjects, he found his freedom in English literature and humanities. Finally, no more formulas or equations; just stories. All those years spent devouring books paid off. Kamal, the boy who had spent most of his school life in the background, was suddenly topping the class in English. His essays didn't just meet the mark; they stood out. His words had weight, and his English teacher noticed. Soon, Kamal was no longer invisible.

It didn't stop there. His talent for storytelling and performance landed him the captaincy of the school's dramatics team. On stage, Kamal became someone else; someone bold, charismatic, and in control. The once-shy, overlooked kid had transformed into a leader. And with that, something else changed. He started jogging in the mornings, cut back on the binge-eating, and swapped his baggy, ill-fitting clothes for something sharper. By his final year, Kamal wasn't just the head of the dramatics club; he was representing his school at state-level drama competitions. For the first time, people; girls—were noticing him.

But beneath the confidence was a wound that hadn't healed. Years of feeling unwanted and unattractive had left scars. No matter how much weight he lost or how many awards he won, Kamal couldn't shake the feeling that he wasn't good enough. This insecurity crept into his personality. He laughed too loudly. Spoke too sharply. He didn't realize it, but his defensiveness became a shield, protecting him from rejection he still feared.

On the outside, Kamal had become a star. But inside? He was still the boy hiding under the blanket, searching for a world where he truly belonged.

CHAPTER - 11

KAMAL - Fun At College (1987)

By the time Kamal returned to Bombay for college, life had shifted in ways he hadn't expected. His hard work at school had earned back his father's approval; something that once felt impossible. At home, though, things were different. His parents looked older, heavier, more worn out by life. His father—once larger-than-life—now seemed smaller somehow, like the weight of his failures had physically shrunk him. The flops at the box office had left them in debt, and diabetes was slowly eating away at him. But maybe it wasn't just the disease. Maybe it was the stress, the constant anxiety. Both gnawed at him, one feeding the other in an endless loop.

College, though—that was a different world altogether. In those days, for most students who weren't chasing medical or engineering degrees, college wasn't about academics as much as it was about freedom. For kids raised under the constant watch of their parents, it was a first taste of independence. Gone were the chauffeured rides and school buses; now, there were crowded local trains and packed city buses. It was about cheap food from the canteen, skipping lectures to catch a matinee show, and sneaking around with your girlfriend or boyfriend, hoping no one from the ever-watching web of family and friends caught you. Back then, a single slip-up could mean disaster—if you were a boy, you'd get a lecture. If you were a girl, they'd marry you off before you knew what hit you. But the risk? That was part of the thrill. Every stolen glance, every secret date—it felt like rebellion, a kind of freedom that tasted sweeter because it wasn't allowed.

When it came to choosing a college, Kamal had options. He could go to the well-established Mithibai College in Ville Parle or St. Andrew's in Bandra. On paper, Mithibai made sense—it had history and prestige. But St. Andrew's? That was in Bandra—a glamorous, upscale neighborhood. And more importantly, his best friends Rinkie and Rahul were going there. Rinkie, the daughter of a famous Bollywood power couple, had a way of turning everything into an adventure. And Rahul? He had a knack for making the ordinary feel epic. With them by his side, how could he say no?

So, Kamal chose St. Andrew's—not for its academics, but for everything else it promised: freedom, adventure, and maybe even a chance to rewrite his own story.

CHAPTER - 12

KAMAL – Mumbai Memories (1988)

By their second year of college, the routine was set—morning lectures, followed by lazy afternoons at Prithvi Café. It was a ten-minute ride from campus, but for them, it felt like an escape.

That afternoon, the low rumble of a Royal Enfield broke through the café's chatter. Rahul pulled up, his black helmet reflecting the sun, while Rinkie slid off the pillion seat, tossing her hair back like she was in a movie. They'd been together for almost a year now—everyone knew it.

As they sipped on iced americanos, the growl of another bike cut through the air. Rajesh rolled in on his vintage Yezdi, Poonam holding onto him, laughing at something only they seemed to share. As they walked over, Rinkie raised a hand.

"Should I get you guys coffee?" she asked, already half out of her chair.

Rajesh shook his head. "Nah, we're in the mood for some kadak chai."

As the waiter jotted down their order, Rahul glanced up, frowning. "Where the hell is Kamal?"

Poonam leaned back, stretching. "I saw him talking to the English professor. Said he'd catch up."

Rahul scoffed. "I keep telling him to get a bike, but no—he's still obsessed with auto-rickshaws. It's like arguing with a brick wall."

Poonam rolled her eyes. "Why do you guys care so much? Maybe he just doesn't want to ride."

"It's not that," Rahul shot back. "The guy's a total sissy—he's scared he'll fall and scratch his pretty little face. His dad's driver still drops him off like he's some newlywed bride."

The table exploded with laughter. Even Poonam, for all her defending, couldn't help but giggle.

"Rahul, you're impossible," she said, shaking her head.

Rinkie grinned. "He's just mad because he's trying to set Kamal up with Anu and doesn't want him showing up in a rickshaw."

"Anu?" Poonam perked up. "Who's Anu? And why am I only hearing about this now?"

Rahul smirked. "Relax, Miss Curious. You'll meet her soon enough—I invited her here. She's in my class, and trust me, she's into Kamal. Something about his 'brooding artist vibe' or whatever."

Poonam clapped her hands, eyes sparkling. "Ooh, this just got interesting!"

Before Rahul could reply, Kamal finally showed up—emerging from a bright yellow-black rickshaw like he owned the street. "Hey, losers," he called, weaving through the tables.

"You're late—again," Rahul snapped. "One day, we're leaving without you."

Kamal rolled his eyes, punching him lightly on the shoulder. "Relax. Traffic sucks. Besides, not all of us want to play Fast and Furious on Mumbai streets."

"Dude," Rahul groaned, "just get a bike already. At this point, I might as well ask your dad to buy you an auto. You can chauffeur us around like a proper driver."

"Please," Kamal retorted. "I'm too classy for that." He signaled to the waiter. "Cold coffee—make it two. I need one to pour on this idiot's head before he explodes."

Before Rahul could fire back, Rinkie's eyes darted toward the entrance. "Look sharp, boys—Anu's here."

Kamal froze mid-sip. And there she was—Anu. Wavy hair falling over her shoulders, dressed in an oversized shirt tucked effortlessly into high-waisted jeans. She spotted Rahul first, but when her eyes met Kamal's, she smiled.

And just like that, his usual cocky attitude vanished.

Rahul, ever the ringmaster, jumped up. "Anu! Over here."

Introductions were made, the group falling into easy banter. But Kamal? He barely spoke, a rare awkwardness settling over him.

By the time the clock struck three, they decided to catch a film at Suburbia on Linking Road. It was a sprawling, retro stand-alone theatre—famous for its butter-soaked popcorn and dimly lit charm. The movie was a buzzed-about indie by Umesh Khosla, starring a breakout actor who'd been blowing up in the media.

As the engines roared to life, the group peeled off toward the theatre—except for Kamal, who hung back with Anu. They slid into the back seat of another cab.

The city blurred past—chaotic, familiar. In the quiet of the car, Anu tucked a stray curl behind her ear. "So," she said softly, "you're the mysterious Kamal everyone keeps talking about."

Kamal laughed under his breath. "Depends. What are they saying?"

"Hmm." She pretended to think. "That you're a theatre genius. And… kind of stubborn."

He tilted his head toward her, their shoulders brushing. "Guilty as charged."

At the theatre, the lights dimmed. Somewhere between the high-energy montages and raw, heart-pounding moments, Kamal realized he wasn't paying attention to the movie anymore. Anu's hand, delicate and warm, kept brushing against his as they shared popcorn. And when their fingers tangled for just a second longer than necessary—neither of them moved away.

As the credits rolled, the group poured out into the neon-lit street, buzzing with post-movie energy. But Kamal? He couldn't stop glancing at Anu—wondering if, just maybe, his predictable world was about to change.

CHAPTER - 13

KAMAL - Teenage Troubles (1989)

By their third year of college, everything seemed settled—at least on the surface. Rahul and Rinkie were inseparable, still tangled up in their intense, on-again-off-again romance. Rajesh and Poonam were just as steady, their flirty banter masking something deeper. And then there were Kamal and Anu—always there, always together, but never quite crossing that invisible line.

They moved through life like parallel tracks on a railway—close, but never touching. Kamal's hesitation frustrated Rahul no end. "Dude, just make a move already," he'd mutter, but Kamal would laugh it off, unwilling—or maybe unable—to explain the tangled mess in his head.

That afternoon, the group squeezed into a cab, heading toward their regular haunt—Suburbia Theatre. The 3:30 pm show was the hottest ticket in town—a love triangle starring Vikram Seth, the reigning superstar, and Madhu, the nation's current obsession. The movie was a cocktail of humor, heartbreak, and longing, the kind of film that left the audience with damp eyes and heavy hearts.

When the lights dimmed for the climax, the group was transfixed. Amid the swirl of emotions, Kamal suddenly realized his hand was in Anu's. His heart slammed against his ribs. For a second, he thought he was imagining it—but no, there it was, warm and real. He froze.

The others noticed immediately.

Poonam squealed, "Oh my God! Finally! You two have been sneaking around and didn't even tell us?" She lunged forward, hugging them both, her excitement filling the air.

Kamal didn't know what to say. His mouth went dry. Anu, on the other hand, glowed—her face lit up like she had been waiting for this moment forever. The energy shifted. Something unspoken passed between them, heavy and electric.

"We have to celebrate!" Rajesh declared.

By evening, they found themselves at the Harbour Bar in the Taj Mahal Hotel, its windows overlooking the glittering Gateway of India. The conversation flowed as easily as the drinks. Kamal sat quietly, his mind spinning. Anu's laughter rang in his ears, warm and inviting—but it also scared him.

Then, out of nowhere, Rinkie blurted, "Let's go to Khandala tomorrow! A quick road-trip. What do you say?"

Rahul, ever the instigator, leaned back and smirked. "Why rush back? Let's stay the night."

Poonam rolled her eyes but grinned. "Yeah, right. I know exactly what you're thinking."

Rajesh laughed. "Come on, Poonam. You're curious too."

The idea took root. Plans were made. Rajesh promised to borrow his dad's vintage Chevy, and they would leave at sunrise. Kamal smiled faintly, but a knot tightened in his stomach.

He had no idea this trip would change everything.

Khandala felt like freedom. The cool air, the winding hills, the reckless energy of being young and a little drunk on the thrill of independence. They spent the day exploring, teasing each other, sneaking glances—until night fell.

By the time they checked into their motel, something had shifted between Kamal and Anu. Maybe it was the lingering effects of the movie or the charged atmosphere. Maybe it was just inevitable.

In their shared room, the silence between them grew thick. Anu sat on the bed, watching him. There was no one else around—just the sound of distant laughter from the others down the hall.

"You don't have to be so nervous," she whispered, her voice soft, coaxing.

Kamal swallowed hard. He wanted to respond—to do something—but his body felt frozen. Anu stood up, stepping closer. She reached for his hand, and when he didn't pull away, she took it as permission. Slowly, she began to undress, her eyes never leaving his

His pulse hammered in his ears. Everything he thought he wanted—everything his friends had teased him about—was right there. And yet, something inside him screamed to stop.

When Anu touched his face, he flinched. The fear in his chest swelled until it drowned everything else. Without thinking, he pushed her hands away—too hard.

"Kamal…" Her voice cracked with confusion.

"I—I can't." His words felt like knives in his throat. Without another glance, he bolted out of the room, leaving Anu behind, exposed and trembling.

He spent the night in the motel's dimly lit lobby, sitting on a threadbare couch, head in his hands. Shame curled around him like smoke—thick and suffocating. He couldn't escape the weight of it.

When the group drove back to Mumbai the next day, the mood was shattered. No one asked what had happened—maybe they already knew. Anu sat silently by the window, staring out at the road. Kamal barely spoke a word.

After that, everything fell apart. Anu drifted away from the group. Kamal pulled back too, drowning in his own confusion and guilt.

He couldn't explain why he froze that night—why he couldn't reach back when Anu reached for him. Maybe it was the years of feeling like an outsider, never quite good enough. Or maybe it was something deeper, something he couldn't yet name.

All he knew was that he had broken something fragile—something that couldn't be fixed.

CHAPTER – 14

AHANA - The Crown (1998)

At eighteen, Ahana Raj had done what millions of girls only dreamed of—she won the Miss India crown. One night changed everything. From a quiet, middle-class girl in Punjab to the face plastered across every magazine cover, Ahana's life was no longer ordinary.

Her father ran a modest hardware store in Ludhiana, and her mother juggled household chores while managing the family's tight finances. Their world was simple—school, home-cooked meals, and the occasional treat of watching a film on their old television. Ahana, however, craved more. She devoured Bollywood movies, losing herself in their glitz and glamour. Her parents often joked that she must have been a film star in her past life, but Ahana didn't laugh—deep down, she believed it.

As a teenager, Ahana spent hours in front of the mirror, imitating the heroines she admired. She wasn't the prettiest girl in her school, but there was something about her—a spark that couldn't be ignored. At seventeen, she entered a local beauty contest in Chandigarh. She walked the ramp like she owned it, exuding a confidence that made people take notice. It wasn't just her looks—it was her fearless attitude, her refusal to be small in a world that tried to box girls like her in.

The contest was aired on local television. That night, Ahana stopped being invisible. The organizers of the prestigious Femina Miss India pageant called. Suddenly, the girl from a small town was flying to Mumbai to compete for a crown that could change her life. And it did.

Victory brought a flood of film offers. Producers wanted her face on their posters, and directors wanted her charisma on screen. But her family was terrified. The film industry was a different world—glamorous on the surface but ruthless underneath. They feared it would chew up their daughter and spit her out.

Ahana, though, wasn't the kind of girl who backed down. Sitting at the dining table, with the aroma of her mother's chai hanging in the air, she made a promise. "I'll take care of myself," she told them. "And if it ever gets too much, I'll come home." Her father didn't believe in fairy tales—but he believed in his daughter. With a heavy heart, he let her go.

In Mumbai, Ahana moved fast. She signed eight films in a matter of months—projects she believed would cement her place in the industry. But there were rules no one warned her about. You were supposed to choose a side—align with a camp, play the game, smile at the right people. Ahana didn't. She valued her independence too much to belong to anyone.

That defiance could have destroyed her career. But when the cameras rolled, Ahana transformed. She wasn't just another pretty face—she was electric. Whether playing the fiery lover or the girl-next-door, she owned every frame. Critics called her a breath of fresh air. Audiences couldn't get enough.

Behind the scenes, the industry tried to box her in—label her, control her. She refused. Producers whispered that her stubbornness would ruin her. She didn't care. Ahana hadn't fought her way out of Ludhiana to be anyone's puppet.

And somehow, against the odds, the girl who came from nothing became everything.

CHAPTER - 15

KIRTI - Dreaming Big (2010)

Music wasn't just a part of Indian cinema—it was its heartbeat. From the golden era of the 50s to the glitzy 2000s, no blockbuster was complete without soul-stirring songs. If a movie had to succeed, it needed chart-topping tracks, and behind those melodies were the voices that became legends. But as technology advanced and reality shows mushroomed across the country, the music industry became a double-edged sword. New talent flooded in, but power remained with the big players—music labels and influential composers—who often saw fresh voices as commodities rather than artists.

Kirti was born into a world far removed from the glamour of Mumbai. In a cramped, two-room house in Jodhpur, dreams were a luxury her family couldn't afford. Her father, a government school teacher, brought home a meager salary while her mother stretched every rupee to feed their three children. There were days when even a new pair of shoes seemed like an impossible wish. Academics never interested Kirti, but music—music set her free. She sang at every school event, her voice raw but mesmerizing. People often whispered that she could rival the greats—maybe even Lata Mangeshkar.

At first, her father dismissed the idea of a singing career. Dreams didn't pay bills. But as the praise grew louder, so did his hopes. He took a loan, risking their fragile finances, and enrolled Kirti in classical music training. Every penny spent on her lessons felt like a gamble, but it paid off. She learned the delicate art of voice modulation, pitch, and emotional depth—a skillset that would soon open unexpected doors.

When a popular music channel announced a nationwide talent hunt, Jodhpur buzzed with excitement. The winners from each city would earn a spot in the Mumbai finals—a ticket to the big league. Kirti's name was whispered with a quiet certainty. At the local auditions, she was electric. Her voice silenced the crowded hall. When the judges called her name as the winner, her father's eyes filled with tears—hope and fear tangled together. But the journey wasn't over. She had to get to Mumbai for the final showdown, and that meant more money.

Desperate to give his daughter a shot at stardom, Kirti's father pawned his wife's gold bangles—the last family heirloom—and borrowed from a ruthless local moneylender. With train tickets in hand, he sent Kirti and her elder sister, Shano, to Mumbai. Shano, sharp-tongued and fiercely protective at 23, promised their parents she wouldn't let anyone take advantage of her baby sister.

Mumbai was everything Kirti had imagined—loud, chaotic, and pulsating with ambition. In the competition's preliminary rounds, she dominated. Judges praised her voice, calling her the breakout star of the season. By the night of the finals, she stood among the top three contestants, the glittering prize just within reach.

The atmosphere crackled with anticipation. The grand prize—₹10 lakh and a year-long contract with "Music World Nights"—could change everything. Even the runner-up prize of ₹5 lakh was enough to erase their debts. Shano clutched the edge of her seat. Winning meant survival.

The first two contestants performed, and scored 26 and 25 points respectively. Kirti needed at least 27 to win. The pressure was suffocating, but when she was handed her song - "Tere Liye" from Veer-Zaara - her heart steadied. It was a timeless classic, and she poured everything into it. Her voice soared, trembled, and held the audience captive. When she finished, the crowd erupted in applause. People rose to their feet. She had to win; how could she not?

The first judge, Ram Batheja, a playback icon, smiled warmly and raised a placard: 9.

"You've got magic in your voice," he said.

Priya Tripathi, a pop sensation, followed suit. 9.

"You're not just a singer—you're a star in the making."

Kirti's heart pounded as all eyes turned to the third and final judge—Rahi Singhal. A legendary composer known as much for his brilliance as for his unpredictable nature. He leaned back in his chair, expression unreadable. Seconds stretched into eternity. Then, without a word, he lifted his score.

A collective gasp filled the room. Kirti froze. The numbers didn't lie—24 points. Third place. No prize. No contract. Nothing. The dream shattered right in front of her. Tears blurred her vision as she stood, trembling, on the stage. All that sacrifice—all for this?

Rahi tapped the microphone, his voice cutting through the stunned silence.

"I know you're wondering why I gave her a 6," he said, his tone calm but sharp. "Kirti, you have been my favorite singer since day one. But tonight—you disappointed me."

His words sliced through her like a blade.

"This song…" he continued, "is a story of pain and longing. You sang it flawlessly—but without the ache it demanded. Technique alone isn't enough. Greatness comes from feeling every note in your bones."

Kirti bit her lip to hold back a sob. Was that it? Had she failed because she felt too much hope?

And then—something changed. Rahi stood, walked onto the stage, and placed a hand on her shoulder.

"But," he said, softer now, "I believe in you. And because I believe in you, I won't let this be your last song."

The crowd held its breath.

"I'm announcing, here and now, that Kirti will sing for my next film—Lehren. She will be the voice the world remembers."

For a heartbeat, the world stood still. And then—chaos. The audience exploded in cheers. Cameras flashed. Shano leaped out of her seat, screaming with joy. Kirti's tears of heartbreak turned to disbelief—then to pure, uncontainable happiness.

As the applause thundered around her, Rahi leaned down and whispered, "Dream big, Kirti. This is just the beginning."

Book – 2

Dealing With Life

CHAPTER - 16

KAMAL - Life Rears Its Head (1990)

The call came in the middle of the night. Kamal knew something was wrong the moment the phone rang—it always is, at that hour. His heart pounded as he picked up, but nothing could have prepared him for the words that followed.

His father was gone. A massive stroke. Dead at fifty-five.

The world shifted beneath his feet.

For the past two years, his father's health had been deteriorating—hospital visits, business meetings missed, the empire he built crumbling at the edges. But death? That felt unreal. One day he was a carefree twenty-year-old with a silver spoon in his mouth; the next, he was the man of the house. No degree. No experience. And no time to grieve.

His mother was drowning in sorrow. She barely spoke. When she did, it was through a fog of sedatives and tears. And the business? On the verge of collapse. Two unfinished films hung around Kamal's neck like a noose—half-shot, heavily financed, and bleeding money by the day. If he didn't find a way to complete them, they'd lose everything.

Kamal had grown up in the gilded world of Bollywood—the flashing cameras, lavish parties, and A-list dinners. The struggles he knew were trivial: surviving bullies at school, curbing his endless cravings for food. Real life had always been a distant shadow, but now, it had kicked down the door.

A few months after his father's funeral, Kamal met with Ramji Dutt, one of the most powerful directors in the industry. The man owed his career to Kamal's father, or so everyone said. Kamal hoped that loyalty would mean something.

"I want to finish the film," Kamal said, forcing steadiness into his voice.

Ramji sighed, leaning back in his leather chair. "I understand, Kamal. I do. But my schedule's packed for the next two years. I can't shift dates for anyone—not even you."

Two years. Kamal felt his stomach twist. In Bollywood, two years was a lifetime. Scripts went stale. Actors moved on. Audiences lost interest. And no financier would throw money at a dead man's dream.

"Please," Kamal tried again, desperation creeping in. "My father—he believed in this movie. I can't let it die."

Ramji's face softened for a moment, but the answer didn't change. "I'm sorry, son. I wish I could help."

Sorry wasn't going to save the company.

The second film was no easier. The lead actor—Shobhit Banerjee—was the biggest star in the country, a self-made icon who had once called Kamal's father his mentor. Together, they had delivered blockbuster after blockbuster. But loyalty only stretched so far when careers were built or destroyed every Friday at the box office.

When Kamal reached out, Shobhit didn't bother with platitudes.

"I've been paid," he said bluntly, "as per contract, but that is only forty percent of the amount. I can complete the shoot, but I need the rest of the money before we re-commence the shoot. There's nothing more I can help you with in this project."

Kamal swallowed his pride. "I'm not asking for charity. I just… I need your time."

"And I need to protect my career." Shobhit's voice was ice-cold. "Your father had goodwill. You? You're just a kid with no money and no clout. No financier will touch you, Kamal. Let it go before you ruin yourself."

Let it go? How could he? If the films collapsed, so did everything his father built. But reality wasn't waiting for him to catch up.

The next five years were hell.

One by one, their assets vanished—luxury cars, vacation homes, even the office that had once buzzed with power. By the end of it, all they had left was the old family house, a battered Fiat, and a bank account that barely covered the bills. Kamal worked day and night, fighting to keep the company afloat, but the losses bled them dry.

And his mother? She was fading. Grief hollowed her out, and her health followed. Each time he looked at her, she seemed smaller, weaker, as if the weight of losing her husband was dragging her towards the same end.

Still, she found the strength to worry about him.

“You need to marry, Kamal,” she whispered one evening, clutching his hand in the dimly lit living room. “I won’t be here forever… You shouldn’t be alone in this world.”

Marriage. The word sent a chill through him.

He had buried his questions about that—the fateful night in Khandala, about the confusion he couldn’t shake—deep inside. He didn’t have time for self-reflection. Survival didn’t allow room for doubt.

But it was getting harder to ignore the truth gnawing at the edges of his mind.

With the family fortune in ruins and no one willing to back him, Kamal was running out of options. The film world, once his playground, had turned its back on him. Friends, who used to flock to their parties, now barely returned his calls. He needed a job—any job.

Becoming a film journalist seemed like the only way forward. He knew the industry inside-out. He had grown up with these people—their secrets, their scandals. Rinkie, his childhood friend, was already making her debut as a leading actress. Rajesh, another boy he had grown up with, was being groomed as the next romantic superstar. Meanwhile, Kamal was about to chase them for interviews.

His mother hated the idea.

“My son—a reporter?” she said, her voice trembling. “Do you know how humiliating that is? You’re supposed to be the one making movies, not begging actors for soundbites!”

But humiliation wasn’t his concern anymore. Keeping the lights on was.

The golden days were long gone. And if Kamal wanted to survive, he’d have to fight for every inch of his future—no matter how far he had to fall.

CHAPTER - 17

KAMAL - Dame Luck Smiles (1995)

Kamal was lounging on his worn-out couch, flipping through an old script for the hundredth time when the phone rang. Probably another debt collector. He sighed and picked it up anyway.

"Hello?"

"Hello, Kamal, son! How are you?"

Kamal froze, his heart slamming against his ribs. That voice—smooth, commanding, impossible to forget. Ramji Dutt.

"Ramji Sir… I—I'm good," he said cautiously, unsure why the legendary director would be calling him after five years of silence.

Ramji didn't waste time on pleasantries. "You wanted me to do a film with you, right?"

Kamal almost laughed. "That was five years ago, Sir. Things… things have changed. We're out of finances, out of business—no one's lining up to give us money."

"You let me worry about the money," Ramji cut in, his voice dripping with confidence. "When I direct a movie, financers queue up. And when they hear that Shobhit is the lead—well, they'll fight to sign the cheque."

Kamal shot up from the couch. "Shobhit? You're saying he'll act in our film? Sir… with all due respect, there's no way he'll give us dates."

"You leave Shobhit to me." Ramji's voice softened into something almost paternal. "I'll handle everything. Just come meet me this evening."

"Yes… yes, Sir. What time?"

"8 p.m. But not at my office—come to my home. You're family, after all."

Kamal's fingers trembled as he hung up. This was it. A second chance. A miracle.

But he knew better than to celebrate just yet. His mother was in Indore, recovering at her sister's house, and he didn't want to raise her hopes. Too many broken promises had already shattered her spirit. He would meet Ramji first—see if this was real. If it was, then he would tell her.

At exactly 8 p.m., Kamal stood outside Ramji Dutt's penthouse. The door opened to reveal a uniformed butler who led him inside.

Kamal had seen luxury before—but this was something else. The marble floors gleamed under the warm glow of crystal chandeliers. Floor-to-ceiling windows framed the Mumbai skyline like a painting. Every piece of furniture screamed opulence—Persian rugs, velvet couches, European antiques. It was as if he'd stepped into a dream.

"Ah, my boy!" Ramji's booming voice pulled him back. Kamal turned to see the man himself, striding in with a dazzling smile. At fifty-something, Ramji still oozed charm and power. He looked nothing like the disheveled genius Kamal remembered from the sets—tonight, he was polished to perfection. Freshly shaved, his silver hair slicked back, a crisp white linen shirt paired with designer Bermudas. He smelled of expensive cologne—heady, exotic, intoxicating.

"How are you, Kamal? You've grown up, haven't you?"

"I'm good, Sir. And you… you look fantastic," Kamal replied, struggling to keep his composure.

Ramji laughed, pleased. "Good boy. What will you drink—whiskey, vodka, wine?"

"Uh… red wine, if that's alright."

Ramji chuckled. "A man who drinks wine has patience. I like that."

He led Kamal to his bar—a masterpiece of dark mahogany with a mirror behind the counter, stocked with the finest liquors from around the world- Jack Daniel's, Crown Royal Canadian, Blue Label, Hennesy, Ciroc, Grey Goose and so on.

Kamal tried not to let his awe show as Ramji poured him a glass of Bordeaux with the flair of a seasoned sommelier-he took out a wine glass hanging from the groove above the bar table. Ramji expertly opened the bottle with the corkscrew, then held the glass to the light, and finally gave the bottle a tilt, so the wine rolled towards its edges. He then swirled the wine in the glass and smelt it, and sighed with satisfaction, "Here you go, my boy, one of the best wines in the world. The French know how to make their wines. Each bottle is a masterpiece, a work of art."

Ramji poured himself a large shot of Chivas with a few cubes of ice, "Cheers," and quickly emptied his glass and went for a refill. The more Ramji drank, the more he talked- about his movies, his shooting experience with different stars, and he was opening up to Kamal. His butler appeared from time to time to serve them the tastiest of snacks in fine expensive crockery. Each time he would come in with a small tray with two square saucers, with a sauce and a freshly cooked snack, just one in each saucer. He would announce the name.

"Ramji Sir, Kamal Sir, please try the corn and cheese enchiladas."

They took the small fork to eat the single snack, and the butler collected their saucers and waited expectantly. Kamal wondered for what. He soon found out.

Ramji announced equally formally, "George, the corn and cheese enchiladas were perfect. They just melted in my mouth."

George said, "Kamal Sir, did you like the corn and cheese enchiladas?"

Kamal complied, "Thank you, George, they were wonderful."

Then George disappeared with the plates.

He reappeared ten minutes later with another dish, and the same ritual followed. And then again, till they had bacon-wrapped dates, honey roast chicken, glazed ham, grilled citrus fish, scotch eggs, and the list was endless.

Apparently, he was very well trained. Kamal was really impressed with Ramji by now. His exquisite taste for food, wine…and yes, they were soon talking women.

Ramji regaled Kamal with his affairs with many of the industry's top girls at one time or another. With so much alcohol in them, they were talking openly now, like two long lost friends.

Kamal was still awaiting discussion about the movie regarding which Ramji had invited Kamal in the first place. But nothing was forthcoming. Instead, he said, "You know Kamal; I have always successfully launched new faces in this industry. Raj Kapoor and Dev Anand started this trend for their movies by starting their own production houses. In fact, if you look at all the established heroines, most were either given a break by Raj or Dev. I am the only other director who has continued this trend."

"Of course, Sir, everyone loves you," sycophancy was as important, if not more, as talent, to survive here.

"You know Kamal, I have the power to make or break the lives of actors and even more so of actresses. You know, when Madhu was struggling to get a foothold in the industry, she had already acted in three mediocre films, and all of them had bombed. When she came to me, she was desperate. After all, she was from a middle-class family trying to make it big in films. Had I not given her a break, she would have been back in some office doing a clerical job."

"How come you gave her such a big role? After all, you could have signed any of the reigning actresses?"

"Well, son, let the truth be told. As the Godfather would say, she made me an offer I could not refuse. You understand, right?"

"Yes sir, yes, of course," Kamal agreed, trying to act glib.

"We had a two-month schedule in Manali, and her room was conveniently connected to mine through a slip door, and we made the most of it. She gifted me heaven, and I gave her a break. She was mine for those two months."

"Hahaha…really, Sir…you are great Sir," Kamal complied.

Ramji continued showing off, "You know that girl Mandira- I launched opposite Amit. During our outstation shoot in South Africa and Agra, we filmed for almost six months. She slept with me every night. After a while, we openly shared the same room."

"Really, Sir, I had heard rumors. But was her mother not on the locations with the unit?"

"Of course. And this was done with the blessings of her mother. She almost became like my mother-in-law for those six months. Sometimes it was so funny. We all would have breakfast in the hotel before leaving for the shoot, Amit, Mandira, her mother, and I. On one occasion, as she was eating her omelette, her mother asked me, 'Ramji, you are not letting her sleep enough, see the dark circles under her eyes.' Amit was shocked. I mean, everyone knew, but it is still supposed to be a sort of an open secret," Ramji laughed loudly, "It's only about give-and-take dear."

Kamal was getting impatient. He wanted to take the discussion to their proposed movie, but he could not initiate it. He knew how whimsical Ramji was, and could change his mind at any minute, he was so moody.

“You see, my boy,” Ramji continued, eyes gleaming. “The rules are simple. I help you—you help me. And if I’m going to direct your film and bring Shobhit on board, I need to know…” He paused, his gaze lingering. “…What do I get in return?”

Kamal’s heart pounded against his ribs. “Sir… I—I don’t have anything to offer.”

"Oh, but you do." Ramji leaned closer, his hand brushing against Kamal's knee. "I've had my share of women. But ever since my time in France, I've discovered… other pleasures." His voice dropped to a whisper. "And, Kamal—you're such a sweet boy."

Kamal froze. His skin crawled where Ramji's fingers lingered. His mind screamed for him to stand up, to leave—but his career, his mother's future, hung in the balance.

"We'll be unstoppable together," Ramji murmured, his breath warm against Kamal's neck. "All you have to do is… say yes."

For a split second, Kamal considered it. How much was his dream worth?

But then he pictured his mother's face—the years of sacrifice, the sleepless nights, the pain she had endured for him. And something inside him snapped.

Kamal was dumbstruck. He felt a tingling where Ramji was holding his hand. He could not speak a word.

Ramji pursued now, taking his silence as consent. "And Kamal, you are such a sweet boy. We will do many projects together," and he pulled Kamal into his embrace.

CHAPTER - 18
KAMAL - He Has Arrived (1995)

Kamal returned home after spending a week at Ramji's penthouse—a week that changed everything. He wasn't the same confused boy who had once stumbled through his desires. That part of him—hidden, repressed—had finally surfaced. Ramji had taken his body with an authority Kamal didn't know he craved until it was too late to deny. His virginity had been surrendered to Ramji's hunger, but what he gained was far more profound—clarity.

The confusion that had haunted him since his school days, the ache that had flared up during that awkward night with Anu in Khandala, was gone. He finally understood. The rejection he had absorbed from women over the years no longer mattered. He didn't need their validation—didn't need them. Why chase after someone who could turn him away when he had found someone who wanted him without question? Ramji's touch had given him more than pleasure—it had given him power.

And with power came opportunity.

As promised, Ramji put his full weight behind Kamal's ambitions. He pulled every string, called in every favor. With the legendary actor Shobhit leading the cast, and Ramji directing, the film practically sold itself. Producers who once wouldn't give Kamal time of the day, now crowded his office, eager to invest in his project. When the film released, it didn't just succeed—it exploded. Overnight, Kamal became one of Bollywood's most sought-after producers.

In three years, Ramji made four more films with Kamal's banner. Each one was bigger, louder, and more successful than the last. By the time the fourth blockbuster rolled out, Kamal wasn't just a name in the credits—he was a force. His phone calls were returned immediately, his decisions could make or break careers, and no one dared to dismiss the boy who had once been a nobody.

And Kamal? He was done living small.

He bought a sprawling 15,000 square-foot office in Bandra—a towering symbol of his arrival. His Juhu bungalow was a palace by the sea, where the waves seemed to echo his triumph. He cruised the streets of Mumbai in a matte-black Range Rover Sport, while his mother traveled in the quiet luxury of an S-Class Mercedes. First-class flights became routine, and when he traveled abroad, only the most opulent suites in the world's finest hotels would do.

With success came a new circle of "friends." The same industry titans who had once sneered at him now vied for his attention. Invitations to exclusive parties flooded in, each host desperate to have Kamal's presence elevate their social standing. In the shimmering world of Bollywood, he was no longer an outsider.

He had arrived.

And he was just getting started.

CHAPTER - 19

KANGNA - The Big Break (1997)

Kangna had never even dreamed of flying business class, but here she was—sinking into a plush leather seat, her heart thudding with excitement. Everything felt surreal. The air hostess smiled warmly as she helped with Kangna's battered suitcase, effortlessly lifting it into the overhead bin. Moments later, she returned with a dazzling tray of drinks.

"Juice, please," Kangna said softly, trying to sound casual.

As the plane soared above the clouds, Kangna gazed out the window. The city she had left behind felt small—too small for the dreams she carried. For the first time in her life, she felt important. By the time the flight landed, that feeling had only grown stronger.

In the arrivals lounge, Kangna scanned the sea of chauffeurs holding placards. She spotted one that read "MS. KANGNA" in bold, black letters. The man holding it, dressed in a crisp uniform, immediately rushed forward when she waved.

"Welcome to Mumbai, ma'am," he said, effortlessly lifting her luggage.

The car—a sleek black sedan—glided through the chaos of Mumbai's streets. Kangna couldn't stop staring. The city felt alive—louder, faster, hungrier. She leaned back against the soft leather seats, savoring the hum of the engine beneath her. This wasn't just a new city. This was the city. Her city.

When the car pulled up to the Novotel, Kangna's jaw nearly dropped. The revolving glass doors, the marble floors—it was another world. Within minutes, she was handed a key card and escorted to a room on the 14th floor.

Alone, she let out a breathless laugh. This couldn't be real. She kicked off her shoes and flopped onto the king-sized bed, sinking into its softness. For a moment, she just lay there, staring at the ceiling's warm golden lights. She fiddled with the bedside panel, trying to figure out which switch did what, but eventually gave up with a chuckle.

That night, she fell asleep with the city lights shimmering beyond her window, her heart pounding with the promise of something bigger.

The next morning, heavy rain slapped against the glass. Kangna stretched and padded towards the window, her breath catching at the sight of the Arabian Sea—wild, endless, and roaring with power. She had never seen anything like it. Her fingertips brushed against the cold glass.

"I'm here," she whispered. "I've made it."

At breakfast, she felt like a kid in a candy store. The buffet stretched on forever—different kinds of fruit, milk, and oats, two types of juices, flavoured yogurt, and chicken sausages. There was a lot of Indian food like idli (steamed rice balls), sambhar (lentil soup), aloo parantha (a stuffed Indian bread), and tens of other food items. There was a station serving eggs to order. She played it safe with an omelet, toast, and fresh orange juice, but everything tasted better here—like success.

She was finishing a cup of coffee on the porch, watching the waves crash against the shore, when her phone rang.

"Hello?"

"Ms. Kangna?" a crisp female voice said. "This is Ayushi from Khosla Productions. Our driver will pick you up at 2 p.m. for your screen test. Will that work?"

"Yes," Kangna replied, trying to sound calm. But the butterflies in her stomach had already started fluttering.

For the next few hours, her mind swirled with questions. What would the test be like? Who was the director? How long would she be here? She had tried calling Wasim Bhai—the man who had promised her this opportunity—but his phone was off. She was on her own.

At 1:55 p.m., the same black sedan pulled up to the hotel. The driver barely spoke, which suited Kangna fine—she was too nervous to talk. When they arrived at The Marwah Studio, her palms were sweaty. The driver led her through a gleaming hallway to a waiting area where three other girls sat—one with an elegant older woman who was fussing over her hair. The other two looked effortlessly stylish, all sharp cheekbones and designer labels.

Kangna felt a sudden twist of insecurity. She tugged at the sleeves of her plain cotton kurti. Was she out of her league?

Time crawled by. Every fifteen minutes felt like an hour. Eventually, a young assistant with a headset burst through the door. "Ramya and Kinjal?"

The two fashionable girls stood and followed her out.

Kangna's heart pounded louder.

When the assistant returned, she called, “Kangna and Rabia?”

Kangna stood, smoothing her hair. This was it.

The makeup room buzzed with energy. Artists swarmed around them, brushes flashing in the light. Kangna barely recognized herself by the time they were finished—her skin glowed, her lips curved in a perfect pout, and her eyes sparkled. She stared at her reflection, stunned.

“You’re up next,” Ayushi said, guiding her into the studio.

The transformation outside was just as dramatic. Bright lights blazed down on a small stage. A massive camera was mounted on a track. The air smelled like heat, metal, and ambition.

A balding man with a bulging stomach lounged in front of a monitor, barking orders at a tall, wiry cameraman. His shirt was wrinkled, and he wore worn-out slippers—but there was no mistaking his authority.

“Who’s this?” the bald man asked, his voice sharp.

“Kangna, Sir,” Ayushi answered quickly. “From Delhi. Wasim Bhai’s recommendation.”

“Ah… Wasim’s girl.” He squinted at her. “Come here, child.”

Kangna stepped onto the stage, her legs trembling.

The wiry cameraman—Suresh, apparently—moved behind the lens.

“Alright, let’s see what you’ve got,” the bald man said. “Smile. No, softer. Now pout. Tilt your head—no, the other way. Suresh, move in—closer!”

The next half hour was a blur. Kangna obeyed every command—smiling, pouting, posing as the lights blazed hotter and hotter. Sweat beaded at her temple. A makeup artist darted in to fix her face between shots. But Kangna didn’t care. This was what she had come for.

Finally, the bald man leaned back in his chair, seemingly satisfied. “Alright,” he muttered. “Send in the next one.”

Back in the waiting room, Kangna felt light-headed. It was over. She spotted Rabia’s mother eating pav bhaji provided by a spot boy. Someone handed her a bottle of orange juice, which she gulped down, her throat dry from the heat.

Before she could process anything, Ayushi leaned close. “By the way,” she whispered, “the bald guy? That’s Umesh Khosla—the director. And Suresh is the director of photography.”

Kangna's breath hitched. She had just performed for the man who could change her life.

"Wait here," Ayushi added. "The driver will take you back to the hotel soon."

Kangna nodded, but her thoughts were miles away. This was only the beginning—and she was ready for whatever came next.

CHAPTER - 20

KANGNA - In Esteemed Company (1997)

Kangna's phone buzzed sharply on the nightstand. She groggily checked the time—4:35 PM. It was Ayushi.

"Kangna," Ayushi's voice was brisk, almost bored. "Umesh Sir wants to see you. The driver's waiting downstairs. Head to the lobby."

Before Kangna could respond, the line went dead.

Her jaw clenched. Typical. No explanation. No update. Nothing. Yesterday, they barely even introduced her to the director—some grumpy middle-aged guy who kept calling her "child," as if she didn't have a name. Now, she was being summoned like a servant. Was she selected for the film? Was this another test? No one told her anything.

Her frustration boiled beneath the surface, but she swallowed it down. Welcome to Bollywood, she thought bitterly. You're not special here. Not yet.

Within twenty minutes, she was in the backseat of a sleek black sedan. The driver, a man in his fifties with salt-and-pepper hair, handed her a thick envelope.

"Umesh Sir asked you to prepare this," he said curtly.

Kangna tore it open, revealing a set of dialogue sheets. The scene was tense—a fiery confrontation between a rebellious daughter and her controlling father. The girl was bold, brash, and utterly unapologetic.

A slow smile curled on her lips. This? This was easy. She had been fighting authority figures her whole life. She skimmed the lines once, letting the words seep in.

The car sped through Mumbai's chaotic streets, but they didn't head toward any film studio. Instead, after thirty minutes, they pulled up outside a sprawling white bungalow—the kind that screamed power and old money. Kangna stepped out, heels clicking on the stone driveway.

In the garden, two men lounged on wicker chairs—one of them unmistakably Wasim Bhai. Relief washed over her. He was the only familiar face in this cut-throat city. She hurried toward him.

"Wasim Bhai!" Her voice wavered slightly as she hugged him tight.

His laughter boomed through the warm evening air. "Hahaha! Look at you! All grown up and ready to be a star, huh?"

She smiled, some of her tension melting away. "I'm trying."

"And this—" He gestured to the other man, who was nursing a beer. "—is Umesh Khosla. Your director. Or did you forget?"

Kangna turned to him, extending her hand politely. But instead of shaking it, Umesh pulled her into a rough bear hug. His earlier coldness seemed to have melted away.

"What'll you drink, Kangna?" he asked, his voice gruff but warm now.

"Oh… um, I'm fine—"

"Nonsense!" He waved a hand dismissively. "I've got something special for you. Picked it up in France—handmade wine from a tiny vineyard in Nice. You'll love it."

Minutes later, a delicate crystal glass appeared in her hand. The wine was rich, smooth, and potent. She took a careful sip, feeling the warmth spread through her veins.

The evening unfolded in a haze of laughter and sharp gossip. Umesh and Wasim seemed to know everyone—actors, producers, even politicians. They traded scandalous stories freely, using intimate nicknames for Bollywood's biggest names.

Kangna listened, wide-eyed, struggling to process how quickly her life had transformed. Just a few months ago, she was being humiliated by small-time casting agents and working behind a grocery store counter. And now? She was sipping imported wine with two industry titans.

The wine dulled her nerves, and soon, she found herself joining in—sharing wild stories from her life back home. When she told them about the ridiculous note, she had left in her school exam papers before running away, they burst into riotous laughter.

"Swear to God," Umesh wheezed, wiping tears from his eyes. "Your life itself is a bloody movie!"

"You better copyright your story, Kangna," Wasim joked, still chuckling. "Or someone's gonna steal it!"

As the night wore on, Kangna felt a strange warmth settling in her chest. For the first time since arriving in Mumbai, she didn't feel like an outsider. She felt part of the fraternity.

Finally, she gathered the courage to ask, "Umesh Sir, when will you take my audition?"

The two men exchanged a knowing glance—and then burst into laughter again.

"This is your audition," Umesh said, shaking his head in disbelief. "You're exactly what I need."

Kangna blinked, confused. "But… I've never acted in a movie before—"

"That's my problem, not yours," he cut in. "I saw your screen test yesterday. You light up the frame, kid. And that mouth of yours? Perfect for a rebellious daughter who won't take crap from anyone."

Wasim clapped a hand on her shoulder. "And I'm playing your father, so you better start calling me Papa. Let's practice, huh?"

The weight on her chest lifted. This was really happening. After all the rejection, the sleepless nights, and the self-doubt—they wanted her.

And for the first time since stepping foot in this unforgiving city, Kangna allowed herself to believe—maybe she belonged here after all.

CHAPTER - 21

KANGNA - On Cloud Nine (1997)

Kangna woke up the next morning with a pounding headache and a heart full of disbelief. For a moment, she lay still, the rich scent of red wine lingering in her senses. Had last night really happened, or was it all a dream? The glittering lights, Umesh Khosla's warm smile, the endless flutes of wine—was it possible she had just signed her way into Bollywood?

Flashes of the evening came rushing back. The lavish party, the way Umesh had introduced her as his "newest muse," and the whispered congratulations from people she had only ever seen on magazine covers. She sat up in bed, a slow smile spreading across her face. She had made it. And it had all happened so effortlessly. What luck to have landed in the good graces of the Khoslas—powerful, influential, and yet surprisingly warm.

Two days later, Kangna's phone buzzed. It was the hotel reception. "A Ms. Ayushi is here to see you," the voice announced.

Kangna slipped on her sunglasses and hurried down to the lobby, her heart racing with excitement. Ayushi stood there—poised and professional—holding a slim black folder in her hands.

"Good morning, Madam," Ayushi said, her tone respectful. "Umesh Sir has sent over the contract for you to review and sign."

Madam. The word hung in the air, sinking deep into Kangna's chest. She wasn't just Kangna anymore. She was someone. She had arrived.

Feigning confidence, Kangna asked, "Can I go through it first?" She had never seen a legal contract in her life, but she wasn't about to admit that.

"Of course," Ayushi said, handing her the folder. "If you sign it by tomorrow, I'll collect it and deliver your copy along with the signing amount."

Back in her room, Kangna spread the papers across the bed and tried to make sense of the legal jargon. Most of it felt like gibberish, but a few things stood out. She would earn ₹2 lakhs for her first film, with 10% paid upfront. The contract locked her in for two years—no working with other production houses. But they promised her more films during the tenure.

₹2 lakhs. Kangna's breath hitched. It was more money than she had ever imagined earning. She considered calling Wasim Bhai—he always had advice—but something held her back. What if he thought she was ungrateful? Umesh Khosla had been nothing but generous, and she didn't want to risk losing his trust.

Without thinking too much, she grabbed a pen and signed the contract. Her hand trembled slightly as she dialed Ayushi's number.

"It's done," she said.

The next day, a driver delivered an envelope with a crisp cheque for ₹20,000. But the money wasn't the only thing that changed. By the afternoon, she had moved into a sleek two-bedroom apartment in Versova. A private driver was assigned to take her to and from the studios. Her wardrobe was measured for custom-designed costumes. Everything felt surreal—like a fantasy she had somehow stumbled into.

A few days later, rehearsals began. Wasim Bhai wasn't there—too busy with his own commitments—but her co-star was. He was a striking newcomer from Delhi, with a cocky smile and an easy charm. In the film, her character, Neeti, falls hopelessly in love with him and eventually runs away from home.

Despite her inexperience, Kangna poured herself into the role. During one particular rehearsal, the energy in the room shifted. The scene was emotionally charged—a rebellious teenager drinking with her boyfriend when her father crashes the bar with his friends. Ram, the assistant director, barked directions while Umesh Khosla observed from the shadows.

Kangna became Neeti. Every word dripped with defiance. Her anger, her pain—it felt real because it was real. The wounds of her own broken relationship with her father burned beneath the surface. When the scene ended, silence fell over the room. Then, slowly, Umesh began clapping.

"Kangna…" His voice trembled with excitement as he crossed the floor toward her. "You are the greatest discovery of Bollywood this decade. I would bet my career—you'll be one of the finest actors this industry has ever seen."

Kangna's vision blurred with tears. She had spent years watching the greats—mimicking their gestures, studying their intensity—but this? This wasn't just acting. It was her soul, laid bare for the world to see.

That night, she lay on her bed, exhaustion pulling at her limbs. On the television, *Guide* flickered across the screen—Dev Anand's brooding intensity filling the room. The scene where the hero's mother disowns him struck something deep inside her. As Lalita Pawar's trembling voice echoed through the room, Kangna's resolve shattered.

A sob escaped her lips—raw, unfiltered. And once she started, she couldn't stop. All the loneliness, the fear, the memories she had buried since leaving home came crashing down. She cried for everything she had lost—and everything she was still too afraid to hope for.

When the tears finally dried, it was past 9 PM. On impulse, she picked up the phone and dialed home.

"Hello?" Her mother's voice was soft, hesitant.

Kangna's throat tightened. "Mummy…"

There was silence—and then the sound of hurried footsteps as her mother called out for her father.

"Kangna?" Her father's voice was softer than she remembered. "Beta, where are you? Are you safe? We've been so worried…"

"I'm in Bombay, Papa." She swallowed the lump in her throat. "I… I signed a movie. They're paying me ₹2 lakhs. I have my own apartment now. I'm fine—really."

For the next half hour, they talked. Kangna told them about her life in Delhi—carefully omitting the darker moments. Her father's sternness melted into relief. Her mother's voice trembled with joy. No one mentioned the day she had disappeared. No one asked why she left. All that mattered was that she was safe.

When they told her Palak was in Dubai on a training program, pride swelled in her chest. Her sister was thriving too.

That night, for the first time in years, Kangna slept peacefully. The weight of her past felt lighter—like maybe, just maybe, she had finally found her place in the world.

CHAPTER - 22
KANGNA - The Roller Coaster (1999)

Notorious was a runaway hit. The edgy plot, slick direction, and chart-topping soundtrack turned it into a cultural phenomenon. Of the seven songs, four dominated the Top 20 charts for weeks. Made on a shoestring budget, the film raked in millions, and the industry buzzed with celebrations.

Just as Umesh predicted, her talent was undeniable—and overnight, she became a sensation. The National Award for Best Debut actor cemented her place as Bollywood's new darling. Her face graced every major film magazine, and prime-time interviews painted her as a small-town girl who had conquered the big city. In her hometown of Babugarh, she became a legend. The girl who had run away with a dream was now living it. Even her old math teacher—once her biggest critic—soaked in the spotlight, giving interviews about the "genius" she had once taught.

In Bombay, about three to four months after the release of *Notorious,* the initial euphoria died down, and slowly reality came to the fore.

Umesh was everywhere, giving more interviews than Kangna; in newspapers, talk shows and magazines. He was already considered an intellectual of Bollywood with his radical but logical views. If anyone had a formula for hit films in Bollywood, it was him. This was another feather in his cap. Another hit film, another new actress he had launched. He became the natural godfather in the process. He was asked, 'How he had taught her to act?', as she was a novice, with no acting experience, no formal training from an acting school, a school drop out, and a run away from home. So, Umesh Bhai, the man with the midas touch, took all the credit. This was okay with Kangna, as he did give her the first break, and he was a father figure in her life. His place had been a home away from home for her. However, she was not the bimbo, as she was made out to be, in some of his interviews. She let that pass. It was a small thing.

More than a year had passed now since they had signed the contract. After Kangna's national award for *Notorious*, many producers and agents approached her to offer her roles in their upcoming films. Kangna knew that she had a contract for another year. But she was offered amounts as much as fifty times what she had received for her movies with the Khoslas. She now understood her real worth, but she still reasoned that she was being offered such amounts because of her hit film with the Khoslas. Otherwise, she would yet be a newcomer, and no one would touch her with a ten-feet pole, let alone offer her such amounts of money.

The Khoslas had been planning another film with her for the last couple of months. This was a larger canvas, and pre-production was on over the previous two months. It was going on sets shortly. The male lead actor, Kiran Kumar, was already, reasonably well established.

Kangna had been approached for an interview with a senior correspondent of *Indian Times* and she had consented. The interviewer was adept at creating controversies and breaking news to boost his paper's circulation, but Kangna was not aware of it.

During the interview, Rajesh Kumar asked her, "Kangna, it is said, that you did not attend any acting school, and that you were a complete novice before Umesh Khosla gave you a chance to act in his film *Notorious*?"

"Yes, it is completely true. Umesh Sir mentored me and gave me a break, and I owe a lot to him."

"But Kangna, in one of the interviews, he said, you did not know the ABC of acting, is it true?"

"As I said, Umesh Sir is my mentor, and I learned a lot working with him. But I was at NSD for a year and picked up a lot of my acting abilities from actors like Wasim Bhai and others."

"So, Kangna, you are saying Umesh Sir, did not teach you the ABC of acting."

"This is what you are saying. What I am saying is that I learned a lot about acting from Umesh Sir, but the basics I learned at NSD."

This was part of a half-hour interview.

The next morning Kangna received a call from Ayushi at 9 in the morning. This was the first time anyone called her this early in Bombay.

"Mam, Sir wants to meet you for breakfast!"

"Regarding?"

"I don't know, but the car is already there to pick you up."

"I am not even fully awake."

"He sounds angry. You better come fast."

What followed at Umesh's house was less of breakfast, more of a blast. He was in a temper like she had never seen him before.

"Good-morning Umesh Sir."

"Who the hell do you think you are, you little bitch? I have made you a star. I can also make you a pauper and make you beg on the streets of Bombay!"

No one had dared to speak to Kangna like this ever before. She had not taken shit even from her own father. Hoiwever, she remembered where her reckless ways had led her to, in Delhi. She controlled her temper and tried to comprehend as to what had happened, "Sir, what have I done? Please let me know. Maybe there is a misunderstanding."

Still, in rage, he threw the *Indian Times* newspaper towards her. The entertainment section was open. There staring back at her was the headline.

'KANGNA CALLS UMESH KHOSLA A LIAR- HE DID NOT TEACH ME ABC OF ACTING'

Kangna was shocked. This Rajesh Kumar had twisted her statements entirely out of context. No wonder Umesh Sir was behaving like a bull in a china shop. Kangna was herself in shock, but she maintained her composure, as a lot was at stake, and tried to explain everything to Umesh Sir. Not that he was convinced.

Three weeks later, they started shooting for the movie, *Jaanu*. This was to be shot mostly in a studio set in Bombay. A set of a college was erected in the Film City studios. It was to be a single schedule shoot of about 60 days. One song was to be picturised at the Ramoji Rao film City in Hyderabad.

Umesh had not spoken to Kangna in the last three weeks, and Kangna was very tense on the shoot's first day. He made no bones about it and continued to ignore her for a significant part of the day. She had known Umesh as the friendly father figure, and she had not seen this side of him. It seemed, he still nursed anger and resentment towards her for having said what she did, although she had explained to him that she had been quoted out of context, and Rajesh Kumar had played him against her. But his ego had been wounded, and he would set her right.

It was the fifth day of the shoot. Kangna was being given the '*treatment*' on the sets. She was scolded for not remembering her dialogues, for her pronunciation, for her body language. Anything and everything that she did was wrong. Her shots were not okayed. So much so that she was now completely fed up, broken, and humiliated in front of the whole unit. She was a spirited girl and started resenting the fact that she was being picked upon unnecessarily.

A shot was under progress. Kangna's character has an argument with her mother about her lifestyle, the usual generation gap thing, while her younger sister is looking on, with a few monosyllables in between. It was actually a simple shot and should have been done in a single take. This was the sixth take.

"Cut! What are you doing? Have you forgotten how to act?" shouted Umesh.

"Sir, I am doing exactly as you explained."

"Really? Listen to her, now she will tell me how to direct my films!" shouted Umesh. The unit staff nodded in agreement, and some sniggered at Kangna.

"Sir, I don't mean that…"

"Surbhi," he pointed to the girl playing the younger sister, "You show her how to do it."

Surbhi enacted the scene. "Perfect! See, she has understood it in one take, and she is a junior artiste. I don't know how they give national awards these days."

Kangna lost it at last. "Sir, I think you are picking on me unnecessarily. I was doing much better than her. I think your ego is not accepting the fact that I can act well."

There was shell shocked silence on the set. Everyone had been seeing the game for the last five days, but no one dared speak up.

The words hung heavy in the air.

Umesh's face turned crimson. "You little bitch—" He lunged toward her, fists clenched.

Kangna froze, heart pounding. She had faced her father's anger before—but this was different. This was power unchecked.

Kangna broke down and started crying. She covered her face and ran out of the set, tears rolling down her cheeks.

When Jaanu released months later, Kangna's screen time had been reduced to three minutes. The movie flopped spectacularly, labeled the biggest disaster of the decade. Umesh used every interview to bury her career—painting her as an ungrateful, arrogant failure.

The industry believed him.

Offers dried up. Her phone stopped ringing. And with four months left on her contract, she was stuck—caged by the very man who once promised to set her free.

A week after the release, Ayushi called.

"Kangna, we need your flat. A car is waiting to move you."

When Kangna reached the parking lot, the sleek BMW she had grown used to was gone. In its place stood a dusty, battered Wagon R.

Rambabu, the driver, avoided her eyes. "Madam, are you ready?"

The new flat was in a cramped building in Azad Nagar—a far cry from the luxury she once had. Faded furniture. No air conditioning. It felt like a prison.

As Rambabu handed her the keys, his voice softened. "Madam… did you eat today?"

The simple kindness broke her.

She shook her head, unable to speak—because if she did, the tears would never stop.

CHAPTER - 23

KANGNA - Finding Her Feet (1999)

For two days, Kangna lay curled up in the dingy, windowless room. No food. No water. Just the crushing weight of humiliation pressing down on her chest. Sleep didn't come—not with Umesh's voice echoing in her ears, mocking her, stripping her down piece by piece. Every sneer, every cold glance from the crew replayed like a broken record in her mind. The same people she'd shared chai and casual conversations with, had avoided her like she was nothing. Less than nothing.

The worst part wasn't the shouting or even the public degradation—it was the silence. The way everyone else just… carried on. Pretending they didn't see her fall from grace. It reminded her of home—of the way her mother would quietly sweep the floor while her father tore through the house like a storm. No one interfered. No one saved her.

And now? The same story, just a different setting.

She let the darkness swallow her whole. What was the point of fighting it? The last time she tried—at Sharma's house—it almost killed her. She had fought so hard to escape the depression back then, only to fall deeper into its trap. This time, she wouldn't resist. She surrendered to the numbness, letting it pull her under. If this was what rock bottom felt like, so be it.

But on the third day, something shifted.

Kangna woke up. Weak. Empty. But the rage that burned quietly inside her was still there—smoldering beneath the surface. She dragged herself to the bathroom and stood under the rusted cold shower. The water hit her skin like needles, but it didn't matter. Water was water—whether it flowed in a luxury suite or from a leaking pipe in a slum. No one could take that from her.

And no one—no one—was going to take her life away from her either.

Kangna changed into a tight pair of denims and a black top and went downstairs. The streets were buzzing with energy. Nothing had changed. She hailed an auto-rickshaw and asked the driver to drop her at Alfredo's, a bar which she knew was nearby. Kangna ordered a Budweiser draught beer as she was thirsty and drank it in one go and ordered a refill. After two beers, she realised she was famished. She called for the menu and ordered a tomato soup with toast on the side and garlic pasta in the mains. As Kangna waited for her food to arrive, she was thinking clearly. She knew that she was in a lot of shit, but she wanted to take stock of her life.

Kangna requested the waiter for a sheet of paper and a pen to note down all her concerns. She started writing whatever came to her mind. It was just like if she wrote down all her troubles, her subconscious mind would automatically help her find solutions to the problems.

Financially, she knew, she was still in the doldrums. Most of the money given to her had been spent in shopping for gifts for her family and herself. She had around 40,000 rupees left which would last for a maximum of one month.

She decided she could not stay a day in that shithole and would move to her own accommodation tonight itself. She also needed to find a new source of income urgently.

And most of all, she needed a real friend in Bombay.

By the time her garlic pasta arrived, Kangna had already downed two more beers. The bill came to ₹2700. She didn't flinch. She tossed ₹3000 on the table and left the rest as a tip. She could afford one indulgence. Tomorrow would be different.

As she stood to leave, a couple nearby hesitated before approaching her.

"Kangna ma'am… could we get an autograph?" the woman asked softly, holding out a paper napkin.

"We loved your work in Notorious," the man added with a smile.

For a second, Kangna froze. She asked their names. After everything, someone still remembered her. Still cared. She took the napkin and scrawled:

To Sapna and Satish – Lots of love, Kangna.

With a final smile, she waved for another auto.

That night, she checked herself into a modest hotel. ₹2000 a night. It wasn't luxury, but it was hers. No one could kick her out this time. And it bought her two days to figure out her next move.

The following morning, she called the only person she trusted—Wasim Bhai.

They met at Alfredo's again. When he walked in—dressed in his usual crisp white shirt, matching trousers, and leather shoes—he was instantly reconised and there were waiters hovering around them; they ordered omellettes and toast with coffee.

Wasim Bhai was a beacon of calm in her chaos. Without a word, he pulled her into a warm hug. And in that moment, she knew—he already knew.

“Bollywood’s newest troublemaker,” he teased, settling into his chair. “You really know how to make headlines, don’t you?”

Kangna laughed—because what else was there to do? “I didn’t ask for this, Wasim Bhai. I tried to play the game, but… I can’t be someone I’m not.”

His smile faded. “Good. Don’t be. This city will break you if you try to please everyone. And you’re not meant to be broken.”

“But Umesh—he’s your friend, isn’t he?”

Wasim chuckled darkly. “Kangna, this is a city of appearances. Everything is make-believe. There are no friends here—only people you haven’t pissed off yet. Everyone’s using someone. The day I’m no longer useful, I’ll be just as disposable.”

Kangna leaned forward. “I need your help, Wasim Bhai. I’m drowning. My contract is a trap. They threw me out of my accommodation. I need a lawyer, a place to stay… and work. I’m not going back home. Not like this.”

"Kangna, I knew that they had made a one-sided contract with you. But I had to play along. Even I have to survive in this industry. In fact, why I am so open with you is that I see a spark in you. You are just like me when I was young. I have learned the ropes the hard way. I am sure you will do better. But do not lose that spark, which is only bestowed on very few people by the almighty."

“Thank-you Wasim Bhai. What do I do now? I need a lawyer, a place to stay and I need work to survive in Bombay. I am not going back, at any cost.”

"Hahaha," laughed Wasim Bhai, "that's my girl. I will get you in contact with my very reliable lawyer Mr. Lonawala. He has been handling my affairs for the last ten years. But my advice is, do not go into litigation for your previous contract. That is already a lost cause.”

“And accommodation?”

“You can crash at my place for now. My wife’s out of town, and there’s plenty of room. But if you’d rather have your own place, talk to Kumar—he’s my guy for rentals. Use my name.”

Relief washed over her, and for the first time in days, the knot in her stomach loosened. “You’re saving my life, Wasim Bhai.”

He shook his head. "I'm just giving you a lifeline. The rest? That's on you. If you're meant to make it here, no one can stop you. And if you're not…" He shrugged. "Not even God can help you."

Kangna smiled faintly. "I'm not leaving. Not until I have everything I came for."

Wasim Bhai laughed, raising his coffee cup in a mock toast. "That's my girl."

And just like that, her issues were resolved. But the fight wasn't over. It was only the beginning.

CHAPTER - 24

KANGNA - Back To Square One (2000)

Kangna moved into a cramped one-bedroom apartment—not exactly her dream home, but it had four walls and a lock on the door. It was a far cry from the glossy life she'd imagined when she first landed in Mumbai.

Days blurred into weeks, and weeks dragged into months as she shuffled from one office to another, chasing auditions that never seemed to materialize. She met every kind of agent the city had to offer. Slick, suited-up ones in corporate offices near Bandra who spoke in rehearsed lines. Greasy, fast-talking hustlers working out of dingy, smoke-filled spaces in Four Bungalows. They all shared one thing in common—empty promises. No one ever rejected her outright. Instead, they dangled dreams, just out of reach, waiting to see how much they could take before delivering… nothing.

Her lifestyle shrank to match her fading hopes. Alfredo's pasta dinners were replaced by greasy dosas at a local Udupi joint called Shriji. Coffee meetings went from the plush lounge at Novotel to coffee shops, then down to the sticky plastic tables at local tea stalls. Her phone, once buzzing with calls, now sat silent. It felt like she had a curse hanging over her head—no one wanted to touch her career with a ten-feet pole.

The only thing keeping her afloat was a handful of ad campaigns. They weren't glamorous, but they paid the bills—barely. Raj, the agent who found her the gigs, always made sure to remind her of his 20 percent cut. It was the industry standard, but every time he took his share, it stung a little more.

One evening, as she stared at her empty fridge, her phone buzzed. It was Raj.

"Kangna ma'am," he said, his voice slick and familiar. "I have news. Big news."

She straightened up, heart pounding. "What is it?

"I spoke to Kamal Thapar's secretary—through a friend of mine. He's open to meeting you."

Kangna froze, her pulse roaring in her ears. Kamal Thapar. The man was a legend—his romantic dramas were box-office gold. Landing a role in one of his films could turn everything around.

“Are you serious?” she breathed, gripping the phone tighter.

“Of course. They’re developing a new script—classic Kamal style. A love story.”

A spark of hope flared in her chest, fierce and hungry. “I’m in. Just tell me when and where.”

“I’ll confirm the time and text you the details,” Raj said smoothly. “You impress him, and we’ll handle the rest from there.”

For the first time in months, something felt real. Tangible.

“Raj… thank you,” she said softly, trying to keep her voice steady.

“Don’t thank me yet, ma’am,” he chuckled. “Just be ready.”

As the call ended, Kangna leaned against the wall, heart thudding. This wasn’t another false promise. This could be her way back—if she played it right.

CHAPTER - 25
Kamal - Big Shot (1999)

At just twenty-nine, Kamal Thapar had already become a force to be reckoned with in Bollywood. Five back-to-back blockbusters had cemented his status as one of the industry's most powerful producers. Under his leadership, the Thapar banner soared, turning every project into gold. Directors lined up for a chance to work with him—but Kamal remained loyal to one man: Ramji.

Ramji had plucked Kamal from obscurity and turned him into a star producer, and he never let anyone forget it. Whether on film sets, in interviews, or behind closed doors, Ramji made it clear—Kamal's success belonged to him. At first, Kamal took it in his stride, always acknowledging his mentor. But lately, the constant reminders grated on his nerves. Kamal was no longer the eager young boy who needed saving. He was a kingpin now—richer, more influential, and no longer content to live in Ramji's shadow.

The Thapar production house was a well-oiled machine with over two hundred employees and a dozen senior executives. And while most feared Ramji, a few ambitious ones had grown tired of his dominance. They saw an opportunity—a growing tension between Kamal and his mentor—and they were more than willing to exploit it.

When it came time to choose their next big project, the team of assistant directors had narrowed the options to two scripts. Kamal and Ramji, after much debate, settled on a youthful, emotional love story set in a college campus—a guaranteed hit with the younger audience. The casting process began with one clear instruction: the lead roles needed fresh faces. Naturally, Ramji would direct the film, meaning his word would be final.

For the female lead, Ramji had already made up his mind. He wanted Kangna—a fiery nineteen-year-old actress who had blown him away with her debut performance in Notorious. "She's raw, but she's got that spark," he told Kamal, instructing the team to arrange a meeting with her.

The male lead, however, was still up for debate.

The next morning, the boardroom buzzed with anticipation. Mahi, a sharp and efficient assistant from the casting department, was leading the presentation. Kamal and Ramji sat on opposite sides of the sleek conference table, with Sanju—an ambitious young assistant director—positioned quietly in between. Sanju was one of Kamal's recruits, and his presence irritated Ramji no end.

Mahi clicked through slide after slide, showcasing the best contenders. Each candidate's headshots filled the massive screen while Mahi rattled off their stats—age, height, training, and previous work. If either Kamal or Ramji said "shortlist," Mahi would flag the name for further review.

They had been at it for hours. Two hundred faces, and nothing extraordinary. The fatigue was beginning to show.

Then, halfway through the second day, Kamal spoke up. "Shortlist him," he said, his voice casual but firm. On the screen was a tall, lean young man with a disarming smile.

Mahi read the details. "Ram Bhatia. Age 24. Height 6'2". Six-month diploma from Whistling Woods. Did a small TV gig—Ram Jane."

Ramji, who had been uncharacteristically quiet, suddenly leaned forward. "Wait. Stop." His eyes narrowed as he studied the screen. "Why does he look so familiar?"

Mahi scrolled back to the actor's stills. "He's only got that one credit, sir. Nothing else on record."

Ramji shook his head. "I don't watch TV dramas. But I know this face."

Sanju, sensing the tension, spoke up. "Maybe he just has one of those faces, sir."

Big mistake. Ramji turned to him, his glare cold and cutting. "When I want your opinion, I'll ask for it."

Kamal shifted uncomfortably, avoiding Ramji's gaze.

"Where did you get his profile?" Ramji's voice was low and dangerous.

Mahi hesitated. "Sanju submitted it this morning."

The temperature in the room seemed to drop.

“Kamal,” Ramji said, his tone sharpening. “Isn’t this the same boy we met at the Bhang premiere in Abu Dhabi?”

Kamal stiffened. “I—I think so. But that was almost two years ago—”

“Don’t play dumb with me,” Ramji snapped. “I remember how you couldn’t take your eyes off him that night. Following him around like a love-struck puppy. And now, you’re sneaking him into my casting session?”

Kamal’s face drained of color.

Sanju, desperate to shield his boss, tried to intervene. “Sir, Kamal had nothing to do with this—”

“Shut your mouth,” Ramji barked. “You think you’re clever? You think you can play games with me in my house?”

Kamal, usually so composed, couldn’t find his voice.

“You, ungrateful little brat,” Ramji spat, his rage boiling over. “I picked you up when you were nothing—a scared, desperate boy willing to do anything to survive. You’d still be groveling for scraps if it weren’t for me. And this—” He gestured to the sleek boardroom; the empire Kamal had built. “—all of this exists because I made you. And now you want to cut me out?”

Sanju stood up, trying to hold his ground. “With all due respect, sir, Kamal doesn’t owe his life to you.”

The slap came out of nowhere—a sharp crack that echoed through the room. Sanju staggered backward, his hand flying to his face.

“Respect?” Ramji sneered, unbuckling his belt with deliberate slowness. “I’ll teach you respect.”

The first lash struck Sanju’s shoulder. The second cut across his back. Kamal—frozen with panic—couldn’t move.

“You think you’re somebody now?” Ramji hissed, striking him again. “You think you can turn against me and walk away unscathed?”

Sanju dropped to his knees, wincing in pain. “Stop—please—”

But Kamal wasn’t there to hear it. Somewhere between the second and third blow, he had bolted—fleeing the room and the chaos he had unleashed.

When the sound of leather on flesh finally stopped, the boardroom fell deathly silent. Ramji fastened his belt, staring down at Sanju with cold disdain.

“You’ll regret this,” he said softly. “Both of you.”

Then, without another word, he walked out—slamming the door behind him.

It was the last time Ramji ever set foot in the Thapar office. And Kamal knew, in the pit of his stomach, that nothing would ever be the same again.

CHAPTER - 26

KANGNA - Destiny (2000)

1:10 PM. Kangna was late—and she knew it. Her heart pounded in her chest as the cab weaved through the chaotic Mumbai traffic. This meeting was everything. The kind of opportunity actresses dreamt of—Kamal Thapar, the man who could turn struggling newcomers into overnight sensations. And here she was, ten minutes behind schedule, cursing the slow, old cab driver under her breath.

By the time she burst through the sleek glass doors of Thapar Productions, her palms were sweaty. The entire seventh floor belonged to them—a kingdom towering above the city. She approached the front desk, trying to mask her panic.

"Hi, I'm Kangna. I had a 1 PM meeting—I'm so sorry I'm late. Can I meet him now?"

The receptionist, a polished young woman in a crisp black blazer, barely glanced up. "And who was your meeting with?"

Kangna froze. His name. Damn it. She scrambled through her memory, drawing blanks. "Uh… your boss. Mr. Kamal," she added quickly, hoping to sound important.

The receptionist raised an eyebrow. "We have three Kamals here—Taneja, Verma, and Thapar. Which one?"

A wave of embarrassment flushed through her. She fumbled for her phone, pulling up the message. "Kamal Thapar. I'm here to meet Mr. Kamal Thapar."

The receptionist sighed, dialed an extension, and after a murmured exchange, said, "He's in a meeting. You can wait."

Kangna exhaled and moved to the seating area. She sank into the plush leather sofa, the cushions swallowing her whole. The reception was like something out of a movie—marble floors gleaming under soft lights, the walls were adorned with framed posters of different movies attributed to this production house and their associates. There were pictures of all leading ladies and actors right from the birth of the industry to the current ones, who had of course worked in movies produced by Thapar productions. There was a beautiful glass display that showcased awards of different shapes and sizes. There were three framed photographs on the wall with names and dates underneath, possibly the founders and the family heirloom. This was no ordinary production house. These were pioneers of the film industry, the torchbearers, the icons.

Kangna was utterly overwhelmed, and she felt out of place. The dress she was wearing suddenly seemed cheap, just not good enough for this place. She thought that the receptionist was better dressed and more presentable than her.

But as the minutes ticked by, awe was quickly replaced by unease.

She watched as others arrived and were swiftly escorted in. A courier boy dropped off a package and left. A trio of sharply dressed executives came and went. Even a guy in ripped jeans and scuffed sneakers—who looked like he belonged at a college dorm, not a film office—was taken in after a short wait.

Meanwhile, she remained stuck in her seat. Invisible. Unimportant.

Thoughts were running through her mind- *Am I being singled out? Am I being punished for being late?* Kangna looked at the receptionist, hoping to catch her attention, but she was busy with her calls.

She stood abruptly and marched back to the desk. “I have another meeting. Let Mr. Thapar know I’m leaving,” she said, her voice sharper than intended.

The receptionist—suddenly much quicker to respond—picked up the phone. After a brief conversation, she looked up. “He’s free. Second door to the left.”

Kangna swallowed hard and pushed the door open.

The first thing she noticed was the smell—expensive cologne, fine leather, and… wine and food! The conference table was still cluttered with half-empty glasses and the remains of what looked like an elaborate lunch. So much for an ‘important meeting.’

Behind a massive white desk, Kamal Thapar leaned back in his chair, all effortless power and arrogance. His tailored suit screamed money, and his manicured hands toyed with a Montblanc pen. He didn't bother to stand when she walked in.

"Ah, Kangna. Sorry to keep you waiting," he said, his tone too smooth, too casual. "Big discussions—you know how it is."

Her eyes darted to a side monitor, where a live CCTV feed still displayed the reception area. He saw me. He knew I was waiting. And he let me sit there for hours while he drank and laughed with his friends.

Her jaw clenched as she shifted her gaze back to him. "Yeah… I can see how busy you were." Her voice was cool, but her blood boiled beneath the surface. "I was so nervous about being ten minutes late. I thought I blew my chance. Guess, I needn't have worried—you clearly didn't care."

"Kangna, I think you are not getting it. We were genuinely discussing a film script."

Kangna replied with tears in her eyes, "Mr. Kamal Thapar, I have no interest in dancing to the tune of any producer.

Kamal's smile faltered. "Relax, Kangna. That's how this business works. Patience is a virtue. You can't walk in with an attitude when you're just one film old." He leaned forward slightly. "Actors sit outside my office for days just to get five minutes with me. You should feel lucky."

Lucky? She felt anything but lucky. She felt small. Like every woman who had ever been made to feel that her worth depended on the approval of men like him. And she was done.

Kangna took a step closer, her voice steady despite the lump in her throat. "I came here because I respected you—because I thought you were different. Turns out, you're just another producer who thinks people should crawl for your attention."

Kamal's expression hardened. "Watch your tone," he said, a warning edge creeping into his voice. His friends, lounging on the couch, exchanged amused glances. One of them snickered under his breath.

Kangna laughed bitterly. "You know what? I'd rather beg on the streets of Mumbai than dance to your tune, Mr. Thapar. You can keep your films—I'm not for sale."

Before he could respond, she turned on her heel, storming out of the office without a backward glance.

By the time the elevator doors slid shut behind her, the tears burning her eyes finally fell—but she didn't wipe them away. Let them see. Let the whole world know; Kangna wasn't the kind of woman who begged.

Not now. Not ever.

CHAPTER - 27

KANGNA - The Struggle Continues (2000)

Kangna slumped onto her couch, tossing her bag aside. She had pinned so many hopes on this meeting, and now it had all fallen apart. She pulled out her phone and dialed Raj.

"Hello, Raj."

"Hello, Kangna mam. I know the meeting was a disaster. It's okay. Don't stress."

"What? How do you already know?"

Raj chuckled. "Mam, haven't you heard? The only thing that moves faster than light in Bollywood is gossip."

Kangna groaned. "Oh my God."

"Listen, don't take it personally. It's not about you. Ramji had a fallout with Kamal Thapar. He's out of the Thapar camp now. He wanted you in the film; he was pushing your name hard. If he was still in, no one could have replaced you."

"Seriously?"

"Yeah. Ramji practically made Kamal what he is today. But he never let anyone forget it, not Kamal, not the whole industry. I guess Kamal finally got tired of it. Plus, Kamal's got a new boyfriend."

Kangna raised an eyebrow. "I didn't know Ramji was gay."

"Ramji was a…let's just say he never discriminated. Anything in pants or out of them, didn't matter to him." Raj laughed. "But Kamal? He's fully into men. And right now, he's all about his assistant director, Sanju."

Kangna exhaled sharply. "God, what a mess. Honestly, I am glad I am out of it."

Raj snorted. "To be fair, it's probably one of the safest sets for a woman to work on."

She rolled her eyes but couldn't help laughing. "You might be right."

"Anyway, don't worry. I am trying to line up a meeting next week with Tejasvi Sinha. He's got a solid reputation. More realistic films, no shady business."

"Thanks, Raj. And in the meantime do you think you could get me any product endorsements? I really need the money."

"I'll see what I can do, mam. But I don't want to put you in any murky situations. You know how this industry works."

Kangna sighed. By now, she knew exactly how things worked. If she was willing to play the game, she could have as much work as she wanted. But she wasn't.

"Thanks, Raj. I appreciate it."

That night, the loneliness crept in again. She picked up her phone and dialed home.

"Hello?"

"Hey, Palak," Kangna said, forcing a smile into her voice.

"Kangna! Oh my God, I was just thinking about you! You're going to live a hundred years."

A little bit of Palak's excitement rubbed off on her. "Really? What happened?"

"Nothing, I just miss you. When are you coming home?"

Kangna hesitated. "I can't right now. I have some meetings lined up and I need to be here in case something comes through. How are Mom and Dad?"

"They're good. Everyone misses you."

Kangna hesitated again, then took a deep breath. "Palak, why don't you come stay with me for a while?"

"Seriously?"

"Yeah. It's a small apartment, but we'll manage."

"Okay, maybe I can, as you know I am in between jobs. Let me talk to Ma and Pa. I'll let you know."

Kangna smiled for the first time all day. She was exhausted from the hypocrisy of this industry, the fake smiles, the endless negotiations. She needed something real. And Palak was the only one who could give her that.

CHAPTER - 28

KAMAL - Lights, Camera, Action (2000)

Kamal leaned back in his leather chair, tapping a pen against the glass tabletop. Across from him, Sanju scrolled through his phone, occasionally glancing up. The office buzzed faintly with voices from the outer corridor—a reminder that the industry never truly slept.

"Sanju," Kamal said, breaking the silence, "now that Ramji is out of the picture, we need a director for our new movie. Any ideas?"

Sanju smirked. "What about Umesh Khosla? He's practically family to you guys."

Kamal rolled his eyes. "Umesh? Come on. The man's a walking soap opera. Worse, he's Ramji 2.0 when it comes to tantrums. And I'm not dealing with another behind-the-scenes love triangle. One disaster was enough."

Sanju laughed, shaking his head. "Alright, what about Shamu Sir? The guy's a genius."

"For thrillers—sure. But romance?" Kamal scoffed. "He'd turn a love story into a crime scene. Plus, you know how he is—one disagreement, and he'll stage a walkout, just to prove a point."

"Let's be honest, Kamal. All directors are a little... unhinged. Occupational hazard."

Kamal chuckled under his breath. "True. The line between their stories and reality blurs after a while. And suddenly, everyone's living in their own movie."

Sanju tilted his head, a sly smile forming. "You know... you've got the mind for this. Why not direct the film yourself?"

Kamal burst into laughter. "Are you saying I'm crazy too?"

"I'm serious," Sanju pressed. "You understand stories better than half these guys. And the technical stuff? Leave that to me—I'll handle the crew, the cast, everything. Your name on the credits will do the magic."

"You're forgetting one tiny detail," Kamal said dryly. "Money. Who's going to finance a vanity project by a first-time director?"

Sanju leaned forward, eyes gleaming with excitement. "We don't need big money. We'll go the indie route—new faces, fresh talent. No star salaries, no ego clashes. We pitch it as your directorial debut and sell the dream. Everyone loves an underdog story—especially when the underdog is Kamal Thapar."

Kamal's fingers drummed against the table as he considered it. "You really think people will buy that?"

"They'll eat it up." Sanju's voice brimmed with conviction. "We start with a small script—there's this writer I know, struggling to make rent. A couple of lakhs and he'll sell us the whole thing. We spin the narrative—Kamal Thapar, stepping into the director's chair with a story straight from the heart. The media will run with it. By the time we roll cameras, the project will be hot property."

A slow smile crept across Kamal's face. The pieces were falling into place. But there was still one more move to make.

"I have a better idea," he said, leaning forward. "Let's cast Rajan Mallik's younger daughter, Umna. She's seventeen—perfect for the lead. And you know how tight the Malliks are with 'MusicWorld.' If Rajan's daughter is headlining, they'll drop six or seven chartbusters to back her debut. By the time we release a teaser, the music alone will make this a blockbuster."

Sanju's mouth was open. "Damn, Kamal. That's brilliant. Plus, fresh faces mean no date dramas, no diva meltdowns."

Kamal grabbed his phone, already dialing. "I'll give Rakhi Dutt the exclusive for Bollywood Prime. She's been dying for a scoop. We'll give her the headline—Kamal Thapar's secret passion project, a directorial debut that's about to shake up Bollywood. She gets her TRPs, we get the buzz."

Sanju grinned, leaning back with satisfaction. "Lights, camera, action."

Kamal laughed, his pulse quickening with the thrill of it. "Let's make history, Sanju."

CHAPTER – 29
KAMAL - The Don (2000)

When Rakhi Dutt spoke, Bollywood listened.

She wasn't just another loudmouthed anchor chasing cheap headlines—she was the real deal. No gimmicks. No recycled news. Her exclusives were fresh, sharp, and always a step ahead. How she got her inside scoops was anyone's guess, but the audience didn't care. As long as the tea was hot, they kept coming back for more.

Rakhi hadn't always been the glamorous, headline queen she was now. When she first appeared on Bollywood Prime, she was just a plain-faced girl next door—relatable, unpolished, and real. But success changes people. And Rakhi? She changed from head to toe. Rumor had it, a few skilled surgeons had worked their magic, sculpting her into a screen goddess. With her bold personality and a wardrobe that screamed power, she was no longer just a reporter—she was a star in her own right.

And that morning, she had a bombshell to drop.

Her voice, smooth and cutting, filled screens across the country.

"Bollywood loves a comeback story—but what about a takeover? Today, I'm talking about the man who's rewriting the rules: Kamal Thapar."

A sleek graphic flashed across the screen - "KAMAL THAPAR: THE DON OF BOLLYWOOD?"

"At just 25, Kamal took control of Thapar Pictures after his father's sudden death. While most young men his age are still figuring out their careers, Kamal was already calling the shots. And not just calling them—he was hitting them out of the park. Five back-to-back blockbusters. Five. Industry insiders say he has the Midas touch. Everything he touches, turns to gold."

The camera cut to a montage—Kamal stepping out of a sleek black Mercedes, paparazzi flashes lighting up his chiseled face. Charismatic. Ruthless. Untouchable.

"But that's not all. Kamal isn't just resting on his success. Word is, he's been secretly working on a project that's deeply personal. A film he's written himself. And here's the kicker—he's making his directorial debut with it."

The screen buzzed with the bold red title: 'FRIENDS' – A Kamal Thapar Film.

"A fresh, youthful romantic musical set against the backdrop of college life. But Kamal's not stopping there. He's using his platform to launch new talent—introducing two newcomers, Ram Bhatia and Umna Mallik, in the lead roles. In an industry obsessed with legacy, Kamal is betting big on the next generation."

Rakhi leaned in, her tone dripping with intrigue.

"Ambitious? Definitely. Risky? Absolutely. But if anyone can pull it off, it's Kamal Thapar. Love him or envy him—he's not just playing the game. He's changing it."

The screen faded to black, leaving one lingering question:

Is Kamal Thapar the future of Bollywood—or its new king?

CHAPTER - 30

VIKRAM - Over The Top (2008)

Vikram Seth was unstoppable. Three back-to-back blockbuster movies had turned him into the biggest star in the country—fans worshipped him, producers lined up outside his house, and sycophants buzzed around him like flies after the rain. With fame came power, and with power came a dangerously inflated ego. Even the media—usually fearless and quick to tear celebrities down—handled him with caution. It wasn't just his superstardom that made them tread carefully. It was the people backing him—powerful names no one wanted to cross.

His days followed an indulgent routine. Mornings were for the gym—a three-hour grind that kept his body camera-ready. Afternoons, when most actors had already wrapped up half their work, was when he strolled onto the set. Evenings? Reserved for a bottle of his favorite whiskey—a ritual he never missed.

That day at Chandiwali Studios, the set was already buzzing by 11 am. Director Ramji was shooting a crucial scene with three of the biggest names in the industry—Vikram, Ganesh, and Sripriya. Ganesh, a method actor known for his no-nonsense attitude, had arrived on time and was growing impatient. By 1 pm, when Vikram still hadn't shown up, Ganesh had enough. Without a word, he left.

By the time Vikram finally arrived—at 3 pm, as usual—the atmosphere on set was tense. Without acknowledging anyone, he slipped into his vanity van. Thirty minutes later, his assistant led him onto the set where Ramji, barely holding back his frustration, was waiting.

"Vikram, you're four hours late," Ramji said, his voice tight. "This isn't the first time—do you realize we're already eight days behind schedule?"

Vikram adjusted his sunglasses and smirked. "Sorry, Ramji Bhai. Had a late night. Needed extra time at the gym to get in the zone."

Ramji's patience was wearing thin. "This is the sixth time, Vikram. What do I tell the other actors? Ganesh already left—he's not going to sit around waiting for you."

Vikram turned to Sripriya, who was quietly observing the exchange. Rumors had been swirling for weeks about their off-screen chemistry, though neither had confirmed it. “You upset, Sripriya? Did I ruin your plans?”

Sripriya, ever diplomatic, gave a small smile. “No, it’s fine. I’m here.”

“See?” Vikram chuckled, turning back to Ramji. “No one’s complaining. You’re the only one losing it.”

That was the last straw. Ramji’s face darkened as he snapped, “This isn’t just about you, Vikram! There are fifty other people on this set. You think everyone’s time is worthless? Your ‘sorry’ doesn’t fix lost hours or blown schedules!”

Vikram’s smile faded. He took a step closer, his voice cold. “I said sorry—what else do you want?”

Before Ramji could answer, Vikram’s hand lashed out. The slap cracked across Ramji’s face, silencing the entire set. No one moved. No one spoke. Even the sound of distant traffic seemed to fade.

Ramji staggered back, his hand trembling as he touched his cheek. For the first time in his career, he was speechless.

Vikram turned and walked off the set, his confidence unshaken. Sripriya hesitated for a moment, then hurried after him.

By the next day, the incident should have been all over the headlines—but it wasn’t. The press, always eager for a scandal, stayed silent. No one dared to report what had happened. Vikram was too big, too connected, and everyone knew it. For now, the story—like many things in the industry—was buried.

CHAPTER - 31

VIKRAM & SRIPRIYA - Temper Tantrums (2009)

The romance between Vikram Seth and Sripriya was no longer a secret. What started as a casual fling had turned into a full-blown, high-profile relationship. They were everywhere—award shows, after-parties, exclusive clubs. Paparazzi loved them. Fans were obsessed. Gossip columns buzzed with one question: When are they getting married?

But behind the glamorous photos and picture-perfect smiles, things were far from ideal.

Vikram had a jealous streak—intense and suffocating. He wanted a say in every decision Sripriya made, especially the films she chose. Certain co-stars—particularly Ganesh, the industry's charming heartthrob—were an absolute no-go for him. Sripriya, however, wasn't one to be controlled. She had worked too hard to let anyone—boyfriend or not—dictate her career. And then, there was his drinking. By evening, Vikram was almost always drunk, unpredictable, and reckless.

Still, she couldn't walk away. Not yet. There was something magnetic about him—the chaos, the passion. The same fire that burned her was the one that pulled her closer.

That night, they were at Opium Den, their go-to spot at The Trident in Nariman Point. Sripriya loved the green apple mojitos; Vikram preferred whiskey straight from the bottle. It was late—1:30 AM—and the place was winding down. They were on their last round, laughing about a recent scandal where Vikram had slapped a choreographer during a shoot.

Out of nowhere, Vikram's voice cut through the laughter. "So… I heard you signed that movie with Ganesh."

Sripriya's smile faded. "Who told you?"

"I have my ways. Answer the question."

She rolled her eyes. "Why do you need me to confirm something you already know?"

Vikram's jaw clenched. His voice dropped, cold and sharp. "Don't play smart with me, Priya. You know I don't want you working with him."

"And you don't ask for my permission when you sign films." She leaned back, arms crossed. "You're doing another movie with Rati, aren't you? Should I be jealous, too? Or is that only reserved for you?"

"That was years ago. I have nothing with Rati now. And don't turn this on me. I said no movies with Ganesh," Vikram snapped, his volume rising.

Sripriya smirked, knowing exactly how to push his buttons. "Aw, is my baby jealous? You know, I love Ganesh's eyes… so deep, so intense. I could stare at them all day."

The waiter chose that unfortunate moment to approach. "Sir, we're closing soon. Would you like to settle the bill?"

Vikram glared at the waiter; eyes blazing. "Is this your hotel? No? Then don't tell me what to do. Get lost before I buy this place and fire you."

Sripriya tensed. She recognized the shift—the sudden darkness in his eyes. She'd seen it before. Felt it before. And she wasn't about to let it happen again.

She grabbed her purse and stood. "I'm leaving."

Vikram slammed his glass down. "Did I say we're done talking?"

Without answering, she walked briskly toward the lobby, hoping to avoid a scene. Behind her, his footsteps pounded against the marble floor.

"Priya!" His voice echoed through the nearly empty corridor. "Don't you dare walk out on me!"

She quickened her pace, heart pounding. By the time she reached the lobby, Vikram caught up, yanking her by the wrist and spinning her around.

"Who the hell do you think you are?" His grip was tight, too tight. "You don't get to leave until I'm finished!"

Her skin burned where he held her, but it was the humiliation that stung worse. Hotel staff froze, glancing discreetly at the commotion. A few guests in designer suits turned to stare, murmuring among themselves.

In a low, urgent voice, Sripriya tried to keep things calm. "Let's go to the car. We'll talk there. Please, Vikram."

But he wasn't listening. Alcohol coursed through his veins, fueling his anger. "No, you'll answer me now! Are you screwing Ganesh? Is that it?"

Her patience snapped. She jerked her wrist free. "Enough, Vikram. You don't own me."

She turned to the concierge, her voice calm but firm. "Please arrange a cab."

"Right away, ma'am."

Vikram grabbed her again, harder this time. And then—slapped her across the face.

The sound echoed through the lobby.

Everything stopped. The concierge stiffened. The night manager exchanged a look with the bouncers, who immediately moved in.

"Sir, that's enough," one of them said quietly, locking his arms behind his back with practiced ease.

"You'll regret this!" Vikram snarled, struggling against their grip. "Let me go, you idiots!"

But no one flinched. No one cared about his celebrity status—not when a woman had just been hit.

The concierge guided Sripriya gently toward the exit, shielding her from the stares. "Your cab is waiting, ma'am."

In the backseat of the cab, as the city lights blurred past, Sripriya felt the sting of his slap linger. But something else settled in—clarity.

This wasn't love. Not anymore. And maybe… it never had been.

CHAPTER - 32

KAMAL —The Empire (2004)

Kamal had arrived. His directorial debut wasn't just a hit—it was a phenomenon. The film had shattered box office records, pulling in over ₹100 crores within the first week alone. Industry veterans called it a fluke. Kamal knew better. It was a calculated move—a fresh script, unknown faces, and a soundtrack that refused to leave the charts. Four songs from the movie dominated the Top 20, with the title track reigning at number one for six straight weeks. And, while the two newcomers in the lead roles were left celebrating their overnight fame, Kamal counted the real prize—a fortune.

But Kamal wasn't the type to sit back and enjoy the view. This was only the beginning. He wanted more—more films, more power, and his name etched in gold on every marquee. "Written and Directed by Kamal Thapar" had to become Bollywood's most valuable brand.

Still, something was missing. The money, the fame—it was all there. But Kamal wanted control. Total control.

He leaned back in his sleek leather chair and pressed a button on his intercom. "Get me Rakhi Dutt from Bollywood Prime," he said, his voice calm but sharp.

Minutes later, Rakhi's polished voice came through the line. "Hello, Mr. Kamal! Congratulations on the blockbuster. Must be feeling on top of the world?"

"Always, Rakhi," Kamal replied, a smirk tugging at his lips. "Listen, I've got a business proposal your company won't want to miss."

"Oh?" Rakhi perked up. "I'm listening."

"I'd rather discuss it in person. Bring your boss to my office tomorrow afternoon. If you're smart, you'll lock it down before someone else does."

Rakhi hesitated for a beat. "A little hint, Mr. Kamal?"

"No spoilers," he said smoothly. "But trust me—this is big. You wouldn't want your competitors to get their hands on it first."

"I'll check his availability and confirm," she said quickly, her tone sharper now.

Kamal hung up, satisfied. The bait was set.

A Month Later:

The Bollywood Prime Awards debuted in spectacular fashion—a glittering, star-studded affair in the heart of Mumbai. The grand venue buzzed with anticipation, and the stakes were sky-high. The event pulled in ₹1 crore from ticket sales alone, but the real jackpot? Music World had snapped up the exclusive satellite rights for a whopping ₹11 crores. Even after shelling out ₹6 crores in expenses—lavish sets, A-list performers, and a media blitz—Bollywood Prime cleared an effortless ₹5 crores in profit.

At the center of it all? Kamal Thapar—the mastermind pulling the strings behind the curtain.

His secret weapon? The musketeers—the fresh-faced leads from his blockbuster, *Friends*. They delivered two electrifying dance numbers, setting the stage on fire. In return, Kamal made sure Umna Mallik walked away with the Best Debut Actress award, while Ram Bhatia claimed Best Debut Actor.

And Kamal? He wasn't leaving empty-handed. He swept the night with Best Director and Best Script, solidifying his dominance over Bollywood.

The awards weren't just a celebration—they were a message. Kamal Thapar decided who won. And who didn't.

Even Shobhit Banerjee, the reigning superstar, knew better than to stay on Kamal's bad side. He gave a show-stopping dance performance that brought the audience to their feet. His reward? Best Actor—a convenient nod for his latest film. Nothing in Bollywood came free, and Kamal made sure everyone knew the price.

Power couple Rajesh and Madhu made a rare appearance, dazzling the crowd with a sultry duet. Rumor had it Kamal had personally negotiated their performance with a seven-figure payout. Madhu, of course, walked away with the Best Actress trophy—another well-placed favor.

Behind the glitz and the glamour, Kamal's empire was expanding. The blockbuster was just the beginning. Now, with a partnership in an entertainment TV channel, he was tightening his grip on the industry.

He didn't just make movies anymore—he made stars. He decided careers. And if you wanted to stay on top in Bollywood, you needed one thing:

Kamal Thapar on your side.

CHAPTER - 33

KANGNA - Clawing Back (2004)

Raj had finally pulled some strings and set up a meeting between Kangna and the elusive director, Tejasvi Sinha. By 3 PM, he was sitting across from her in his modest office—a dimly lit space that still smelled faintly of fresh paint and desperation.

"Kangna," Tejasvi began, his tone calm but direct, "I'm working on a film—*Cockpit*. It's a gritty, realistic take on the lives of air hostesses. No gloss. No sugar-coating."

Kangna leaned back, crossing her arms. "So… you want me to play an air hostess?" Her voice was steady, but the flicker of hope in her eyes betrayed her. "It's the lead, I assume?"

Tejasvi's lips curved into a faint smile. "Not exactly. There are two leads. I want you to play an air hostess who spirals into addiction—alcohol, drugs—the works. She loses her job, her dignity… but she fights back. The film also digs into the murky side of the airline industry—exploitation, corruption, the whole underbelly. Your character is raw, messy, and painfully human. I saw you in Notorious. You're the only one who can pull this off."

No screen-test. No hoops to jump through. Just a straight offer.

The paycheck? A measly 20 lakhs. For a moment, her pride wanted to reject it outright—but she couldn't afford pride anymore. Not with the bills piling up. Not with her career hanging by a thread. At least this role would keep her working and give her something else to think about—something other than the wreckage Umesh had left behind.

"I'm in," she said, her voice firm.

The catch? The other lead was Ahana Raj—the reigning queen of female-driven blockbusters. And Kangna knew from experience—two actresses sharing the spotlight was a recipe for war.

The production moved fast. Tejasvi ran a tight ship—no chaos, no tantrums. Everything was planned down to the minute. And unlike the industry's starry directors, he wasn't interested in playing power games. Maybe because he was an outsider himself—someone who had clawed his way into the business without a famous last name.

The shoot lasted 40 days. Kangna was on set for 17 of them. Most of her scenes were solo—angry, broken, high on substances, or clawing her way back to sanity. Only three days required her to share the frame with Ahana—and the tension between them was as thick as the makeup on their faces.

It didn't help that Ahana traveled with an entourage and her personal makeup artist, while Kangna made do with the overworked unit team.

One evening, after a particularly intense scene together, the two women walked back toward their vanity vans. The silence between them was heavy until Ahana spoke—her tone deceptively casual.

"I liked your work in Notorious. You were impressive," she said, her voice smooth but unreadable.

Kangna glanced sideways, trying to gauge her angle. Compliments in this industry always came with strings attached. "Thanks. It was… an experience," she replied, keeping her guard up.

Ahana didn't miss a beat. "Though… from what I hear, things with you and Umesh weren't exactly smooth sailing."

There it was—the dagger hidden in silk. Kangna felt her pulse quicken but refused to let her face betray her. She let out a bitter chuckle. "Yeah, well… these guys think they own the industry. A few hits, and suddenly, they're kings. But I don't play by their rules."

Ahana stopped walking, turning to face her fully. "Good. Don't. I've never played their game either, and trust me—they don't forget it. They'll try to freeze you out if you don't fall in line." Her smile was tight, but there was something almost… genuine beneath it. "Watch your back, Kangna. They hit hard when they want to."

Kangna held her gaze. "I'm tougher than I look."

"Good," Ahana said softly before disappearing into her luxury van.

That was it—the extent of their truce. In Bollywood, two actresses could share a frame, but never real friendship.

At least one thing was finally going right—Palak had moved to Bombay. Having her sister back was like having a piece of home again. The loneliness that had gnawed at Kangna for months, began to fade.

And when the final payment from *Cockpit* hit her account, Kangna wasted no time. She packed up her crumbling apartment and moved to a modest but comfortable two-bedroom flat in Goregaon. It wasn't glamorous, but it was a step up—a sign that maybe, just maybe, she was clawing her way back.

For the first time in months, she felt something like hope. And this time, she wasn't letting anyone take it away from her.

CHAPTER - 34
AHANA - Beyond Control (2010)

Ahana's career was at the peak—on her terms, by her rules. No shortcuts, no handouts. She had landed a dream project—Mafia—a high-octane thriller with none other than Bollywood's biggest superstar, Ramesh Bajaj. Most of the shoot was in Hong Kong, a city that sparkled like a dream—and one where dreams could spiral out of control.

Ahana arrived a week earlier with the crew, throwing herself into rehearsals. Ramesh, tied up with a reshoot in New York, was set to join them later. The director, Yasim, wanted to make the most of his absence—songs, solo scenes, everything that didn't need the superstar.

The day Ramesh finally landed; the set buzzed with a restless energy. Ahana, lost in her lines, snapped when two spot boys clattered noisily nearby.

"You idiots—can you shut up and let me work?" she barked, frustration simmering beneath her polished exterior.

A warm, teasing voice cut through the tension.

"You idiots, clear out! Madam doesn't need amateurs—I'm here to serve. Tea or coffee, ma'am?"

Ahana froze. She turned to see Ramesh standing behind her, his signature smile in place—a mix of charm and mischief that made hearts skip.

Yasim laughed, calling, "Cut!" before pulling Ramesh in for a hug.

Feeling sheepish, Ahana walked toward them, extending a hand. "Ramesh Bhai… sorry, I didn't—"

He cut her off with a quick, playful hug. His voice dipped low, just for her. "Ahana, call me anything… just not Bhai."

The air between them shifted—subtle, electric. For the first time, she felt the weight of his presence. He wasn't just a superstar. He was Ramesh Bajaj.

By five o'clock, the day's shoot wrapped. Ramesh and Ahana left in separate BMWs, heading back to the Ritz-Carlton, where the stars stayed. The rest of the crew? Scattered across budget hotels. Privilege has its perks.

At 8 pm, they met in the lobby. Ramesh, effortlessly suave in a tailored black jacket, leaned in with a smile. "So, has Hong Kong been kind to you?"

“Haven’t seen much of it,” Ahana admitted. “Yasim’s kept us locked in rehearsals.”

“Unacceptable,” he declared. “Come on, I’ll show you the real Hong Kong. I promise—back by ten, no puffy eyes tomorrow.”

She hesitated. “You sure? I don’t want Yasim breathing down my neck.”

“Trust me,” he said, offering his hand. “I’ve got you.”

They slipped into his car and sped through the neon-lit city, arriving at the sleek, sky-high Tenkū restaurant. From the 101st floor, Hong Kong sprawled beneath them—a glittering sea of lights, bridges cutting across the harbor, mountains in the distance. It was breathtaking.

“Wow…” Ahana whispered.

“I told you,” Ramesh said, watching her reaction more than the view. “I don’t do half-measures.”

"Now, let's order. I promised to have you back by ten!"

Ahana scanned the menu and gasped. "What am I supposed to eat here? It's all seafood!"

"Don't worry. They have Southern fried chicken and black pepper chicken. I recommend the fried chicken. Depends how hungry you are."

"I'm starving! I could eat both," she laughed.

"Okay, then. A bottle of champagne and a mountain of chicken for the lady!"

Ahana, true to her word, devoured most of the chicken. She was a real foodie, and no one would guess that so much food could fit into her toned stomach. Ramesh ate very little by comparison.

At exactly 9:59 pm, they returned to the Ritz. As they stepped out, Ramesh pointed to his watch.

“Right on time,” he said, bowing theatrically. “Your perfect escort.”

“At your service, madam,” he quipped, voice warm against her skin.

Before she could react, he leaned in and brushed a soft kiss against her cheek. “Goodnight, Ahana.”

In the quiet of her room, Ahana lay awake—heart pounding harder than it should. Ramesh was everything—charming, funny, and dangerously easy to fall for. But she couldn’t afford to fall for a married man.

And yet… she wasn’t sure she could stop herself.

For twelve days, the pattern repeated. Long shoots, glamorous nights. Every evening, Ramesh would whisk her away to a different restaurant, each one more impressive than the last: Caprice for French cuisine, Bo Innovation for continental, Lung King Heen at the Ritz for harbor views, Duddell's for Cantonese. When they started craving Indian food, Ramesh took her to Bombay Dreams, Namaste Kitchen, and Bindaas Bar, making her feel right at home.

And, like most Indians presented with kebabs and curries, Ahana abandoned her fork and spoon and dug in with her hands, regardless of social class. She devoured galouti kebabs, chicken tikkas, murg makhani, dum biryani – the works.

When the schedule cleared for two days, Ramesh suggested an escape. “Macau,” he said, eyes glinting. “Vegas of the East. What do you say?”

She hesitated—only for a breath.

“Let’s do it.”

An hour’s drive later, they arrived in a whirlwind of lights and luxury. By afternoon, they were at the Venetian, gambling like it wasn’t their money. Ahana, too cautious at first, lost fast. Ramesh played like he always lived—bold, reckless—and won big before luck turned.

When their last chip vanished, they laughed like conspirators, half-drunk on free casino cocktails and the thrill of letting go.

“We need more wine,” Ramesh declared, leading her to Fernando’s, a rustic Portuguese bar where the air was thick with salt and temptation and they ordered a bottle of red wine, potato wedges, and fried chicken.

By the second bottle, the world outside blurred. They talked—about everything and nothing. Dreams, regrets, the price of fame. With Ramesh, Ahana felt seen—not as a rising star, but as a woman.

In the car ride back, the air grew heavy. His hand brushed hers—once, twice—and then there was no going back.

The kiss ignited like a spark to dry tinder. Heat, hunger, the kind of desire that burned away reason. By the time they reached the hotel, they barely made it to his room.

The moment the door clicked shut, everything unraveled. Clothes hit the floor. His mouth found hers—demanding, urgent. She pulled him closer, losing herself in the heat of his body, the taste of his skin. Nothing else existed—no rules, no consequences—just the ache they both needed to satisfy.

They didn't stop. Not that night. Not the next morning.

By sunrise, tangled together in the sheets, the frenzy softened. Ramesh traced lazy patterns on her bare back, his voice softer than she'd ever heard.

"I never do this," he admitted. "But with you..."

She knew what he meant. Whatever was happening between them—it was real. Dangerous, maybe. But real.

Ahana should've felt guilty. She should've walked away.

Instead, she stayed. And by the time they left Macau, it was already too late to turn back.

CHAPTER - 35

SRIPRIYA - Grounded (2010)

Sripriya hadn't slept all night. Her pillow was still damp from the tears she had cried. This was the fourth time. The first three times, Vikram had slapped her behind closed doors. This time, it was in public—a five-star hotel lobby, in front of strangers, flashing cameras just a breath away.

He wasn't the same Vikram she had fallen for—playful, charming, with that easy confidence of a star kid who had the world at his feet. Back then, his protectiveness felt intoxicating. It made her feel safe, special. But somewhere along the way, his warmth had hardened into control. He didn't treat her like a girlfriend anymore—more like something he owned. Something he could break.

In the beginning, being Vikram Seth's girlfriend had its perks. Doors opened faster; creeps backed off. In an industry where a young actress was treated like a commodity, his name was her shield. Without it, she knew the reality—directors, producers, even male co-stars thought sleeping with them was just part of the job description. An unspoken price of survival.

She had brushed off his possessiveness as love—until it turned into something darker. The first slap came when she playfully mentioned a male co-star during dinner. She had laughed it off. A jealous boyfriend—it happens. But the second time? The second time, he wasn't joking.

It was the night they first talked about marriage.

"You know, Vikram, the brand value of a married heroine tanks in this industry," she had said lightly, curling up beside him in bed.

He smiled, but it didn't reach his eyes. "Finish your pending films first. Two years. Then we'll get married."

"And after marriage? What happens to my career?"

His voice sharpened. "What career? My family doesn't let their women work—especially not in films."

Sripriya sat up, stunned. "What are you talking about?"

"What if our kids grow up watching their mother wrapped around other men on screen? What kind of mother does that?"

She tried to keep the mood light. “I don’t know—what kind of father kisses women on-screen and goes home to his wife?”

He laughed, a loud, forced laugh, and she knew he was uncomfortable.

"Seriously, though – no work after marriage. Let's be clear about that," Vikram said, his tone hardening.

"Come on, Vikram! You don't expect me to just sit around the house. I'm as big a star as you are."

He laughed even louder. "Star? If I hadn't come into your life, they would have turned you into a whore. You’d have to sleep your way through every director and producer to get work."

Now she was furious. "I'd rather be a whore to many by choice than a concubine to one by force."

His eyes turned red. He slapped her so hard she fell off the bed.

The next morning, a reporter got wind of the incident, and it was splashed across the papers. After a week, he'd charmed her back, and she'd given in.

She then remembered the third time. She was shooting a film with Ganesh—a modest-budget film where she and her male lead shared a vanity van divided by a thin partition. They'd returned from a shot, and she was changing costumes. Her costume assistant was helping her. Suddenly, Vikram barged in. "Hey, what's up?"

"Hey. What are you doing here, on my set?"

"Was shooting nearby, thought I’d drop by."

"Great. Let me just finish this shot. Then I'll come with you."

"Why are you sharing this vanity van? Why don't you have your own?" He looked at her suspiciously.

"Can we talk about this later? We're losing daylight."

"No, I want to know now," he insisted.

She looked around helplessly. "Priti," she said to her assistant, "can you wait outside for a bit?"

Priti quietly left.

Sripriya was angry. "How dare you come on my set and interrogate me like this? Especially when I told you we're losing the light! What's gotten into you?"

"Listen, I know there's a connecting door between the compartments. So, I want an answer."

"You came here to check up on me? You don't trust me? You're jealous of Ganesh, aren't you?" she yelled, not caring if Ganesh or the crew outside could hear. The damage was already done.

His face darkened. And then—another slap. Harder than before. She crumpled to the floor as the door swung open behind him. Everyone outside heard. Everyone knew.

She should have walked away then. But she didn't.

And now—this.

Her hands trembled as she touched the red, angry mark blooming on her cheek in the bathroom mirror. The imprint of his hand burned into her skin. She knew the drill—ice packs, makeup, long scarves. But this time, it wouldn't be easy to hide.

Her reflection blurred as fresh tears welled up. She couldn't do this anymore. She wouldn't.

Without thinking, she grabbed her phone and dialed the one person who had always stood by her—her mother.

When her mother picked up, Sripriya broke down, her voice cracking under the weight of everything she had held back for too long.

"Maa… I can't take this anymore."

And for the first time in months, she felt something shift—although she felt as if she was looking at a dark, uncertain future, however she knew she had regained her soul, her freedom.

CHAPTER – 36

RAMESH & AHANA - Cupid Strikes (2010)

Ramesh barely had time to breathe. After wrapping the high-octane Mafia shoot in Hong Kong, he flew straight to Los Angeles for another grueling schedule. But even in the chaos of film sets and endless retakes, his mind refused to stay in the present. It kept drifting back—to her.

By the time he returned to Bombay, he should've felt relief. His sprawling sea-facing apartment, the sound of his daughters' laughter, and Tina's warm embrace—this was the life he had built. A life others envied. But something had shifted. A restlessness gnawed at him, a void that none of this could fill. Because he had left his heart behind—with Ahana.

It was absurd. Ramesh had everything—a thriving career, a beautiful family. He had seen co-stars get tangled in messy affairs during outdoor shoots, but he always stayed away from that chaos. Until now. Until Ahana.

And now, he was trapped. Calling her would be crossing a line, a line that could destroy the family he loved. But every day without hearing her voice was torment.

Ahana wasn't doing any better. She had everything she had ever dreamed of—back-to-back blockbusters, a skyrocketing career. Cockpit had smashed the 100-crore mark, cementing her place at the top of Bollywood. But none of it mattered. Not anymore.

All she wanted was him.

But wanting Ramesh meant walking a dangerous path. He wasn't just any man—he was Ramesh Bajaj, beloved superstar, devoted husband, and doting father. His picture-perfect family was plastered across every magazine cover. She wasn't naïve—she knew what people would say. The "other woman." The "homewrecker."

Yet, none of that stopped her heart from aching for him.

She told herself to stay strong. If he wanted her—truly wanted her—he would call. But he didn't. Days turned into weeks, and the silence stretched between them like an open wound.

Until that night.

It was 11:00 PM. Alone in her high-rise apartment, Ahana stared at her phone, her heart pounding. Her rational mind told her to let it go—but her heart wouldn't listen. Before she could stop herself, she dialed his number.

One ring. Two. Three. She cursed herself for being weak. What was she doing?

By the fifth ring, she was ready to hang up—

"Hello."

His voice. Low. Familiar. And it shattered her resolve.

"Hey," she breathed, trying to sound casual.

"What's up?" he asked, his tone unreadable.

"Nothing… Just—wanted to check how your LA shoot went."

A pause. Then a soft, knowing chuckle. "Really? Liar. You've been dying to talk to me."

A blush crept across her face. Even through the phone, he disarmed her. "Don't flatter yourself. I was just—forget it. It's late. I should go."

"Wait." His voice dropped, rough with something deeper. "This attitude… It's why I can't stop thinking about you."

The air shifted. She closed her eyes, feeling a mix of relief and longing wash over her. "I missed you, Ramesh. More than I should have."

"You think I didn't?" His words came fast, raw. "I missed you every damn day. And I don't know how to stop."

"Then why didn't you call?" Her voice trembled. "I thought I was losing my mind. I couldn't focus—I've been drowning in this… in us."

"I wanted to. God, I wanted to." He sighed, the weight of his turmoil bleeding through the line. "But I'm not that guy, Ahana. I've never cheated on Tina—never. And yet, here I am, breaking every rule I ever set for myself."

Tears burned in her eyes, but she held them back. "I hate myself for this too. I never wanted to come between you and your family. But I can't help it—I love you, Ramesh. And it's tearing me apart."

Silence. Heavy. Fragile.

"I don't know what the future holds," he said finally, his voice barely above a whisper. "But this—us—it's real. I've never felt anything like it. And I don't want to lose you."

A sob caught in her throat. “I feel the same. Like I was meant to find you. But how do we do this? How do we keep from falling apart?”

“We’ll figure it out,” he promised, though his voice wavered. “But no one can know. Not here. Not in Bombay. It would destroy everything.”

Ahana bit her lip, torn between love and fear. “Okay,” she whispered. “We’ll be careful.”

“Goodnight, babe,” he murmured, softer now. “Dream of me.”

“I already do,” she confessed.

As the call ended, Ahana leaned back against the wall, heart pounding, the city lights blurring outside her window. She had crossed a line tonight—one they could never uncross.

And there was no turning back.

CHAPTER - 37

KANGNA - Time For Revenge (2010)

The success of *Cockpit* had changed everything for Kangna. Despite being the second lead, her performance had stolen the spotlight. Critics praised her raw intensity, and the audience couldn't get enough of her. The industry was finally paying attention—but Kangna knew better than to trust the glittering smiles. In Bollywood, loyalty was rare, and power games were the norm.

Through it all, one person remained constant—Raj. Once just her agent, now her manager, he was one of the few people she could trust. Straightforward and no-nonsense, Raj had her back in this shark tank of an industry. And if Kangna wanted to survive in Mumbai, she needed people like him.

Offers poured in after *Cockpit*, but Kangna was careful. She and her sister Palak sifted through scripts late into the night, rejecting the glossy, shallow roles. She wanted characters with depth—women who had stories to tell. By the end of the month, she'd signed seven films, securing a hefty advance of over a crore. Palak, ever practical, took charge of Kangna's finances, ensuring they would never struggle again.

The new apartment in Juhu felt like a dream—a sprawling three-bedroom with a sea-facing balcony where Kangna could breathe. In the evenings, she and Palak would sit there with glasses of wine, watching the sun melt into the Arabian Sea. For once, life felt good. Secure.

One of the films she signed was *Baazi*, a big-budget thriller starring Rajesh Raj. The 45-day shoot in Manali was grueling, but Kangna thrived under pressure. Long nights, biting cold, and scenes that demanded vulnerability—it was exactly the kind of challenge she craved. Somewhere between takes and stolen glances, things heated up between her and Rajesh. The chemistry that sizzled on screen slipped behind closed doors. It didn't matter that he was married. In the cocoon of Manali, nothing felt real. But by the time they returned to Mumbai, it was over.

Baazi was a blockbuster. Suddenly, Kangna wasn't just a rising star—she was a force to be reckoned with. She chose her next five films carefully, including two where she was the lead—no male hero towering over her. *Didi Ki Shaadi* and *Another Day* shattered box-office expectations and the long-held myth that women-led films couldn't draw crowds.

For years, Bollywood's elite had dismissed her—a small-town girl with no industry connections. But Kangna had done the impossible. She had made it without bending to anyone's will. And some people didn't like that.

The whispers began. Doors that had once opened easily started closing. Power plays were in motion.

One afternoon, Raj walked into her living room, his face unreadable. "Kangna Mam, Kamal's office called."

Kangna arched a brow. "Kamal Thapar? The Kingmaker?"

"Yeah. Thapar Productions wants you for their next big project. Vikram Seth is the male lead."

She let out a low whistle. "Vikram Seth. Big fish."

"I can arrange a meeting if you're interested," Raj said carefully. He knew her well enough to tread lightly.

Kangna leaned back on the sofa, a slow smile curling her lips. "Sure. Let's meet. Friday, 11 AM."

Raj hesitated. "Kamal doesn't get to the office before noon."

"Then he'll learn to be on time," she said, eyes gleaming with something colder than amusement.

By the time Kangna strolled into Thapar Productions at 12:50 PM, the receptionist was practically vibrating with nerves.

"Good afternoon, ma'am. Kamal sir's been waiting since 10:45," she blurted.

"Oh," Kangna said breezily. "I had an interview. You know how it is." She remembered the hours she'd once spent in this very lobby, invisible and unimportant. Not today.

Kamal rose the second she entered his office. Polished and diplomatic, he masked his irritation with a smile. "Kangna! What a pleasure to see you."

"Likewise," she said, settling into the leather chair across from him.

He wasted no time. "I have a role that's perfect for you. It's a war epic — three army officers leading India to victory. Vikram plays the commanding major, and you'd be his wife."

Kangna tilted her head, feigning interest. "His wife?"

"Yes," Kamal nodded, missing the edge in her voice. "It's a high-profile project—huge cast, major studio backing. This could be your ticket to the big league, Kangna. You work with stars like Vikram Seth, and suddenly, you will be part of the inner circle. You understand how the game works."

She laughed softly, shaking her head. "Kamal, you really think I need this to make it?"

His smile froze. "I'm offering you an opportunity."

"No," Kangna said, leaning forward. "You're offering me a consolation prize. A wife? Standing around in the background while your heroes play soldiers? I don't do background roles anymore. I carry films. My name sells tickets."

Kamal's jaw tightened, but his tone remained smooth. "Careful, Kangna. This industry runs on relationships. You can't just break the system."

Kangna looked him in the eye. "If you're trying to scare me, Kamal, try harder. Your 'system' is built on nepotism and old-school power plays. And guess what? Audiences are changing. People are tired of watching the same five faces recycled in every movie. You've spent years pulling the strings, deciding who gets to be a star. But here I am—without your blessings. And I'm not going anywhere."

He leaned back, his expression hardening. "You're ambitious. I respect that. But don't forget who still controls this town. Careers can be made—or broken—with a single phone call."

Kangna stood up, smoothing her dress. "I'm not scared of your phone calls, Kamal. And just so we're clear—I never wanted your film. I came here today for one reason—to make you wait, just like you made me wait years ago."

She turned on her heel and strode out of his office without another word.

In this city, revenge wasn't loud. It was quiet, calculated—and sometimes, it looked like success.

CHAPTER - 38

SRIPRIYA - On Her Own (2010)

The aroma of homemade sambhar filled the air as Sripriya scooped a handful of rice with her fingers, savoring the familiar warmth. Her mother sat across from her, eyes fixed on the faint yellowish bruise along Sripriya's cheekbone. It had been three days since Vikram had slapped her—three long days of silence, tension, and flashing cameras. The swelling had faded, but the sting of humiliation still burned.

Outside their apartment complex, three journalists had made the front gate their second home. Cameras slung over their shoulders, waiting—hoping—for a glimpse of her. Sripriya and her mother hadn't even dared to step onto the balcony. The news had exploded across TV channels and tabloids, dragging their lives into a public spectacle. Everyone had a theory—some painted her as a victim, others as an opportunist. The truth, as always, was lost somewhere in the noise.

Her mother broke the silence, her voice firm. "You have to break up with him, Priya. Enough is enough."

Sripriya kept eating, but her appetite faded. Deep down, she knew her mother was right. The fairytale romance with Vikram—the flowers, the gifts, the whispered promises—was long gone. In its place stood a man who used his power like a weapon. The slap wasn't the first sign, but it was the loudest.

"You hear me, Priya?" Her mother's voice trembled with urgency. "This boy—he will destroy you. I warned you from the beginning. He will never marry you, and he will never change."

Sripriya set her plate aside and wiped her hands, frustration flickering across her face. "I know, Ma." Her voice was quiet but heavy. "You've said it a hundred times. But let's not pretend he hasn't helped me. Without him, do you think I'd be here? He opened doors no one else would. And in this industry…" She let out a bitter laugh. "Without a powerful man behind you, they'll eat you alive before you even get a chance."

Her mother sighed; pain etched into her face. "If only your father were still here," she murmured.

Sripriya's heart tightened at the mention of her father—the man who had believed in her dreams long before the world had. "Even Papa couldn't change this, Ma. Girls like us; middle-class backgrounds with no connections; we're always at their mercy. Either you play their game, or you get crushed under it."

Tears welled up in her mother's eyes. Sripriya stood up and wrapped her arms around her. "Don't cry," she whispered. "We've come too far to break now. I'll find a way out. I promise." A new determination flickered inside her. "I'm ending it with him. For good."

She pulled away and walked to the mirror, reaching for her makeup kit. With practiced precision, she brushed a subtle streak of red across her cheek—just enough to make it look fresh, raw. A reminder of what he'd done. If Vikram wanted to play dirty, she could play smarter.

As their car pulled out of the gate, the waiting journalists pounced. Two cameramen lunged toward the window; lenses hungry for the next headline. Sripriya lowered the glass—just enough for them to catch the angry flush on her cheek.

The reporters swarmed closer. "Sripriya Ma'am! Is it true Vikram hit you? Are you breaking up? Did he threaten you?"

She raised a hand, silencing their chaotic questions. Then, in a voice steady and sharp, she delivered the words she knew would dominate every news cycle:

"Yes, the reports are true. I was assaulted by Vikram. I've decided to end our relationship. I will not tolerate a man who disrespects me. We're done—forever. I deserve better."

The cameras flashed relentlessly as she rolled the window back up. The car glided forward, leaving the frenzied media in its wake. Inside, Sripriya leaned back, heart pounding but steady.

By the time they reached the highway, her words had already hit every major news channel. Screens across the nation played her statement on loop, dissecting every expression, every syllable. Only a handful of people had witnessed Vikram's slap—but now, the entire country watched as she struck back in the most public way possible.

A cold smile touched her lips. He thought he could break her. Instead, she had turned his power against him.

Let the world watch. She wasn't hiding anymore.

CHAPTER - 39

SRIPRIYA - Crash Landing (2011)

A month had passed since Sripriya's explosive statement about Vikram Seth shook the industry. In just four weeks, her entire world had flipped upside down. What once felt like a dazzling, unstoppable carousel of movie sets, premieres, and paparazzi flashes had ground to a cold, silent halt. The phones had stopped ringing. The invitations dried up. And her name—once plastered across every headline—was now being carefully erased.

Before she spoke out, Sripriya had twelve films in various stages of production—two of them completed and primed for release. She had been unstoppable. Untouchable. But now, everything had changed.

The first movie, *One Two Ka Four*, was supposed to be a blockbuster. It was a glitzy, big-budget Thapar home production—produced and directed by Kamal Thapar himself—starring Vikram Seth and her. The release date was set, the posters were up across the city, and the trailer was breaking records online. But days after her statement, everything shifted.

The studio pulled the movie back into post-production without warning. First, the posters vanished. Then, the trailer was quietly taken down. When the new trailer dropped a week later, it was as if Sripriya had never existed. She was cut out of every frame. No close-ups. No credit. No trace. She knew exactly what was coming next—her role would be butchered, her best scenes deleted, and whatever scraps were left would be her weakest moments.

And that's precisely what happened.

When the movie finally hit theatres, she barely had three minutes of screen time—awkwardly edited and out of context. The industry knew why. Everyone knew Kamal and Vikram were more than just colleagues. They were co-conspirators, gatekeepers of a world, in which power always trumped truth. Sripriya had laughed along when they'd played these games on other actresses—blackballing careers over bruised egos. But now, she was the target. And there was nothing funny about it.

The second film—*Rain*—was different. It wasn't flashy or star-studded. It was a small-budget, indie gem produced by Mr. Kher, an old-school filmmaker with a heart for storytelling. The script was raw and intimate—a character-driven drama where Sripriya shined. For once, it wasn't about box-office numbers. It was about art.

Ganesh had been excited too—he believed *Rain* could surprise everyone. The plan was simple: a low-key release in 600 theatres, banking on word-of-mouth to build momentum. If the film found its audience, Mr. Kher even hoped to pitch it for the Oscars. For Sripriya, it was a lifeline—a chance to reclaim her career on her terms.

But that hope shattered on release day.

Her phone buzzed early that morning. It was Mr. Kher. She answered immediately, heart pounding with anticipation.

"Hello, Kher Sir?"

His voice trembled. "Sripriya… we're finished."

Her stomach twisted. "Why? What happened?"

"They blocked us," he said, his voice heavy with defeat. "The multiplexes—they've shut us out. We're only screening in 50 standalone theatres."

For a moment, she couldn't speak. The words didn't make sense.

"But… but the contracts—"

"It doesn't matter," he interrupted softly. "We're wiped out before we even got a chance."

She wanted to scream. She knew exactly who was behind it. The Khilji group—a shadowy empire that controlled 350 multiplexes across the country—had pulled the strings. And Kamal and Vikram? They had ties everywhere. One call was all it took to bury her and destroy Mr. Kher in the process.

By noon, reality hit hard. Without multiplex screens, Rain was doomed. It wouldn't reach the audience who would understand it. There would be no Oscars, no second chances—just silence.

And it didn't stop there.

One by one, her other films crumbled. Productions stalled without explanation. Scripts were "being rewritten." Budgets mysteriously vanished. Every excuse led back to the same brutal truth:

No one wanted to touch Sripriya.

The message was clear. She had broken the industry's unspoken rule—you don't go against the powerful. And now, they were making her pay.

A month ago, her career had soared like a kite on a clear, blue sky. Now, the string had been cut, and she was plummeting—faster than she could catch herself.

And there was no one left to break her fall.

CHAPTER - 40
AHANA - Loose Control (2011)

The Bajajs knew how to throw a party—and when they did, Bollywood showed up. Their lavish soirées were the stuff of industry legend, a magnet for stars, producers, and power players. Tonight was no different. It was their sixteenth wedding anniversary, and Tina Bajaj had pulled out all the stops. The sprawling terrace of their sea-facing Juhu penthouse gleamed under fairy lights, with servers from the Taj Group weaving through the crowd, offering crystal flutes of champagne and delicacies curated to perfection.

Tina ran her home like a seasoned director—no detail too small, no mistake unnoticed. She called the shots while her husband, Ramesh Bajaj, played the charming superstar everyone adored. On-screen, he was Bollywood royalty. Off-screen, he was the ever-doting husband and father. At least, that's how it seemed.

By 11:30 pm, the party was in full swing. The elite of the industry—directors, actors, influencers—danced under the stars while vintage jazz floated through the night. At midnight, a five-tier cake from The Boston Cupcakery took center stage. It was a masterpiece—red velvet, frosted with smooth white cream, topped with a miniature figurine of a man on a bended knee, offering a ring to a woman in a glittering gown. Everyone cooed over it, capturing it for their social media feeds.

Ramesh played the perfect host—smiling, laughing, ensuring every guest felt special. But the performance faltered the second his eyes locked onto hers.

Ahana.

She had slipped in quietly, dressed in an emerald-green satin dress that clung to her curves like temptation itself. Her dark hair fell over one shoulder in loose waves, lips painted the color of sin. She stood a few rows behind Tina, and for a split second, the noise faded. The air grew heavier.

Ramesh froze with the first slice of cake still in his hand. A wildfire of longing tore through him. It had been weeks—weeks of stolen moments and unsaid words building into something uncontrollable. But here, with his wife inches away, Ahana was untouchable. And yet, he couldn't tear his eyes away.

The night wore on. By 4 am, most of the guests had trickled out. Only a few close friends remained, lounging in the dim glow of the post-party haze. It was the dangerous hour—the time when masks slipped, and truths surfaced.

And that's when it happened.

In a quiet corner of the study, Ramesh found her. Or maybe she found him. It didn't matter. What mattered was the heat between them—unspoken but electric. Without a word, he pulled her close.

"Ramesh, no," she whispered, hands pushing weakly against his chest.

"You don't mean that," he murmured, his lips grazing the side of her neck.

God, she didn't. Weeks of restraint shattered as she tangled her fingers in his hair, dragging his mouth to hers. It was desperate—hungry—like they were both starving. For a few reckless minutes, nothing else existed.

Until the door swung open.

Tina.

Ramesh reacted fast—too fast. With a sharp pivot, he stepped away from Ahana and pointed at the painting on the wall. "I was just telling Ahana how this piece reminds me of Tuscany," he said, his voice steady, heart pounding.

Tina, bleary-eyed and exhausted, barely glanced at them. "Mmm… you're still entertaining guests? I'm going to bed," she said, yawning as she shuffled away.

When the door clicked shut, Ahana let out a shaky breath.

"That was insane," she whispered.

Ramesh smirked, but his pulse hadn't slowed. "You drive me insane."

4:30 am.

When Ahana finally reached home, her phone buzzed.

Ramesh: "Hey! That was close. What got into you?"

Ahana: "You kissed me first, superstar. Care to explain yourself?"

Ramesh: "A wild cat's spirit possessed me. I can't think straight anymore."

Ahana: "Careful. This cat has claws. And I'm not afraid to use them."

Ramesh: "I'm begging to be tamed, your majesty."

She laughed softly to herself, fingers dancing over the keyboard.

Ahana: "You're reckless. Tonight was your anniversary, Ramesh. What if she caught us for real?"

A long pause. Then—

Ramesh: "Maybe I wanted her to."

Ahana's heart slammed against her ribs.

Ahana: "Don't joke about that."

Ramesh: "I'm not. Hiding this… it's exhausting. I want you all the time. And sometimes, I wonder—what if it all just came out?"

Ahana: "You're crazy."

Ramesh: "Only for you."

Their affair burned hot and fast—messages at midnight, stolen phone calls between shoots, a love too fierce to contain. Ahana lived alone, but for Ramesh, balancing his double life was becoming a dangerous game.

And the game was about to get more complicated.

A week later, over brunch, Tina casually dropped a bombshell.

"You know, Ramesh," she said, slicing into an avocado toast, "you do all these endorsements. Why don't you recommend Ahana? She's so talented—and sweet. You said you needed a girl for that toothpaste ad next month."

Ramesh froze mid-bite, struggling to keep his face neutral. Where was this coming from?

"She's become such a good friend," Tina added, smiling. "She's all alone in the city. We should help her out."

The irony burned in his chest. His wife—his innocent, trusting wife—was asking him to boost his mistress's career.

Later that day, he called Ahana.

"Hey," he said, his voice tight. "What kind of game are you playing with my wife?"

Ahana laughed softly. "Relax. I didn't plan this. We were just talking, one thing led to another… and well, your wife thinks I deserve a break."

"Unbelievable."

"Don't worry," she purred. "I'm not going to expose us. But I won't apologize for wanting more of you."

Ramesh exhaled sharply. "I'll get you the ad."

"You'd better," she teased. "It's our perfect excuse to be together."

For now, the secret held. But the line between love and disaster was razor-thin—and they were both dangerously close to crossing it.

CHAPTER - 41

TINA - Woken Up With A Jolt (2013)

The toothpaste ad shoot was scheduled at the breathtaking Catherine Falls in Ooty—a two-day affair that felt more like a secret getaway. Ramesh and Ahana occupied two lavish presidential suites at the Savoy, side by side, while the rest of the crew bunked in a nearby cottage. Ahana's suite remained untouched—except for the rumpled sheets they intentionally left behind each morning, a calculated move to keep the gossip at bay. If Hong Kong had been the spark, Ooty was the wildfire. They were consumed by each other—urgent, reckless, insatiable. Every stolen moment intensified their hunger, making it painfully clear—this wasn't just an affair. It was something much greater.

A year had passed since Ooty, and the fire hadn't died down. Ramesh and Ahana had shot three more campaigns together—always choosing remote locations where no one could intrude. Ramesh had even started pulling strings to get Ahana roles in his projects, especially if they involved outstation shoots. Whispers followed them everywhere. People in the industry weren't blind— and tongues had started wagging a wee bit, but wagging nevertheless. The smoke had not reached Ramesh's home as yet.

Maybe it was the thrill of danger, or maybe they just stopped caring—but Ramesh and Ahana were getting reckless. She wasn't just his co-star anymore—she was everywhere. At industry events, in his productions, even in his home. Under the pretense of being Tina's friend, Ahana had practically become part of the family. The lines between wife and mistress blurred, and Ramesh didn't seem to mind. If anything, he fed the illusion—his love for Ahana growing louder, bolder, drowning out everything else.

On Ramesh's birthday, their dangerous game hit a new level. The house buzzed with energy—an exclusive guest list packed with Bollywood royalty and cricket legends. The India-Australia series was in full swing, and Ramesh, ever the showman, had three Australian players over, along with Indian cricketers. The air was thick with laughter, whisky, and the sharp scent of secrets.

Tina floated through the crowd, the perfect hostess—smiling, chatting—but her eyes never left her husband. She saw the exact moment it happened. Ramesh, standing tall and proud, called Ahana to his side. Without hesitation, he took her hand—held it a beat too long—and introduced her to the Australian cricketers like she was someone important. Someone who mattered.

From across the room, Tina felt it—an ache that curled cold and sharp in her chest. For the first time, she felt invisible in her own home. But she said nothing. Not yet.

A month later, the façade cracked. A phone call changed everything.

"Tina… I don't know if I should be saying this—but there are rumors," her friend's voice was heavy with concern. "People are talking about Ramesh and Ahana. It's not just work—he's recommending her for everything. They say—"

"I know how this industry works," Tina cut her off, forcing a lightness she didn't feel. But as she hung up, her hand trembled.

The cracks widened. Ramesh was barely home before midnight anymore—always busy, always elsewhere. And when he did come home, his touch was colder. His excuses thinner. Suspicion gnawed at her sanity, growing louder each day.

One night Ramesh came in at 2 am. Tina lay awake when she heard the front door click shut. The soft shuffle of his feet across the hardwood floor. The faint scent of cologne mixed with something else—something foreign.

When he slipped into bed, she didn't wait.

"Where were you?" Her voice cut through the dark.

Ramesh froze. Then, chuckling softly, he turned towards her. "Awake? Damn. I was trying not to wake you."

"I asked—where were you?"

His smile faltered. "What is this—an interrogation?" He tried to make a joke of it. "Do I need a lawyer?"

"Cut the act, Ramesh," her voice trembled, anger barely held in check. "Where the hell were you?"

He sighed, shifting back against the pillows. "At the office. I needed some quiet space to think."

"At 2 a.m.?" She didn't blink. "Or were you with Ahana?"

The room turned ice-cold.

His jaw tightened, eyes flashing. "Are you really serious right now? What would Ahana be doing in my office?"

Tina pushed herself up, heart pounding in her chest. “Don’t treat me like I’m stupid. I know what people are saying. My friends. The media. Hell, even Google has an opinion on it!” She grabbed her phone, shoving it toward him—headlines glowing in the dark.

‘Ramesh Bajaj’s New Muse? His Growing Closeness to Rising Star Ahana Kapoor!’

He took the phone from her hand, tossing it aside. “Jesus, Tina. You’ve been reading gossip columns now?” His voice dripped with condescension. “You know how these tabloids work—anything for TRPs. I thought you were smarter than this.”

Her throat burned. “I’m not imagining things. At your birthday party—you held her hand. In front of everyone.”

His heartbeat thundered in his ears. He hated how sharp she was—how much she noticed. “I introduce hundreds of people. What’s your point?”

“You don’t hold their hand like they’re your wife,” she snapped.

His facade cracked—just for a second. But it was enough.

When he leaned over and pulled her into his arms, the warmth felt hollow. “Sixteen years, Tina. Have I ever given you a reason to doubt me? Ever?” His breath was hot against her skin. “I love you. I chose you.”

The fight drained out of her, leaving something more painful—hope.

“I’m sorry,” she whispered, tears stinging her eyes. “I’m being ridiculous. I love you, Ramesh.”

She wanted to believe him—wanted to feel close again. With quiet desperation, she reached for him, pulling his shirt over his head, peeling away the distance between them.

But when she kissed him—he pulled away.

“Tina… I’m exhausted,” he said, voice flat. “Can we do this tomorrow?”

She laughed softly—but it didn’t reach her eyes. “Tomorrow…”

But deep down, she knew. Tomorrow would never come.

And for the first time in sixteen years—Tina realized she might already have lost him.

CHAPTER - 42

SAHIL - Starry Eyed (2010)

Sahil Deb grew up in the bustling city of Guwahati, Assam. Born into a middle-class family, life wasn't easy, but Sahil was never one to back down from a challenge. His parents, both government employees, instilled a strong work ethic in him. He excelled in school, and after years of relentless effort, he graduated from the Guwahati School of Engineering. But while his classmates dreamed of stable corporate jobs, Sahil dreamed in technicolor—of bright lights, red carpets, and seeing his name in bold letters on the big screen.

Bollywood was calling. And Sahil was ready to answer.

With nothing but a suitcase full of dreams, he landed in Mumbai—wide-eyed and hungry. The city was a beast, unforgiving and chaotic, but he didn't care. He shared a crammed 1BHK apartment with seven other struggling actors, surviving on cutting chai and stale vada pavs. Days blurred into nights as he hustled—visiting casting offices, standing in endless audition lines, and chasing the faintest whisper of an opportunity.

What set Sahil apart, though, was his undeniable presence. Tall, with sharp features and an easy charm, he quickly caught the attention of casting agents. Within a year, he landed a string of endorsements—watches, colognes, even a popular energy drink. His face started appearing on billboards, and his effortless charisma made him a favorite with the masses. Yet, he wanted more—he wanted to be a movie star. And in Bollywood, good looks were only the opening act.

His break came when an independent production house was casting for a film based on a bestselling novel, *Shikara*—a heart-wrenching love story set in a sleepy North Indian town. The producers wanted fresh faces. Sahil auditioned, gave it everything he had, and walked out without any expectations. Days later, his phone buzzed. He had the lead role.

When *Shikara* hit the screens, it exploded. Critics raved about his raw, authentic performance, and fans couldn't get enough of him. Overnight, Sahil Deb was Bollywood's newest obsession. He earned a Best Debut nomination at the National Film Awards, and soon, the offers poured in. Among them was one from the formidable Amar Gehlot—a powerhouse producer known for launching careers and controlling destinies.

Sahil, still riding high on his newfound fame, signed a three-year exclusive contract with Amar's production house. It seemed like a dream come true. Until it wasn't.

To cash in on his popularity, Amar's team fast-tracked another movie, *Pure Soul*—a romantic comedy that showcased Sahil's easygoing charm and sharp comic timing. It smashed box office records, cementing his position as Bollywood's golden boy. But behind the glitz and glamour, there was a darker game unfolding—one that Sahil never saw coming.

Amar's contract wasn't just about movies—it was a stranglehold. Hidden in the fine print was a clause giving Amar the power to "loan" Sahil out to other producers. On the surface, it seemed harmless—until Sahil realized that these deals came with strings attached.

The real test came when Amar called him into his sleek, glass-walled office, one afternoon.

"There's a project with Kamal Thapar," Amar said, lighting a cigar. "It's a big-budget movie to be shot in international locations. You'll be the lead."

Sahil's heart raced. Working with Kamal—one of Bollywood's biggest directors—could skyrocket his career. "I'm in," he said, without hesitation.

Amar smiled thinly. "Good. But you know how it works, right?"

Sahil frowned. "What do you mean?"

Amar leaned back, exhaling a cloud of smoke. "Kamal… you know about him right…he has his preferences. You play the game, or you're out." His meaning was clear—and revolting.

Sahil's stomach churned. He knew about Kamal's sexual orientation and had heard many stories about the casting couch. Yet it was a bit too much to be proposed so directly.

He had worked too hard to sell himself like a commodity. "I'm not doing it," he said, his voice firm. "He can find someone else."

Amar's smile vanished. "Careful, Sahil. It's a once in a lifetime offer. No one says no to Kamal."

But Sahil walked out, dignity intact. He had no idea he had just signed his own death warrant in Bollywood.

The fallout was swift and brutal. Amar handed the role to Rajvir—a desperate, pliable actor who knew how to play by the industry's unspoken rules. Within months, Rajvir's star shot past Sahil's. And Amar? He made sure Sahil would never get another break.

Doors that had once swung open now slammed shut. His phone stopped ringing. Directors who had once fawned over him, refused to take his calls. He was still under Amar's contract—trapped—and the industry had blacklisted him.

After a long wait, the contract with Amar Gehlot was over, and Sahil heaved a sigh of relief. But it was too soon. He had already been blacklisted, and no one was prepared to work with him.

Even after two hit films, Sahil was struggling. He had no godfathers in the industry to support him at the time of his need. But thanks to his girlfriend Shamita, Sahil was still managing to survive. Sahil and Shamita had worked together in an endorsement in the first year, and they had started dating. They had been together for almost four years now, and were in a committed relationship. And with Shamita's moral support, Sahil kept trying his luck. He had understood that these bigshots were not going to give him any work. He started approaching independent producers for films, like a fresher. The agent, whom he had appointed a year ago, on a monthly retainer plus commission based on signed projects, had not managed even a single contract for Sahil.

The months of forced idleness gnawed at him. Every day, Sahil watched Rajvir's face plastered on magazines, while his own career crumbled before his eyes. The depression crept in, slow and heavy.

Through it all, the only person who stood by him was Shamita. One evening, as Shamita walked in after a long day on her TV set, she found Sahil sitting in the dark. His face was shadowed with frustration.

She could not see him in this state."Sahil, what is this Reddy doing for you. You are paying him 30,000 rupees a month, and he has not given you a single project in a year."

"You know Shamita how these big producrs have got the word out against me. No one dares to give me work."

"Yeah, but then what is the point of continuing with Reddy. I heard at the studios that he is quite close to Umesh Khosla."

"Really?"

"Yes, I think you should get rid of this Reddy guy and look for some other agent. In fact, I know this girl, Usha Biswas. She is representing Nidhi and came to meet her on the set. Seems like a very sincere girl."

"I think you are right, Shamita. Can you set up a meeting with her? Let us talk to her, and if it works out, we can let Reddy go."

"Cool, let me talk to her tomorrow and set up a meeting with her soon."

Sahil had brightened up a little, Shamita had given him some hope and hope is what keeps one alive and kicking.

Sahil and Shamita were waiting for Usha the next evening at the Love & Latte coffee shop in Lokhandwala.

She spotted them and came over. "Hello Shamita," She extended her hand.

Shamita introduced them, though Sahil needed no introduction, "Hello Sir!"

"Just call me Sahil."

Sure, Sir."

They all laughed, and immediately a rapport was stuck.

Shamita was right. Usha was bright and sincere. She was an MBA degree holder and worked in a PR agency before being approached by a few actors to handle their work, and she had become an independent celebrity manager.

Sahil found Usha to be a sharp, no-nonsense woman with a reputation for hustling hard. She agreed to represent him for half of what Reddy charged. It was a gamble, but Sahil had nothing left to lose.

Within a month, Usha worked her magic. Fox Studios was casting for a biopic on a boxing legend, and she got Sahil in the door. He nailed the audition.

When the movie released, it shattered expectations. Critics who had once written him off now hailed him as a “force to be reckoned with.” The box office numbers soared.

Sahil was back. And this time, no one could ignore him.

He signed twelve new endorsement deals and became the face of a top athletic brand. Producers—corporate and independent—lined up with scripts. The old guard tried to block him out, but the audience had spoken. Sahil Deb was no longer a passing sensation.

He was a threat.

And he wasn’t going anywhere.

CHAPTER - 43
KAMAL - Sky Is The Limit (2010)

The All-India Prime Awards—AIPA—had evolved into the most glamorous, exclusive, and prestigious event in Bollywood. What started as an opportunistic project by Kamal Thapar and his sharp-witted journalist friend, Rakhi Dutt, had become a power hub where careers were made, secrets were traded, and fortunes shifted. Now in its seventh edition, AIPA was no longer just an awards show—it was a statement. And this year, it was making the boldest one yet.

Monte Carlo; playground of the ultra-rich; a glittering jewel on the French Riviera where luxury wasn't just a lifestyle—it was the law. The tiny country of Monaco, second smallest in size; next only to Vatican City, housed a population where millionaires were the average and billionaires were the elite. It was a tax haven where wealth moved silently, and so did secrets. This was where Kamal had decided to host the most extravagant AIPA yet. And if the rumors were true, he wasn't footing the bill.

Word on the circuit was that a Saudi Sheikh—infamous for his decadent tastes in women, wine, and everything in between—was the mysterious benefactor behind the spectacle. He wasn't just a guest; he was part-owner of the iconic *Hotel de Paris*, the venue for the weekend's debauchery disguised as an award ceremony. For the cameras, it was about celebrating cinematic excellence. Behind closed doors? It was a power summit—deals worth millions brokered over vintage champagne, alliances formed in private suites, and desires indulged in, without consequence.

Everyone who mattered was on the guest list. The dynasties of Bollywood—Vikram Seth, Ramji Dutt, Shobhit Banerjee, Ranjan Raj, and the Rajesh Raj empire—were present in full force. Business tycoons with their checkbooks open, music moguls eager to strike new partnerships, and international media barons looking to claim a piece of the Indian entertainment goldmine—this was where the real business happened.

Of course, Kamal was at the center of it all—host, orchestrator, and puppet master. Sharing the stage with him was Amna, Bollywood's rising princess, whose allure had only grown stronger. Kangna, once the industry's rebellious outsider, was not only invited but was nominated for a major award. It was Kamal's way of signaling that no matter how far you tried to stray, eventually, you had to come back to the empire he had built.

But not everyone got a seat at the table. Actors who refused to play by the industry's unspoken rules found themselves conveniently excluded. Actresses, on the other hand—whether A-list stars or rising starlets—were always welcome. Their presence wasn't just encouraged, it was expected. They were the sparkle that masked the shadowy deals taking place in the back rooms.

Beyond the flashing cameras and designer gowns, the real power players were arriving. Sheikhs from Saudi and Dubai, their eyes sharp and wallets deeper than imagination. Indian underworld figures—silent, invisible, but always present. Politicians who shaped laws by day and bent them by night. And the fixers—the ones who made problems disappear and dreams come true, for the right price.

This wasn't just Bollywood's biggest night. It was a chessboard, and Kamal Thapar was moving the pieces. Here, under the dazzling lights of Monte Carlo, the lines between glamour and power blurred—and everyone was playing for keeps.

CHAPTER - 44

KAMAL - At Cannes (2010)

The black stretch limousines glided through the glittering streets of Monte Carlo, pulling up one after another in the grand circular driveway of the Hotel de Paris. The air buzzed with an electric mix of power and extravagance. As the doors swung open, a parade of the world's elite stepped out—business magnates, movie stars, and political heavyweights—each arrival more opulent than the last.

Inside, the marble-clad lobby gleamed under cascading chandeliers. The hotel staff, polished and discreet, anticipated the crush of VIPs. Whenever the crowd swelled, guests were quietly ushered into private lounges—a world of crystal flutes filled with vintage champagne, handcrafted cocktails, and delicate hors d'oeuvres served on silver trays. Nothing was off-limits. This wasn't just an awards ceremony—it was an exclusive playground for the global elite.

The guest list read like a billionaire's club directory. Private jets touched down at the Nice Côte d'Azur Airport in quick succession—Gulfstreams, Bombardiers, even the occasional Airbus ACJ. But it was the arrival of a certain Indian business tycoon that turned heads. He didn't just arrive—he made an entrance. His personal Boeing 737, a flying palace retrofitted with a nightclub-worthy bar, velvet lounges, and two opulent bedrooms, soared in with a guest list as outrageous as his lifestyle.

Onboard, the party was already in full swing. Bollywood's brightest stars mingled with high-profile politicians and top-tier industrialists. Vintage whisky poured freely, and crystal glasses clinked in mid-air to the pulse of a live DJ. By the time the plane touched down, the guests were already flushed with alcohol and high on the thrill of the night to come.

CHAPTER - 45
KAMAL - Power Play (2010)

Once they had settled in their rooms, Kamal picked up the intercom and dialed Kangna's room.

"Hey, Kangna. Hope I'm not disturbing you."

"No, Kamal. What's up?"

"Can you come to my room? There's someone I want you to meet."

A pause. Too long.

"If it's a problem, we can meet in the lobby," he added, his voice smooth but knowing.

"No, it's fine. I'll be there."

When Kangna walked into Kamal's suite, she expected to see Vikram Seth, who was there nursing a drink—but it was Umesh Khosla; the unexpecrted guest, sitting there, legs crossed, expression cold. The atmosphere shifted the moment she stepped in.

Kamal stood up, smiling. Vikram, already a couple of drinks in, greeted her with an exaggerated hug. Umesh? He barely nodded.

"Hello, Sir," Kangna said quietly, her voice laced with caution.

Kangna said, "Kamal, thank you for inviting me to this function."

Kamal, ever the charmer, leaned back against the sofa. "You should thank the organizers for inviting you. I'm just a guest like you."

Kangna let out a soft, knowing laugh. Everyone in the room was too seasoned to believe that. These awards were never just about talent.

Vikram, his voice louder than necessary, raised his glass. "Kamal, this is insane! I've never seen an award function like this—not even in Hollywood! Private jets, designer outfits, a freakin' royal treatment!"

Kangna arched an eyebrow. "And who's footing the bill? I mean, satellite rights can't be that profitable."

Vikram waved her off. "Who cares? As long as we're treated like kings and queens, baby, that's all that matters."

She tilted her head. "Nothing's free, Vikram. Someone's always paying—and trust me, they expect their pound of flesh."

A tense silence slipped between them. Kamal shifted uncomfortably, but Umesh was the first to break it.

"Bollywood's a global powerhouse now," Umesh said, his voice clipped. "Bigger than Hollywood in sheer volume. And those who understand that—well, they know how to play the game. It's all about cooperation, dear. It's about give-and-take. You take care of people, and people take care of you."

Kangna's eyes narrowed. "What do you mean by cooperation? Spell it out for me."

Umesh's mouth curled into a thin smile. "Why don't you just read between the lines?"

She leaned forward, her arms crossed. "I had rather hear it from the horse's mouth. Why don't you tell me clearly without beating about the bush?"

Kamal glanced toward Vikram, who suddenly found his drink more interesting. Umesh, however, wasn't one for subtlety.

"Your performance in *Another Day*—I liked it. You've got talent. But talent's not enough in this industry. It's connections, loyalty—the right kind of loyalty—that matters." He locked eyes with her. "If you cooperate with us, the Best Actress award is yours. Simple."

A chill crept up her spine, but her face stayed impassive. "Cooperate how?"

Umesh didn't blink. "You work in the films we offer. You back us—publicly and privately. No stray comments. No controversies. And when we call, you answer."

Her fists curled in her lap. "And the fine print?"

"You already know," Umesh said coolly. "You stay in line. You keep your mouth shut when it matters. And you don't bite the hand that feeds you."

Kangna felt her blood boil, but her voice was cold. "Let me get this straight. You want me to lie when it's convenient for you? Be a puppet who nods along while you rig the game? Sell out the people who actually believe in me?"

Umesh's patience cracked. "Don't be naive. This is how it works, sweetheart."

She stood up, her chair scraping loudly against the floor. “Sweetheart?” Her voice cut through the room like a knife. “Is that how you buy your way out of this conversation—with cheap words and expensive bribes?”

Kamal shifted in his seat, uncomfortable. Vikram’s jaw clenched, but he stayed quiet.

“You’re right about one thing, Mr. Khosla,” she continued, her tone razor-sharp. “It’s a game. But I’m not your pawn. You think I’ll sell my dignity for a trophy? I’d rather burn it to the ground.”

Umesh’s face darkened. “I told you.” he muttered, turning to Kamal. “She’s too stubborn. A lost cause.”

“Better stubborn than spineless,” Kangna snapped. “You can keep your award—I’m not for sale.”

Without waiting for a reply, she turned on her heel and stormed out of the room.

By the time they could react, her suitcase was packed. Five minutes later, she was out of the hotel—leaving the glittering façade and their dirty deals behind.

CHAPTER - 46

KAMAL - Seven Seas (2010)

At 9 PM, the awards ceremony promised to be a spectacle. A custom-built venue on the French Riviera sparkled under a canopy of lights as paparazzi swarmed the red carpet. Inside, the crème de la crème settled into their velvet-draped seats, champagne flowing as smoothly as the evening's carefully orchestrated schedule. The awards? Almost an afterthought.

No scandals, no awkward moments, just an ocean of glittering smiles and carefully curated charm. The biggest names in Bollywood basked under the limelight, clutching their golden trophies while cameras flashed like fireworks. Everyone said the right things. Actors gushed about the "visionary filmmakers" who shaped their careers. Directors raved about the "once-in-a-generation" talent they worked with. It was a symphony of mutual admiration—and everyone played their part to perfection. This night wasn't about trophies—it was about power moves, whispered deals, and being seen.

But the real event began after the awards. As the clock inched towards midnight, an exclusive after-party sprawled across the rooftop terrace. Ice sculptures glistened beside fire pits, and world-renowned chefs curated a midnight feast of truffle-laden delicacies and fresh Mediterranean seafood. Conversations swirled—some about million-dollar investments, others about scandalous affairs. For the right people, nothing was out of reach.

And for the select few—the inner circle—this was only the beginning.

The next morning, while most guests nursed their hangovers in silk-sheeted suites, a private convoy escorted 200 of the most powerful attendees to the marina. Awaiting them was the Seven Seas, a six-star luxury cruise liner, gleaming under the Riviera sun. For five days, they would drift through the sapphire waters of the Mediterranean—no press, no rules, only endless indulgence.

Stops in Cannes and Nice promised days of boutique shopping and sun-soaked beaches, but on the open sea, the real parties would unfold—champagne baths, secret rendezvous, and deals sealed under the cover of night. For those aboard, it wasn't just about luxury—it was about living in a world where no desire was too extravagant, and no boundary was unbreakable.

Though it boasted 350 opulent suites and a staff of 550, this voyage catered to an exclusive guest list—where fame and fortune were the only currencies that mattered.

At the heart of the ship was the Regent Suite, a sprawling kingdom of indulgence. Walls wrapped in genuine leather, a private terrace with uninterrupted views of the ocean, a golden bathtub glinting under the soft glow of imported Italian lights. It even had a private spa—a sanctuary for those who needed to wash away their sins.

Five world-class restaurants offered anything the palate craved—from hand-rolled sushi flown in from Tokyo to aged Wagyu beef carved tableside. In the wine cellars, over 3,000 bottles of the rarest vintages waited to be poured—each glass more expensive than the last.

The Constellation Theatre was a jewel in itself—a venue with velvet seats for 700, promising live performances every night. But the real entertainment? That would happen behind closed doors.

As guests stepped aboard, they were greeted with a chilled glass of Dom Pérignon in a lobby that dripped with excess. Above their heads hung a million-dollar crystal chandelier—an unapologetic symbol of the wealth floating through the room. This wasn't just a cruise. It was a statement.

Moments later, a sleek voice crackled to life across the ship's private TV network. Darren, the Seven Seas' charismatic entertainment director, flashed a dazzling smile from the screen. "Welcome aboard," he drawled, promising a week where boundaries would blur and reality would feel like a distant memory.

As the sun dipped below the horizon, the guests gathered on the main deck—flutes of champagne shimmering in their hands. Golden light melted into the dark sea, casting a glow over the crowd as laughter rang out like music. This was just the beginning—a week where night bled into day, and every desire would be indulged.

Out here, far from prying eyes, anything was possible.

And the party was just getting started.

And at the heart of it all—Kamal. Always watching, always calculating. This wasn't just a party. It was a stage, and he knew exactly how to play the game.

CHAPTER – 47

AMELIA - Rags To Riches (2010)

Amelia Manu leaned back on the sun lounger, the salty breeze brushing against her skin as the luxury cruise sailed across the Mediterranean. The deck shimmered under the golden hues of sunset, but her eyes drifted to the crystal chandelier hanging in the lobby—a sparkling reminder of how far she had come.

The chandelier was probably so expensive that her family could have bought a few houses in that much money. Water had been used more carefully in her middle-class home in Delhi, compared to the way wine and champagne flowed here on this ship. The amount of money they spent on flower decoration in a day would be enough to feed her entire family for a year. She had come a long way, Amelia reflected, as she sipped her champagne, watching the sky turn red, as the sun was setting on the other side.

Her thoughts went back to her earliest memories of her walking to school with her little sister in tow. She must have been around seven years old then. They studied in a government-funded public school, as that was what her father could afford with his modest salary. Her father was employed as a bank clerk. Her mother did all the housework- cooking, cleaning, stitching their clothes to save money, washing and ironing the clothes, and so many other little chores. Her father left for work at 7 in the morning and had to take two buses to reach his bank. He would be back only by 8 at night, tired from all the work. They would eat their dinner together after her father came back from work, and then he would watch some TV, and be off to bed. The rat-race continued all over again the next day, and the next.

She sometimes wondered as to how she had managed that journey from that space to this esteemed life that she was leading now. It was unbelievable. At that point in time, she never could have imagined that such a life, or even one-hundredth of what she was leading right now, would ever be possible for her.

But of course, there was a price she had to pay, and sometimes she regretted it; at other times, she justified it in her mind that there was no other way to achieve all this.

She was a good student and always stood in the top three ranks in her class. She got into the government college, based on her grades. In the third year of her college, she had participated in a fashion show in an intercollegiate event, and she won the Miss Technology beauty contest with her good looks, winning smile, and wit. She became the college heartthrob.

A month later, she got an offer to endorse a fashion apparel retail brand based out of Delhi. The money was handy for the family, and she gladly accepted it. One thing led to another, and by her final year, she was doing an endorsement every couple of months. She was now supporting her father in the household expenses. Instead of being pleased, he repeatedly told her to focus on her engineering degree and then get a suitable job in a multinational company for a professional career ahead. She did clear her engineering final exams, but with passing grades only. This did not leave much scope for a job, but she got modeling assignments frequently now.

She also had constant arguments with her father, who blamed her for spoiling her career by getting into this modeling thing. A year later, she was performing at a fashion show for an international brand in Hyderabad. After the show, a man in a white shirt and a white lungi approached her as she came backstage. She was wary of these types of characters. By now, she knew the score and understood why her father had always been against the modeling career, as she would often get approached by dubious characters who would offer money to the models to sleep with them. In time, she understood that many of the girls were looking for such opportunities, as that is where they made the big bucks. The endorsements were not so important to them for the money, but for face value-the moment they appeared in an endorsement, their asking rate went up about 5 to 10 times for a night. Usually, the quality of clientele would also go up, as only the rich could afford to pay so much money for the pleasures of a night. So, it was vital to get the right endorsements. It was a dirty game, but Amelia kept away from all of this. As she tried to go past the man, he blocked her way. She looked up, and he said 'Namaste' with folded hands.

She stopped to listen to him, "Yes, please, what can I do for you?"

"My boss is a film producer in Telugu films. He is making a film. He was watching the show and wants to cast you as the main lead."

"Oh, I see, but I have never acted in films."

"That is ok. He needs a fresh face to launch. It is a love triangle."

A movie-role offer! It sounded absurd. She wasn't even an actress. "I don't speak Telugu," she replied, half-hoping that would end the conversation.

"No problem, Madam. We will teach you Telugu. Even if you don't learn, we can dub all your dialogues."

"I see," she was still wondering if all this was some sort of a trick. After all, she was in a strange town and didn't want to get trapped in any shady deal.

He thrust a card in her hand. "This is my card. I will call you in the morning and arrange a meeting in our office." And he was gone as quickly as he had come.

The next morning, sharp at 11, she was sitting in Mr. Naga Rao's large but functional office. She had googled the credentials last night and had come to know that this was no small-time production company. They were one of the biggest production houses in Tollywood, as the film industry here was nicknamed.

Mr. Naga Rao was also in a white shirt and a white lungi. It was in complete contrast to his dark features and a thick mustache.

The only problem was, he did not know English or Hindi. He could understand both but could not speak in either of them, and she did not know Telugu, the local language. But his secretary, sitting beside her, who was called Kumar, did all the talking on behalf of Mr. Naga Rao. He even understood every nod of his boss's head, his silence, his grunts, and translated everything to Amelia in meaningful English.

They wanted to know how much she would charge. She said it was up to them. But they still insisted. So, she gave the first figure that came to her mind, "Twenty lakhs?"

Mr. Naga Rao shook his head vehemently. She cursed herself for asking such a big amount.

Kumar said, "That is ok."

They wanted to start her training right away, which would take a month for her to pick up the language and the diction. She was confident she could easily pick up the language.

She said, "Can I go home and come back in three days?"

Again Mr. Naga Rao shook his head, even more violently this time, shaking it from side to side, "Amma, something, something…"

She wondered why he denied her this too, and who the hell was this 'Amma'? She thought, *'why did he want to ask his mother about this?'*

Kumar said, "Sir says, no problem." Then she realised that shaking the head was a supplement to the affirmation he gave in words and the 'Amma' that he was referring to was none other than her.

She did not want to convey the news to her parents on phone, but wanted to break it in person. She reached home from the airport minutes after her father had come back from work.

She shouted in glee, "Mamma, Papa, I want to give you a great news." And she took out the envelope containing the cheque of Rs. 5 lakhs and handed it to them, "I have signed a film with a famous Telugu film director and producer Mr. Naga Rao, and they will pay me rupees 20 lakhs to act in it. This is the advance of rupees 5 lakhs."

Her sister jumped in delight, and her mother was beaming. But she wanted to please her father, as in the last couple of years he had been upset and angry with her for choosing this career of modeling. She felt that this money and the break would make him happy and he would accept her decision wholeheartedly.

He was glaring at the cheque, not looking at her directly, "So you took this decision without consulting us first? You did not think that you need our permission anymore?"

"Pappa, it all happened so suddenly, I did not have time to ask your permission."

"Was that director running away somewhere? What would happen in one day?" He looked up at her angrily. Her mother's facial expression had become grim by now.

Amelia was looking at the floor, not knowing what to say.

He continued, "Amu, I have always dissuaded you from this line of work for the last two years. We go out in the world, and we hear stories as to how girls are treated in this profession. I have worked hard all my life, day in and day out, only for the reason that all of you can lead a life of dignity and respect. I do not want you to compromise on our values. Why do you think they are paying you so much money?"

Amelia still not dared to look him in the eye. She knew by now how the modeling industry worked, and she knew that her father was right. But she could not discuss these issues with her father. These were taboo subjects in their simple middle-class home. "Papa, films are different. They can pay us so much because they are earning in crores. So, they can easily pay me rupees 20 lakhs."

"But have you thought why they need to take only you? They can get anyone to act in their films."

"Naga Sir said my face suits the role in the film."

"Amu, I want no further discussion on this. My knowledge is limited to my bank, but we meet so many people who talk about how they exploit young girls. You have to return the cheque and start looking for a job."

Amelia did not want to let go now. She had landed the chance of a lifetime. Dame luck had smiled upon her, and she would not let the opportunity slip by. She did not want to toil for the rest of her life, like her father. "Papa, I cannot return this cheque. I have to do this film."

As her father had said earlier, there was no further discussion on the subject. He got up and addressed his wife, "I am going to wash up and will have my dinner in 15 minutes. See to it, she is out of the house by the time I am at the dinner table."

That was the last time Amelia had seen her family.

Amelia had picked up Telugu in 20 days, and she would perfect it in the coming weeks. She was talking to everyone in Telugu by now. Be it the bell boys, the waiters, taxi drivers, strangers, Kumar, and Naga Sir. She had adopted the language completely. That was the easy part. The tricky part was getting the colloquial accent. She rehearsed the film dialogues and learnt them all by heart.

She had been put up at the Hyatt Palace, Banjara Hills in Hyderabad. The trainer would come at 10 am and give her a four-hour lesson in Telugu until she broke for lunch. Afternoons, she would watch Telugu hit movies to further improve her language, understand the culture, and familiarise herself with their sense of timing.

She spent the evenings rehearsing her dialogues.

One evening, a week before the shoot was to start, she got a call from Kumar, that 'Sir' was coming to see her and wanted to personally check her dialect, her understanding of the character she played in the film.

Sharp at 8 pm, the bell rang. She was happy to see Naga Sir walk in with his trademark white shirt and lungi, holding one end of the lungi in his right hand, as if signifying that it was casual attire now, suitable for the evening. Amelia was growing fond of the culture, and she realised people were very punctual and generally meant what they said, unlike what she had encountered elsewhere.

Naga Sir called the room service and asked them to serve a bottle of wine, peanuts, and salad. Amelia knew that he drank in the evening. She had no problem with it. She would give him company as he drank, and they could chat and relax.

The waiter came and poured the wine into two glasses. Naga Sir handed her a drink, despite her protests, "Only grape juice, Amma."

Amelia said, "Sir, I have never tried it before."

"Amma, you never acted in a movie before, but now you are going to."

She could not refute his logic. She sipped the wine. In fact, it was like grape juice, a little more pungent and perhaps not so sweet.

They were conversing freely in Telugu. They had emptied the bottle of wine, giving Amelia a heady feeling. The waiter brought another bottle, refilled their glasses and discreetly left.

"Amma, I am thrilled with you. You have picked up Telugu very well. You speak like a Telugu girl only." He said to her in Telugu and laughed.

"If you also act well enough, then I will make you a huge star in Telugu cinema."

"Thank you, Sir."

"No need to thank me, Amma. Now only one week for shooting, I need to understand you very closely, I need to know how you think, how you feel, how you react, so I come here every day for one week and sit and talk with you."

"Yes, Naga, sir, that will be very nice. I am also bored and lonely the whole day."

"I need to know your mind, your body, every part of your body, very closely," and he kept his hand on hers and started caressing it.

She pulled her hand away, looking confused.

"Don't be shy Amu, I need to know you very intimately. You need to understand me fully. Only then can we have a full connection. Then without talking, we can understand each other. This will show on screen." saying this, he again took hold of her hand, this time more firmly.

She knew what he meant. She also noticed that he progressed from Amma to Amu. She knew what was coming. Her mind was working. There was no way he would let her act in the movie without him having her. That is what they wanted in the modelling world too. And every director would want this.

This was a small price to pay for what she wanted. She had already made her choice. Amelia leaned into Naga's open embrace.

Today sitting on this deck, amongst these rich and famous people, having the most incredible luxury at her feet, her mind went back to the simplicity of her father. That simple life was so pure and truthful, uncomplicated and beautiful. She compared her father's character to that of the men here. Her father was prepared to work all his life for his meager pay and willing to provide for his family and his daughters through his hard work. In comparison, these rich, powerful and famous men were so greedy. What wouldn't they do for just a little extra pleasure? Tears rolled down her face. But it was too late now. She had made her choice, and she was part of this filthy system. She had lost her honour and freedom. Whatever interviews she gave to the press were not her independent views. They were the lines fed to her by the scriptwriters in this circus. Everything here was scripted. Even what and who she liked on social media like Facebook and Twitter was defined for her. She had no freedom to speak her mind. She had to fake her smiles. She was acting more off-screen than on-screen.

Amelia recoiled at the thought that she had allowed the fat, ugly man from Saudi to take her three times last night. He was so full of lust; he had not left a part of her body untouched; biting her all over. But she had no say in the matter, as he was investing in the two movies, in which she was given the lead role. And these lustful nights were part of the deal, along with many more to come through the next year, till the movies got produced and released.

The money would not be invested directly in his name but would be routed through the production company of Khoslas. Umesh Khosla, would of course get to direct the movies. The music would be composed by Salim and Rajesh duo, both of whom were very much part of this party.

Book – 3

CLIMAX

CHAPTER - 48
ANKITA - The Last Voyage (2010)

It was the second night of the trip, and the party by the infinity pool was in full swing. The private yacht, anchored off the coast of Monaco, was a floating paradise of excess, exclusivity, indulgence, and secrets. The crowd, a mix of Bollywood actors, European film technicians, and high-profile guests, had been drinking all day. The air was thick with the scent of expensive liquor, salt water, and something more illicit.

Ankita, a rising actress from a modest background, had been invited as a 'special guest' by Kamal Thapar. He had insisted this party was important for her career; a chance to meet the right people. Ankita, eager to make her mark, had hesitated at first. But , her mentor and friend Seema, had reassured her: "Just network, be seen, and leave before things get messy."

The evening started harmlessly. People lounged around in swimwear, sipping cocktails, playing poker, and drifting on inflatable floats. Laughter echoed across the deck. The energy shifted when someone suggested a high-stakes game of strip poker. It was meant to be playful, nothing serious, but as the alcohol flowed, so did inhibitions.

Ankita wasn't a gambler, but she felt the pressure to fit in. She joined, thinking it was all in fun.

In strip poker, all players are required to have equal number of clothes to begin with, and the one they would discard if they lose the given hand, is declared as 'ante' before each hand is dealt. To equate the clothing, each one had a top, shorts, and an accessory-either a piece of jewelry, or hat, or a wrist band. It was also decided that the first ante would be the accessory, whatever it may be, the second would be the top, and the third one would be the shorts along with the underwear, if any.

The first hand was dealt with five cards to each player. They could look at two, while three remain face down in front of them. Then the 'flop' was dealt. Looking at the flop, the players had the option of discarding any of the cards and replacing them with an equal number of the face-down cards in front of them, if they so chose. Then the 'turn' was dealt, and the players had the option to replace one of their cards with one of the face-down cards. Now the 'river' was dealt, followed by a show of cards by all players. The player with the worst hand loses their 'ante' declared earlier, or predefined-as in this game today.

The first few rounds were lighthearted; accessories, bracelets, hats removed. Next would come the tops, the shorts. The game wasn't about winning or losing anymore; it was about control, about who would submit to the night's unwritten rules.

Things were getting out of hand for Ankita, as she lost another hand, and had to pull off her top. Ankita had never experienced public nudity and felt shy and embarrassed, especially as she was the only one with her top off. Now all eyes on the deck had turned towards the poker table. Something interesting was happening here.

The next few hands got Raj and John down to their shorts, and then Zoya also had to take her top off.

Ankita lost yet another hand she thought she had in the bag, with a pair of Aces. The group cheered as she hesitated. Someone teased, "Come on, Ankita, don't be a bore." With flushed cheeks, she forced a smile, slipped off her shorts, and instinctively wrapped her arms around herself. She felt all eyes were on her, watching, evaluating.

Trying to escape the moment, she dove into the pool, thinking it would provide some refuge. But inside the water, things were worse. Hands brushed against her; accidental at first, then deliberate. She turned to leave, but Zoya, also nude now, appeared beside her.

Ankita was being heckled by three guys, and Zoya, who was now behind one of them pulled off his trunks. One of the other girls pulled off the trunks of the other guy. Now there was a commotion, and the others playing poker also jumped into the fray and started denuding the others. In a short while, most of the people were naked in the pool.

News must have floated back to the others, and in about ten minutes, the Chairman of the airline company along with the bevy of beauties that he had flown into Monte Carlo, joined the party. Alcohol was not the only thing everyone was high on. Cocaine and meth were equally free flowing in the party.

"Relax," Zoya whispered, pressing a small pill into Ankita's palm. "Just let go. It's all fun."

Ankita hesitated. She had never taken drugs before. But her head was spinning, her anxiety mounting. Everyone else seemed so carefree, so alive. Against her better judgment, she swallowed it.

The world changed within minutes. The music pulsed through her veins. Her body felt weightless, electric. The water shimmered like liquid gold, and suddenly, everything felt good. She laughed, danced, let herself be pulled into the rhythm of the night. . Her body was now on fire and responding to the touch of the guy beside her. He was surprised by her passion and became excited. John was directly in front of her. Ankita put her arms around his neck, pulled his face to hers, and kissed him. The fat guy kissed her neck from behind, and she moaned and pulled him to her with one free hand.

Ankita woke up to the sound of waves lapping against the yacht. Her head throbbed. Her mouth was dry, her body sore. She was lying on a carpeted floor, naked, covered only by a thin blanket. Around her, other bodies lay, sprawled; some unconscious, some stirring. The air reeked of alcohol, sweat, and something more sickening.

She sat up, disoriented. Her clothes were nowhere in sight. Panic clawed at her chest as flashes from the night before hit her in jagged pieces; her hands on someone's shoulders, a man whispering in her ear, the sensation of being lifted. Then came the blurred fragments of memories that didn't quite fit. A kiss. Hands on her waist. Laughter ringing in her ears. Someone leading her to a private cabin. Her own voice, slurred, whispering, "I need to lie down."

Her stomach lurched. What the hell happened?

She spotted Zoya, half-dressed, lying nearby. Ankita crawled over, shaking her awake. "Zoya, what happened last night?"

Zoya stretched lazily and smiled. "You had fun. You finally let loose."

Ankita's skin crawled. "I don't remember." Her voice caught. "Did I …?"

Zoya exhaled, rubbing her eyes. "You were amazing. Everyone loved you."

The words sent ice through Ankita's veins.

She saw a bottle of water lying nearby-she got up and drank from the bottle. The water felt good. Perhaps, some coffee would do her good. She wanted to vomit, and her hands were trembling. She was feeling so helpless and uneasy. She saw John lying nearby. There was someone's trouser lying on the floor. She wore them. They were too wide but would have to do for now. She took a table cloth and wrapped it around her top.

Later, in the evening, they were on the deck again. Ankita had been feeling drained the entire day. She didn't want to eat anything. She had Aspirin and coffee, but the headache would not go away. She came to know more sordid details about last evening from Zoya and the others, and was shocked at her own behaviour. As the evening progressed, Ankita felt worse. Zoya gave her some wine to relax, but it did her no good. Finally, she popped another pill on Zoya's advice. Within minutes her troubles disappeared and she felt better. She relaxed into the evening. The music that was hurting her eardrums had now turned into a beat, and she wanted to dance to it. She felt alive and happening and kissed Zoya for making her feel better and they danced together. Other couples joined them and the party had begun. And not long after, it was orgy time. She had discovered a new life. She was now part of the gang.

It was later that night, must have been almost morning. Ankita had again passed out. As she woke up, it was the same feeling of exhaustion and confusion. She was in some strange room. She looked around; there were two other guys and a girl on the bed with her. The effect of the drugs had subsided. Her hands were shaking, and her whole body was trembling.

She staggered to her feet, she needed to get out of here, find her phone, call someone, anyone. She stumbled into the hallway, trying to gather herself.

She heard music. Voices. Laughter.

Following the sound, she reached a door, slightly ajar. She pushed it open just enough to see inside.

Her breath caught in her throat.

The room beyond was dimly lit, but what she saw was unmistakable. A gathering of high-profile guests, including Kamal – completely nude. Only one man was fully dressed in a crisp suit, his face obscured by shadows. But what made Ankita's blood run cold were the others in the room. Children.

Young girls and boys, barely in their teens. Some younger. Their eyes empty, their bodies limp. Some sitting on laps, others being held too closely. The adults whispered to them, touching them in ways that made Ankita's stomach turn.

The realization hit her like a punch to the gut. This wasn't just another party. This was something else; something darker.

A choked sound escaped her lips before she could stop it.

Heads turned. The man in the suit stood up, abruptly. Kamal's eyes locked onto hers, widening in shock.

"Who let her in?" someone shouted.

Panic surged through Ankita's body. She turned to run, but her legs wobbled, her body betraying her. Hands grabbed her arms. She screamed, but a rough palm covered her mouth. She kicked, struggled, but the drugs had dulled her movements.

"Shut her up," Kamal barked.

Someone slapped her. Hard. Stars exploded in her vision. She was dragged through the hallway, past empty champagne bottles, past unconscious bodies, past everything that once seemed glamorous but now felt like a waking nightmare.

They pulled her onto the deck. The sun was just beginning to rise, casting a soft golden light over the horizon. For a moment, she thought of home; her mother, her old life, the dreams she once had.

She knew what was coming.

The men lifted her, dragged her toward the edge of the ship. She struggled weakly, but she was outnumbered. As she looked down at the dark, endless water below, a cold calm settled over her.

She had been naive. She had walked into this world thinking she could play by her own rules. But the game had always been rigged.

And now, she was just another casualty.

As they shoved her overboard, the last thing she saw was the face of the man in the suit. Recognition flickered.

She knew who he was.

But did it even matter now?

The cold water swallowed her whole.

CHAPTER - 49
TINA - Paranoid (2013)

It had been almost two years since the Mafia shoot in Hong Kong, and by now, Ahana and Ramesh's affair was practically an open secret. Industry circles whispered, tabloids speculated, and yet, Tina had tried everything to shut it out. For six months, she had cut Ahana off; banned her from their home, distanced herself from mutual friends, even refused to acknowledge her existence.

None of it worked.

Ahana and Ramesh were still working together; films, endorsements, ad shoots. Their chemistry wasn't just professional; it was visible. They were in the same spaces, traveling for the same events, and thanks to Tina's own complacency, they had all the time in the world to be together.

But what could she do? She wasn't the first woman in Bollywood to face this humiliation, and she wouldn't be the last.

Ramesh had recently bought a massive seven-bedroom villa on a private island in Hawaii. A sprawling 18,000-square-foot property with its own beach, an infinity pool, and manicured lawns on both sides. It was luxury on a level even Tina hadn't experienced before. They had spent the last New Year's Eve there as a family; Tina, Ramesh, and their daughter. At the time, she had convinced herself it was just another investment.

Now she wasn't so sure.

Lately, Ramesh had been making more frequent trips to Hawaii, always under the guise of 'endorsements' or 'promotions.' Tina was secretly relieved whenever he was away. At least that way, he wasn't with the bitch.

Last night, he had left for yet another trip. This morning, she sat alone at the dining table, picking at a bowl of oats and fruit. She needed to lose weight, she reminded herself. Somewhere between dealing with all this mess, she had stopped caring about her body.

Her phone buzzed. Unknown Number.

She ignored it.

It buzzed again. And again. The fourth time, she put her phone on silent.

But it didn't stop.

Whoever it was, they were persistent. For the next half an hour, the calls kept coming; 18, maybe 20 in total. Annoyed, Tina finally grabbed her phone and answered.

"Who the hell is this?" she snapped.

A calm, steady, female voice responded, "This is important. It's about Ramesh and Ahana. If you want to hear it, I'll continue. Otherwise, I'll hang up."

Tina froze.

The woman's voice was soft, unhurried. Not gossipy or dramatic; just firm.

"Who are you?" Tina managed.

"That doesn't matter," the caller said. "Think of me as a well-wisher. Or a fan. I just thought you should know; Ahana is on a flight to Hawaii right now. She'll be staying with Ramesh in your villa for the next two days."

The line clicked.

"Hello?" Tina's voice wavered. "Hello??"

Silence.

She looked at her screen. Private Number. She couldn't call back.

Her heart pounded. Was this a prank? Some random troublemaker stirring things up? But something about the woman's tone made Tina believe her.

Her mind raced. She couldn't confront Ramesh; not without proof. She couldn't even talk to her friends; things always leaked in Bollywood. And telling her mother? No way. The last thing she needed was for her mom to call Ramesh in panic and blow everything up.

Then an idea struck her.

She went to the kitchen, where Gita, the nanny, was cleaning up.

"Gita, can I borrow your phone for a second?"

Gita handed it over, without question.

Tina quickly dialed Ahana's secretary. She disguised her voice slightly, making it sound businesslike. "Hi, I am an independent producer working on a new film. I'd love to set up a meeting with Ahana. Could you let me know when she's available?"

"Madam left the country today for Hawaii," the secretary replied. "She'll be back in two days."

Tina felt the blood drain from her face.

So, the woman on the phone was telling the truth.

Tina clutched the edge of the kitchen counter. Her brain started connecting the dots; Ramesh's sudden obsession with Hawaii, his frequent trips, the private villa instead of a hotel. Hotels meant documentation; passports, check-in records. A villa? No paper trail. No evidence.

She had been such a fool.

Tina took a deep breath. She needed a plan.

She picked up her phone and dialed her mother.

"Mom, can you come stay with the kids for a few days?" she said, trying to sound casual. "Ramesh is in Hawaii, and I want to surprise him."

"When should I come?" her mother asked.

"Right now. Book the earliest flight."

"Oh God, Tina! Always in such a hurry. I need to pack, sort out things.

"Just do it, Mom. And don't tell anyone. It's a surprise."

A pause. Then, a sigh. "Fine."

Tina hung up.

Her hands were shaking, but she felt something she hadn't in months; Control.

If Ramesh thought he could play her for a fool, he had another thing coming.

CHAPTER - 50

TINA - Nightmare (2013)

Tina rang the doorbell. It was 2:30 a.m.

Her heart pounded in her chest, her fingers cold and stiff around the handle of her suitcase. She could hear the waves crashing somewhere in the distance, the soft rustling of palm trees in the night breeze.

The door creaked open after a few minutes. Doby, the houseboy, stood there, bleary-eyed and confused. He rubbed his face, struggling to process what was happening.

Before he could speak, Tina pushed past him.

She took the stairs two at a time, her breath sharp, her vision tunneling.

She didn't knock. She didn't hesitate.

She shoved open the bedroom door.

And there they were.

Ahana lay naked in her bed, wrapped in Ramesh's arms. His body curled around hers, skin against skin, their breaths slow, deep; completely at peace.

For a split second, everything froze.

Then Ahana's eyes flickered open.

She blinked, confused. Then she saw Tina.

Tina saw the recognition hit her. Saw her face change. She jolted up, grabbing the sheets to cover herself.

"Ramesh!" Ahana shook him hard.

Ramesh stirred, groggy, confused. He rubbed his eyes, mumbling something incoherent before he registered what was happening. His gaze landed on Tina, standing in the doorway, and his face drained of color.

A thousand emotions crashed into Tina at once. Rage. Shock. A sick, twisted sort of satisfaction that she had been right. But beneath all of it was something far worse; heartbreak so deep it felt like she was being hollowed out from the inside.

Ramesh just stared at her, like he couldn't believe she was real.

Ahana was the first to speak. Her voice was sharp, cold. "Get out."

Tina blinked, as if she had misheard her.

Ahana sat up straighter, her grip tightening on the sheets. "I said, get out. If you have any dignity left."

Tina didn't move.

Ahana's eyes narrowed. "Are you deaf, or just pathetic? Get the fucking hell out of here, you stupid bitch."

Tina sucked in a sharp breath.

Something inside her shattered.

She turned on her heel and walked out.

She barely remembered rushing down the stairs, registering Doby's horrified face as she passed him.

The moment she stepped outside, the humid air hit her like a slap. The taxi that had dropped her off was still there, the driver leaning against the hood, scrolling through his phone.

She yanked the door open and got in.

"Where to, Madam?"

"Hyatt Palace. Waikiki Beach."

She couldn't go to The Aston. Ramesh knew people there. He could find her.

Not that he would.

She stared blankly out of the window as the cab pulled away, the villa shrinking in the distance.

She should have screamed. She should have dragged Ahana out of bed, by her hair, thrown her onto the floor, made a scene. But she hadn't.

She had walked out. Like a fool.

Like a woman who had already lost.

She checked into a suite, ignoring the receptionist's polite questions, brushing past the bellboy, kicking off her heels the moment she shut the door behind her.

Her hands were shaking as she called room service.

"A bottle of vodka," she said. "Now."

Minutes later, the bottle arrived. She poured herself a shot, neat, and downed it in one go. Then another. And another.

The alcohol burned, but not enough.

The TV blared in the background, some mindless late-night show. She wasn't watching.

Her fingers clenched around the glass, and suddenly, she hurled it against the wall. It shattered, tiny shards glittering against the carpet.

How dare she?

How dare Ahana speak to her like that? How dare she throw her out of her own house?

And Ramesh; he hadn't even said anything.

No explanation. No denial. No guilt.

Just silence.

Tina drank from the bottle; Gulping down the liquid as it burned her insides.

Had he done it in their Mumbai home too? Had Ahana slept in their bed, touched their sheets, laughed in their space?

Tina's stomach twisted.

Another shot.

She wanted to scream. To burn everything down. To erase the last few years of her life.

But instead, she slumped onto the sofa, the bottle slipping from her fingers.

And then, everything went black.

CHAPTER - 51

TINA – On Her Feet (2013)

A soft voice pulled her out of the abyss.

"Madam? Are you okay?"

Tina groaned, her head throbbing as she forced her eyes open. A young Filipina housekeeper in a blue uniform stood over her, concern etched on her face.

"Do you need help, madam?"

Tina blinked, struggling to piece together where she was. Her throat felt dry, her body heavy.

"What time is it?" she rasped. "Where is Ramesh?"

The girl hesitated. "Madam, was someone else with you? It's 2 PM."

"2 PM?" Tina's stomach twisted. She had blacked out for nearly twelve hours.

"Oh." She sat up, wincing at the sharp pain in her temples. "Where am I?"

"You're at the Hyatt Palace, madam," the girl said gently, handing her a glass of water.

Tina gulped it down, the cool liquid reviving her slightly. As her memory flooded back, she noticed that the broken glass she had thrown last night was gone, the carpet was spotless. The staff here had seen enough guests like her to know how to handle a situation discreetly.

"Can I get you some coffee, madam? Maybe some Aspirin?"

Tina exhaled. "Yes. Please."

A few minutes later, she was sipping strong coffee, the painkiller slowly kicking in. The caffeine and sugar steadied her, making her feel almost human again.

Tina forced herself into the shower. She let the hot water run over her face, washing away the remnants of last night; tears, rage, and humiliation. Afterward, she threw on a sundress and sunglasses and went down to the poolside cafe. She ordered a late breakfast; scrambled eggs, toast, and another coffee, heavy on the sugar.

As she sipped, her mind cleared.

When she left for Hawaii, she had prepared herself for the worst. If she caught Ramesh cheating, she had thought she would walk out; no questions, no drama. Take her daughter, file for divorce, and never look back.

But now, seeing the situation for what it really was, she realized that was exactly what Ahana wanted. That girl wasn't just having an affair; she wanted to replace her. She wanted Tina's life.

And Ramesh? Well, he had let it happen.

Tina clenched her jaw, replaying Ahana's voice from the night before.

"Get out."

The audacity. The sheer disrespect.

No. She wasn't going to just walk away. She had too much to lose. She had to fight.

But how?

She had no illusions; Ahana had Ramesh wrapped around her little finger. Even if Tina threatened to leave with her daughter, what if Ahana convinced him to let them go?

No, she needed leverage. Something real.

She picked up her phone and dialed.

"Where the hell are you?" Ramesh's voice was frantic when he picked up. "Tina! I've been calling you all night! I called home, they said you weren't there either."

"I am at the Hyatt Palace," she cut him off. "Come here at six."

"Hyatt Palace? Waikiki Beach? You're still in Hawaii?" He sounded shocked. "Tina, we will come right now."

"Not we, Ramesh. You. Leave your little harem behind. And not now. I am going to take a nap. Come at six. Room 1101."

She hung up before he could respond.

At exactly 6 PM the doorbell rang.

"Come in."

Ramesh walked in wearing jeans and a white T-shirt, looking exhausted. Tina smirked internally. The little bitch must have given him hell today. Good. Serves him right.

He stepped toward her, reaching as if to hold her.

She put up a hand, stopping him cold.

“You don’t get to touch me anymore, Ramesh,” she said evenly, her voice devoid of emotion.

He swallowed hard, his eyes pleading. “Tina, I am so sorry. I still love you. Please, forgive me.”

She tilted her head, studying him. “What exactly are you sorry for, Ramesh?”

He hesitated.

She took a step forward, her voice sharpening.

“Are you sorry that I caught you? That she insulted me in our home while you lay there and did nothing? That you lied to me for two years? Or are you sorry that you turned me into a joke, made a fool of me in front of the whole industry while you paraded around with her like some lovesick fool?”

His face darkened with shame. He looked down at the floor, silent.

“Don’t feed me some bullshit about being sorry,” she continued. “You’re not sorry. You’re just sorry you got caught.”

Ramesh ran a hand through his hair. “Tina, I’ve never cheated on you before. We’ve been married for 16 years. It was a mistake. Please, can’t we move past this?”

Tina narrowed her eyes. “That’s exactly my point, Ramesh. You never cheated before. So why now? What’s so special about her?”

He had no answer.

“You played me for a fool. You humiliated me. You gave her stature; and that’s why she dared to speak to me like that. That’s what I can’t forgive.”

Ramesh exhaled, defeated. “What do you want me to do, Tina? Just tell me.”

She crossed her arms. “Tell me the truth, first. How deep are you in this? What is she to you?”

Silence.

Then, barely above a whisper; “She’s pregnant.”

Tina blinked. For a second, she thought she had misheard him.

“Ahana and I got married in a secret ceremony in Las Vegas. A few months ago.”

Tina’s face turned red in rage and as Ramesh came towards her to hold her to calm her down, she slapped him hard, one more, and then another and so on…until she was exhausted from the effort and collapsed on the floor.

The ordeal had shaken Tina.

She cried out her tears bitterly.

She looked at him with loathing, "Get out, Ramesh. Get out of my room and my life.

The next morning, Tina sat in her suite, drinking black coffee, her suitcase packed. She had spent half the night drinking and thinking. Now, she was clear. She dialed Ramesh and told him to come over.

When he arrived, she didn't bother with small talk.

"You wanted to know what I want," she said.

He nodded cautiously.

"She has to leave Bollywood."

His eyebrows shot up. "What? You can't be serious."

"Oh, I am very serious," she said, taking a sip of coffee.

"Tina, she's one of the top actresses right now. I can't just tell her to quit."

She smirked. "You're her husband. The father of her child. If anyone can tell her, it's you."

"Tina, be reasonable. What will she tell the media? That she just vanished?"

"You're great at spinning stories, Ramesh. Figure it out. Maybe she wants to explore Tollywood." She let out a small, humorless laugh.

Ramesh ran a hand through his hair, thinking.

Tina glanced at her watch. "I have a flight to catch. Make a decision."

Ramesh exhaled. "Fine. But there's one condition. I keep the child."

Tina considered it. Their marriage was already over; only the facade remained. But she needed to protect her own child.

"Okay," she said. "But I want two things. First, your will; irrevocable; giving our daughter her rightful share of everything."

Ramesh nodded. "And the second?"

"You go back to Vegas and divorce her. Quietly. Just like you married her."

He had no choice.

On the flight home, as the plane took off, Tina stared out of the window at the endless ocean below.

She thought about the past. The early years; before the money, the fame. They had been a middle-class couple, grounded in reality. Ramesh had been just a man, her man, before he became a star.

They used to have a ritual; a joke, really. Two empty pots stood by their front door, labeled ‘Glamour’ and ‘Ego’. Every time they came home, they would pretend to wipe off the glitz of the industry, throw it into the pots, and only then step inside. It was their way of keeping the madness outside.

At some point, Ramesh had stopped doing it. Maybe that was when everything had changed.

Tina sighed. That world; the one they had built together; was gone.

Now, she had to focus on her daughter. On her future.

And once she no longer needed her?

She would find a new purpose. Maybe it would be in helping others. Or maybe she would finally start living for herself.

But one thing was certain.

She was done being the woman waiting in the shadows.

CHAPTER - 52

KIRTI - Broken Dreams (2010)

Kirti had gone back to Jodhpur along with her sister, Shano. Rahi had assured them that he will require her services soon enough. He'd asked them to call him after about a month or so, and gave them his mobile number.

Her family was a little disappointed that Kirti could not get the award, which would have meant an end to their financial woes. However, Rahi's promise kept them going.

Shano called Rahi after precisely one month, but he did not answer her call. She used the public phone to call his number as they did not have a phone at home. She called him up again after a few days, and then again. He did not answer.

This went on for a few more times, and now Shano, Kirti, and the whole family were losing hope and getting very desperate.

Shano and Kirti reached the phone booth one evening and dialed his number, and he immediately answered, "Hello?"

"Sir, this is Kirti. You asked us to call..."

"Who Kirti, from where?"

"Sir, from Jodhpur. I was in the third position in the *Classic talent hunt* programme. You said you will give me a song for your movie."

"Yes, yes, yes. Kirti, why you did not call earlier. We have already recorded that song."

"Sir, we have been calling since the last 20 days, but you did not answer the phone."

"Oh! Okay, Kirti, I don't answer calls from unknown numbers. Anyway, let me see. I am composing for another movie. You can come in about 15 days."

"Okay, Sir. Where should we come?"

"Note this number. It is of my secretary, Ganesh. He will give you all the details. 88756..."

Shano looked at Kirti angrily, "Why didn't you ask the other details regarding where we will stay, etc.?"

Kirti said, "How can I ask all that, and moreover, he gave Ganesh's number, we can speak with him."

"At least you should have asked him for some money. How will we go to Bombay? You know Papa is already struggling with so many loans."

"He will think we are so cheap. He is trying to help us; we can't suck his blood like leeches."

Shano was still angry, "I will talk to Ganesh tomorrow. You stick to your singing."

Kirti and Shano reached Bombay in 15 days. Her father took another loan from the moneylender after keeping his wife's gold chain and rings as security. And arranged second-class train tickets for both of them, and gave them some cash for their expenses, till Kirti got paid for her services.

Her father had also told Shano that if there is any problem, they should just return home. He assured them that he would manage everything, and they need not worry about the repayment of loans. But Shano knew that her father was just consoling them, and he was worried about his debts.

Ganesh was good on his word and arranged for them to stay in a *Kholi* (a one-room tenement) with a small kitchenette and a shared toilet and bathroom in Jogeshwari East. Still, at least they felt safe and secure and gave the phone booth owner in their town, a call about their well-being, a message to be conveyed to their father.

Kirti would go to Rahi's studio on Veera Desai Road, which was nearby, for her training and rehearsals. Shano, having nothing better to do, would accompany her sister. In about a month, the sisters had become comfortable in Bombay and had started enjoying the vada pav, Bombay's local snack. The only problem was that they had almost run out of money, which their father had given to them.

One afternoon Kirti had come to the studio alone, as Shano was not feeling well. By now, they were comfortable with Rahi and the staff. Rahi had informed Kirti that the recording would be next week, and she had to be ready with the song. Kirti was rehearsing by herself in one of the rooms and was waiting for Rahi to do a final check. He had some visitors, and there was a meeting on, so she did not disturb him. It was around 7 pm, and he was still not free, so she went to his cabin and knocked.

Rahi said, "Come in."

Kirti pushed open the door and was taken aback to see three other visitors, and said, "Rahi Sir, I think you are busy. I have finished the rehearsal, maybe you can check it tomorrow, as today Shano is not well, and I need to go back to be with her."

Rahi said, "Kirti, come in. Let me introduce you to the producer Abbas Bhai and the director Mukesh Bhai, and she is the singer I told you about."

She said a polite hello to them.

Rahi said, "We were discussing about you only, Kirti. Anyway, we are almost done. I will call you in ten minutes. We need to record this song."

"Okay, sir," she felt elated. Now things were really falling into place.

She waited for about half an hour, when he called her into the 'Riyaas Room,' as he called it. The room was wall to wall carpeted, with low seating for four people. There was a piano and some other musical instruments. On the other end, towards the wall was a low couch with round cushions. A projector was suspended from the ceiling. Video songs from a Hindi movie were playing and projected onto the opposite wall. There was a fridge in one corner and a large glass cabinet beside it, stacked with liquor bottles. It was the first time Kirti had enterd the Riyaas room and she found it luxurious.

As he entered, Rahi turned off the projector. He sat on the low couch and asked Kirti to pick up a mike and start singing. Kirti was very nervous but she started with the song.

"Kirti, stop. First, I want you to relax. Feel the song. This is a love song. I want you to feel it and then sing."

"Okay, sir."

She sang again.

"No, Kirti, you are not getting the feel. Have you ever been in love?"

"No, Sir."

"Okay, no problem. Imagine the situation. You are missing your lover, and you want him to touch you and feel you, and are pining for his love. Can you feel that now?"

"Yes, Sir."

"Okay, sing now."

She sang again.

"No, Kirti. You are not getting it. Come here."

She hesitated, but walked over.

He took her hand and made her sit beside him.

“Close your eyes. Feel the song,” he whispered.

She began to sing.

His fingers trailed over her hand, then up to her shoulder. She stiffened.

“You’re doing good,” he murmured, his breath warm against her ear.

She flinched as his lips brushed against her neck. His hand moved to her chest.

“Sir, please…”

He ignored her, his grip tightening. She struggled, but he overpowered her easily. His hand clamped over her mouth, muffling her screams as he forced himself on her.

It was over in minutes.

Kirti felt the pain and humiliation of her ordeal. This man, whom she and her family had been treating like God's messiah, was a wolf in sheep's clothing. The ever so sweet and benevolent Rahi had lured her into this well-planned trap. She saw the bloodstain on the couch, proof of her soiled virginity, lost to this dirty, lecherous man. She felt ashamed, and tears flowed down her cheeks in fresh torrents.

He put his hand on her arm, "You are very beautiful, Kirti…"

She recoiled at his touch, and pushed him away viciously, took her clothes, and ran to the bathroom. She dressed and ran out before he could stop her, even as he shouted after her.

She walked home in a daze, her body aching, her mind numb.

When Shano opened the door, Kirti collapsed into her arms, sobbing.

At first, Shano panicked, thinking she was hurt. But as she listened, her expression turned to horror, then rage.

The sisters did not sleep a wink. It was almost 3 in the morning. They lay in bed, and tears rolled down as and when the shock of what had transpired came back into their minds. When they had cried themselves out and the tears had dried up and they still could not sleep, they went up the stairs to the small shared terrace, where the water tanks and the dish antennas were laid out. They sat on a ledge, and the stillness of the night gradually calmed their nerves.

Finally, Kirti spoke up, "What will we tell papa?"

Shano had grown up a lifetime in these few hours, "We cannot tell papa. He will be broken if he hears about this."

"How do we go back?"

"Kirti, we cannot even go back. Papa has already taken so many loans. If we go back, how will he repay them? At least, till we are here, the lenders have a hope that their money is coming back."

"Should we go to the police?"

"We cannot even do that. With all his money, connections, and power, no one will believe us, and Rahi will only wipe us out. They might ruin Mano and mummy and papa's life too."

Kirti started crying again, "So what do we do now?"

Shano hugged her little sister. Gently, she told her, "Kirti, we have to accept what has happened to us. We were such gullible fools. People like Rahi would be laughing at us, at our stupidity, and they want to take advantage of our weakness. God has given Rahi everything one can ask for; riches, fame, and talent. But he is so greedy and cheap. He will never be equal to us, as he does not respect himself, and he does not respect God. We are much better off than him. We can earn money in due course, but he will not respect himself for the rest of his life. So, be brave, my little girl, you can hold your head high, and you can love yourself as you are still pure as a flower."

The next day, Kirti and Shano reached Rahi's office. Before that, Shano had gone out and found the nearest police station and done some research.

As they entered, Rahi was sitting with a few people. Rahi greeted them with his fake smile, "Oh, nice to see you, Kirti! I was missing my ace singer. Can you wait at the reception; I will finish this meeting and call you dear."

Shano said, "No problem. Take your time. We are waiting in the Riyas Room." They walked out before he could protest.

Within five minutes, he entered the Riyas Room, looking irritated.

Shano had decided to take the bull by the horns, as that was the only way she could salvage their desperate situation; otherwise, he would finish them off.

"Rahi, we went to the Amboli police station on Veera Desai Road. The lady police inspector will be on duty by 7 pm. They have asked us to come back. I have also kept Kirti's clothes with your semen stains to prove the rape."

Rahi was, as expected, a hard nut to crack.

"No problem, I know everyone right up to the police commissioner of Bombay. And by the way, it was your sister's fault. She was the one who seduced me."

Shano was prepared for this. She knew by now what Rahi feared. "Rahi, I also have a friend of mine in Times Now. I have called her, and she will be reaching your office shortly. You can give her the bytes. Your fans will love it."

"And I have prepared a statement for the press, starting from how you fooled and trapped us, right from the beginning, by giving Kirti fewer points in the contest, and then offering her a film. Everything is in there. Let us see how the police cannot register this case." And she placed the sheaf of papers in front of him.

Rahi knew he was trapped. The image that he had built up so carefully over the years would be shattered, and people, including his children, would despise him.

He immediately changed color. "Shano didi, please let it go. Actually, I had no such intention. My conscience is clear. But your sister is so beautiful, I just fell for her." And he crouched by her feet.

"No, Rahi, scum like you need to be exposed. Otherwise, you will keep exploiting innocent young girls all the time. Let us set an example of you. Let everyone see your real face."

For the first time, Rahi paled. He looked around, paranoid.

Shano did not want to push her luck too far. She continued in her stern voice, "Fall at Kirti's feet, not mine."

As he bent down to hold Kirti's feet, she hit his face hard with her foot, "Don't touch me, scoundrel."

Shano said, "I will come to your office by 11 am tomorrow. I want the signed contract in Kirti's name. She will be singing all the songs for the movie *Naach,* at a price of Rs. 11 lakhs. So, keep the contract and the cheque ready. Otherwise, the police and the press will be here before noon."

As they left, Shano stopped at a pharmacy and got a morning-after pill for Kirti.

CHAPTER - 53
SRIPRIYA - Bleak Sky (2012)

Two months had gone by, and Sripriya had not moved out of her house. Where could she go? The movies were out of her kitty. The endorsements had evaporated. If she called earlier, reporters who would appear even at midnight, seemed uninterested in her story anymore.

What hurt her more was that most of her so-called friends of the film world had even stopped taking her calls or replying to her messages. It was like she was the pariah, with the plague. She was suddenly an outcast and very lonely.

Money, she was not worried about, as of now. She had earned enough in her career of 14 years in the industry so far, and she had hardly had the opportunity to spend any of it. The most significant expense in the debit column of her accounts was the income tax that she paid every year.

But she was wary of getting rusted. Another few months like this, and she would forget how to face the camera. Besides, she had entered her 30s. The prime period of the life of a heroine is well before that. She knew that she was on the downhill now. She wanted to retire at some time in her life, but not like this, not forgotten altogether.

At dinner, as her mother poured more sambhar onto the rice, she said, "Priya, I think you need to stop eating rice at night. Just stick to salads."

Sripriya knew what her mom was getting at. She had been putting on weight. But she could not control her craving, and the depression and loneliness were not helping.

The mother and daughter were so close to each other that they could read each other's minds without the need for words. Her mom knew that she needed to get back to work, to break this jinx.

CHAPTER - 54

SRIPRIYA - Back To The Top (2013)

Sripriya had been lying low for a while, waiting for the right opportunity to reclaim her place in the industry. Then, through a reliable source, she heard that Ramaswamy, a celebrated director from the South, was looking for a North Indian actress for his next big film.

Without wasting time, she got hold of his secretary's number in Chennai. Instead of calling herself, she asked her mother to make the first move; it always helped when things came from a senior person. The secretary was polite but non-committal. He said he would check and revert.

To her surprise, he called back the very next morning. Sripriya still had star power down South. Despite her South Indian roots, she had grown up in Delhi and worked exclusively in Bollywood. She fit the profile. The production house wanted her to fly to Chennai for a screen test the following week. Ramaswamy, or Rama Sir as he was fondly called, had a rule; no matter how big the star, they had to audition.

Sripriya didn't mind. She knew she was right for the role.

Shooting for *Peria Thalaivar* was a refreshing experience. The sets were well-managed, with most scenes shot in Gemini Studios. A rural schedule was efficiently completed in a nearby village, and train sequences were filmed at Ramoji Film City in Hyderabad. Everything ran like clockwork; no tantrums, no unnecessary delays. The discipline of the Southern industry was a sharp contrast to the chaos of Bollywood.

Sripriya thrived in this environment, and her performance was one of the best of her career. The film was a blockbuster.

Then came an even bigger opportunity; Rama Sir decided to remake the film in Hindi and wanted her to reprise her role. Sripriya gladly accepted. After all, it would give her an excellent opportunity to reopen Bollywood's closed doors, albeit in style.

For the male lead, he was considering actors from the Hindi film industry. Sripriya suggested Sudhanshu Banerjee; someone she had worked with in the past. Their on-screen chemistry had been strong, and she knew he had the talent. Rama Sir trusted her judgment, and after a screen test, Sudhanshu was signed.

The movie was an even bigger hit in the Hindi version, putting Sripriya right back in Bollywood. Even Sudhanshu Banerjee gave the best performance of his life and really came into his own.

The film also changed something else; her relationship with Sudhanshu. She had never looked at him that way before, but now, seeing him evolve into a confident performer, she found herself drawn to him. He was nothing like Vikram. While Vikram was controlling and complicated, Sudhanshu was easygoing, fun-loving, and refreshingly straightforward. His childlike enthusiasm made her feel light, something she hadn't felt in years.

Before long, they were inseparable. Their relationship deepened, and after almost a year of dating, Sudhanshu proposed.

Sripriya was ecstatic. She liked him, and his family was influential enough to ensure Vikram stayed out of her life for good.

There was only one catch. In the very early days of Sripriya's career, when in her teens, she had met Shobhit, who was in his prime at that time. Any actress was more than willing to have a fling with him and she had done precisely that.

She recollected it was her second year in the film industry. She was naïve, fresh and bubbly. They were shooting in Switzerland and had been put up in the Alpina Hotel in Gstaad. They came back to the hotel, tired, on the fourth day of the shoot. As they entered the lobby, they were surprised to see Shobhit, then a big star of Bollywood, right in front of them, just checking in. He greeted them warmly as she and her co-star Vicky were introduced to him. She was dumbfounded to see the man of every woman's dream right in front of her. She had grown up watching his movies, she'd idolised him.

The next evening, when she returned from the shoot, she hoped to catch a glimpse of Shobhit Sir again, but she could not find him. On that day, Vicky had gone to see one of his relatives who lived in Gstaad. She was roaming around aimlessly in the lobby when someone tapped her from behind, "Are you looking for someone?"

"Yes, Sir, you," she blurted out. And as her face turned crimson with embarrassment and nervousness, she tried to gain composure and said, "No, no Sir, I mean…"

"Shh…there is no need for words," Shobhit gently took her hand, and with ease and confidence, guided her to the bar adjoining the lobby. She was so conscious and nervous; she couldn't open her mouth. He let her be.

He ordered a bottle of champagne. The waitress arrived with a bottle in an ice bucket and two glasses. The waitress expertly opened the bottle and poured the drink into their glasses, "Enjoy," and she left.

He picked up his drink, looking her in the eyes, and made a toast, "To the most beautiful woman in the world," clinked his glass with hers and drank it in one shot. She followed suit. The waitress quickly appeared from nowhere and refilled their glasses.

They had finished off the bottle in an hour. The champagne had loosened up her inhibitions. She was now bubbly and effervescent, just as the champagne flowing in her system.

They had another bottle of champagne. After a while, she was enjoying herself so much that she had lost track of time. She was having the best evening of her life. Next morning, she woke up in his bed, lying naked with him under the sheets. She never remembered how and when it happened, but it was a glorious night.

She spent three such nights with him—each, better than the last. On the fourth evening, when she came back from the shoot and checked for him, she came to know that he had already left the country. No goodbye, no promises, nothing. He left as quickly as he had come into her life.

After that, they had met each other many times in Bombay, during film parties, functions, but there was no hint of recognition or acknowledgment that they knew each other so well. Sripriya had also played along.

Now, this was a different matter altogether. Sripriya was planning to get married to his son. She wanted to see his reaction and if he would still play along. So, Sripriya told Sudhanshu that she would like to meet his parents, and only if they approved would she give her consent. Sudhanshu was thrilled that Sripriya had such a good upbringing that she wanted his parents' blessings before accepting his proposal.

The following week, she arrived at the Banerjee family mansion. As the car pulled up, she was taken aback. The sheer grandeur of the estate, right in the heart of Mumbai, was staggering.

Inside, they were ushered into an enormous lounge. It was bigger than most banquet halls, tastefully done in muted tones of beige and gold.

At precisely 11 AM, Shobhit Banerjee descended the grand marble staircase, looking every bit the king of his empire. Dressed in an immaculate white kurta, with matching white leather loafers and a silken shawl, he exuded authority. His wife, Suma, walked beside him, radiating quiet elegance.

Even Sudhanshu, usually carefree, straightened up and spoke with careful respect, “Papa, this is Sripriya.”

Sripriya folded her hands in a soft Namaste and looked straight into his eyes.

These were the same eyes that had once smiled at her across a champagne glass, and had effortlessly pulled her into a world of indulgence. But now?

Now, they were impassive.

Powerful.

Unreadable.

“So, you want to marry Sudhanshu?” Shobhit’s voice was steady, almost detached.

It felt like a scene from Mughal-e-Azam, with him as Emperor Akbar and her as the audacious woman seeking his son’s hand.

“Yes, Sir,” she said evenly. “If we have your permission and blessings.”

For a moment, there was silence. Then, in a voice that betrayed nothing, he said, “Welcome to the family. We shall be delighted.”

And just like that, it was done.

No recognition. No acknowledgment. Nothing from the past mattered.

As she bent to touch Suma’s feet, she heard Shobhit’s footsteps retreating up the stairs.

Sripriya let out a quiet breath.

She was finally free.

CHAPTER - 55
KANGNA - Clipped Wings (2014)

Kangna was back in Mumbai. After the massive success of *Another Day*, her career had skyrocketed. She was no longer just another actress—she was a phenomenon. Big directors wanted her, brands chased her, and the media couldn't get enough. With over five million followers on social media and millions of views on every interview and post, she was the industry's new obsession.

Money was pouring in. She had signed over twenty brand endorsements—each worth ₹1 crore to ₹1.5 crore—securing hefty advances. She upgraded her lifestyle, buying a sleek Mercedes S-Class for herself and an Audi for Palak. The crown jewel? A sprawling piece of land in Manali, a quiet retreat away from the chaos of Bollywood. Everything she owned was funded by the advances from her films and endorsements—ambitious, but carefully balanced.

Power came with a price tag. She was leveraged—heavily. Her assets were secured against future earnings, and while it seemed like a calculated risk, the underbelly of Bollywood was a dangerous place to play with debt.

And the vultures were watching.

If the industry had one unshakable truth, it was this—no one rises without making enemies. Kangna wasn't just rising; she was soaring. And that made her a target.

It started with an interview. A casual mention—just a passing reference—to her past affair with Rajesh. Rajesh was old money and an even older friend of Kamal's.

The phone rang in Kamal's plush, dimly lit study. He leaned back, cigar smoke curling through the air as he listened.

"Kamal, did you watch Zen TV tonight?" Umesh's voice was smooth, dangerous.

"I don't waste time on that crap," Kamal grunted.

"You should. Kangna finally spilled about Rajesh."

A pause. Then, "So what? Everyone knows."

“Not like this. Not out loud,” Umesh said, his tone sharpening. “And here’s the fun part—she’s sitting on twenty endorsements and ten films. She’s leveraged to her last rupee. Imagine if… something shook her foundation.”

Kamal exhaled, realization dawning. “A case. Defamation.”

“Exactly. One lawsuit, and those endorsement contracts collapse like a house of cards. The refund clauses alone would bleed her dry. And I’ve got one more trick—something that’ll make her choke on her morning coffee.”

A slow, cold smile crept across Kamal’s face. “You’re ruthless, Umesh Bhai. I love it.”

A week later, Kangna's secretary, Raji, met her for the morning update, as Kangna sipped her coffee on the balcony, "Mam, there is a certain Deepak from Bhasin Properties who wants to meet you."

"What about?"

"He has an offer for a villa in Pali Hill. He was saying, it's a great deal."

"But we have already invested in the Manali property. I think we don't have scope for any further investment as of now."

'That's what I told him, but he is very insistent. He was saying it's a deal of a lifetime. Some industrialist needs funds urgently, and is offering the property at a 30% discount from the market rate."

Just then, Raji received a call on her cell phone. She looked at it and whispered, "It’s him again."

Kangna said, "Okay, answer the phone, and if he is willing for a 40% discount, maybe we can meet him."

Raji spoke on the phone and then informed Kangna that the property dealer was prepared to meet in the evening. Kangna asked Raji to arrange a meeting between Mr. Lonawala and Deepak in the former’s office in the evening.

A week later, the Pali Hill Bungalow deal had been signed. It was a beautiful property in a 1000 square metre plot, with a lovely lawn and swimming pool in the backyard. The constructed area was about 20,000 square feet built over three floors. It would be a perfect place for Kangna and her team to live, and she could have an office on the ground floor. The property was worth around Rs. 54 crores, but the deal was being struck at Rs. 35 crores. Kangna liked the villa so much that she just had to do it. Although they were leveraged very dangerously with this new investment, the endorsements would be done in a few months. It would be tight for a while, but they would be okay after that.

It had been a month after Kangna had signed for and paid the advance for her Pali Hill villa. She had been out with Palak and some friends from her hometown, celebrating Kangna's recent success. They came home in the evening.

Raji approached her with a sheaf of letters, just as Kangna came in and settled on the couch.

"Raji, you know we do the mails in the morning."

"Mam, I thought this was important."

"Raji, I have been signing contracts left, right, and centre. I am done now. Cannot do any more endorsements. And anyway, bring it up in the morning. I am really pooped now."

"Mam, it's a cancellation notice on the Videocon contract."

"What! How can that be?"

"And also, Mam, there are three other cancellations."

Kangna was alarmed, "Show me. It's not possible."

She went through the bunch of papers, "Call Mr. Lonawala immediately. I need to see him right now."

By the time Mr. Lonawala, her legal counsel, arrived, the situation had spiraled. Twelve out of her twenty endorsement deals—gone. Six movie contracts—pulled. All citing the same reason: a pending criminal defamation suit filed by Rajesh.

Lonawala, his face grim, nodded. “Someone planned this. Someone who knew exactly how to strike.”

Kangna’s blood turned cold. Umesh. Of course, it was him. This was his signature—calculated, surgical destruction. She wasn’t just fighting for her career. She was fighting to survive.

Mr. Lonawala continued as Batliwala joined them. "We have received notices for 12 endorsement cancellations out of the 20. We could receive a few more or even all of them. We will have to wait and watch till next week."

"Go on," said Kangna.

"We have 30 days to reply to these notices. Assuming the worst-case scenario, that all the contracts get canceled, we will have a maximum time of another 45 days to return all the money that we have received as advance and used to pay as an advance for the two properties and payments for the cars." He looked up at Kangna to see how bad she was taking it, as it seemed like a hopeless situation to him.

Palak was scribbling on a sheet of paper in front of her, quite impassive. Kangna said, "Mr. Batliwala, where do we stand with our fund flow. What are our commitments for the next six months, and what impact will cancellations have on the fund flow. Besides, what is the outflow related to such cancellations, and when would it be due?"

Mr. Batliwala was well prepared. He made a click on his open laptop. He started rattling off figures like he was a machine himself, "Ms. Kangna, We had 20 endorsements for Rs. 25 crores, out of which we had received six crores as advance, and the balance would have come in, within three to six months depending on the execution of the contracts. We had signed eight movies for a total contract value of 88 crores, out of which we have already received eight crores as advance, and the balance would come in different stages, based on completion of the films. The amounts have been rounded off to the nearest crore for easy understanding." He looked up at her. She looked back at him with comprehension.

Mr. Batliwala continued, answering the second part of her question, continuing with his 'we' as if he was also acting in the movies. "We bought the Manali farmhouse for a price of Rs. 30 crores, out of which we made a down payment of 20%, which is Rs. six crores. The balance of Rs. 24 crores will be payable in four interest-free, six-monthly installments. That means, in five months from now, we will have to pay another Rs. 6 crores and so on. The villa we bought for Rs. 35 crores, with a down payment of Rs. 5 crores, and the balance Rs. 30 crores will be payable in 120 days from the date of the deal, and since a month has elapsed, that means three months from now the amount is due. The cars we had bought on a down payment of about Rs. 2 crores, so there is no further liability on them."

Palak looked up and read from the notes she had been making, "So the major outflow is Rs. 30 crores in 3 months from now, and Rs. 6 crore five months from now, am I right, Mr. Batliwala?"

"Perfect. Also, in case of cancellation of all the endorsements, that is in the worst-case scenario, we have will have to refund Rs. 6 crores to the companies/agencies who had given us advance for the same."

Mr. Batliwala continued, "Ms. Kangna, if we are not able to pay the balance amount of Rs. 30 crores for the villa in the three-month time frame, they will forfeit our advance of Rs. 5 crores, and we will have to pay an additional penalty of Rs. 10 crores."

"Oh my God, why so?" Palak intervened

Mr. Lonawala answered her, "We had struck a bargain deal for a property worth Rs. 50 crores; the owner was selling at a discounted price of Rs. 35 crores, as he needed the money urgently, and hence we had agreed to the penalty clause. Moreover, we were not anticipating any problem in paying the balance amount."

Palak continued, "That's a lot of money to be paid out in the next six months. There is no way that we can pay that out, in case we do not have the endorsements."

Mr. Lonawala said, "I have another bad news for you. Would you like to hear it in private?" looking at Raji.

Kangna said, "Mr. Lonawala, you may continue. This is my team and my family." Raji looked at her gratefully.

Mr. Lonawala, who was making contracts for many of the film folks, said, "I am privy to information that the Pali Hill deal was done to trap you. There was already a plan to file a case against you so that your endorsements would get cancelled, and since you would not be able to fulfill the deal, you would have a monetary loss of Rs. 15 crores."

Palak stared in anger on hearing the shocking news. Kangna said, "I had figured that they filed the case to get my endorsements cancelled. But even I had not thought that Pali Hill was a trap."

As the others stared helplessly, Kangna said, "Whoever initiated Pali Hill would have invested at least Rs. 10 crores towards advance. With the thought that we will be unable to meet our commitment and will suffer a loss, thereby hurting us, but also making a big profit in the bargain. Now, if we can pay off the Pali hill amount, not only we get a premium property at a discount, but the person who had paid the advance will lose what he has invested. Am I right, Mr. Batliwala?"

“That’s right, Ms. Kangna,” Batliwala confirmed.

Palak summarized, “That means we have to arrange Rs. 36 crores within five months, assuming the worst happens, and we lose all our endorsements.”

Kangna leaned back in her chair, her mind already churning through solutions. “Whatever happens, even if I have to sell off all my other assets, I will not let go of the Pali hill bungalow. Let's take the fight into their court. Have you taken the cost of legal expenses into consideration?

Mr. Batliwala nodded. "Yes, but if the defamation case lingers, there could be further legal expenses. Plus, if the producers decide to pull out, we may face additional penalties for contract breaches."

Kangna remained quiet for a moment, absorbing the enormity of the situation. Palak, sitting beside her, felt a growing knot of anxiety in her stomach, but Kangna's steady demeanor reassured her.

Finally, Kangna spoke, her voice firm and decisive. "We're not going down without a fight. First things first, we need time. Mr. Batliwala, I want you to negotiatc with the property sellers—request an extension on both payments. Use my track record, my name, and if needed, offer a small penalty fee to buy us a couple more months."

Mr. Batliwala nodded, making notes on his laptop.

"Mr. Lonawala," she turned her attention to the lawyer, "I want you to draft responses to these cancellation notices. We'll challenge every single one of them. Use any legal loophole, every technicality. Delay, dispute, and drag it out as long as possible."

"I can do that," he agreed. "But you know the pressure will increase."

"Let it. I'm not here to make their life easy," Kangna said with a glint in her eye. "And we're going to counterattack."

Palak leaned forward. "What's the plan?"

Kangna's face hardened. "They want to destroy me quietly, but I'll drag them into the light. We'll give Umang Chaturvedi all the ammunition he needs—exclusive interviews, evidence of industry bullying, and how powerful figures sabotage anyone who won't bow to them. Let's expose their dirty tricks."

Lonawala raised his eyebrows. "You're taking a big risk, Kangna. They could retaliate harder."

"They already are," she shot back. "I'm not a helpless girl from Delhi anymore. I know the game, and I know where to hit back." She turned to Palak. "I want our social media team to craft a strong narrative. No victim talk—we focus on resilience, on truth. We show my fans the reality behind the glitz and glamour. If the mainstream media won't support us, we'll create our own wave."

Palak's face brightened with resolve. "Consider it done."

"And one more thing," Kangna continued. "Find out everything on Umesh—his dealings, his weaknesses, and his secrets. If he wants to play dirty, we'll show him we're not afraid to get our hands dirty too."

Mr. Lonawala hesitated for a moment. "Are you sure you want to escalate this? There's no going back after this point."

Kangna's gaze was unyielding. "I'm sure. I've worked too hard to let them tear it all away. If they want war, I'll give them one."

Kangna leaned back, deep in thought. The pieces were falling into place. The financial hit was severe, but not impossible to recover from. The real challenge was time. She had to secure funds fast. The big players had assumed she would crumble under pressure, but they had underestimated her resilience.

She looked up at Mr. Batliwala. "We need a financial strategy. If we liquidate some assets or find an investor, how much time can we buy?"

Mr. Lonawala jumped in, "If we can show a structured repayment plan, we might be able to renegotiate the terms of the endorsement clawbacks. Some brands might be willing to reinstate the contracts if we can handle the legal crisis quickly."

Mr. Batliwala continued, "I can look into alternative financing; perhaps a short-term loan against your existing assets. But lenders will hesitate unless we prove your earning potential is intact."

Palak said, "What about international brands? You've built a global image after *Another Day*. Maybe we can tap into endorsements outside India?"

Kangna's eyes lit up. "That's an idea. Raji, contact our PR team in London and LA. See if they can arrange meetings with brands that don't care about Bollywood politics."

Mr. Batliwala added, "And what about your social media? You have millions of followers. Why not monetize it aggressively? Sponsored content, direct brand partnerships; cut out the middlemen."

Kangna smiled. "Yes. If traditional endorsements drop me, I'll create my own brand. Fashion, cosmetics, wellness; my fans trust me more than any brand ambassador. Let's explore launching my own label."

Mr. Lonawala looked impressed. "This is risky but brilliant. If you can sustain your image and finances for the next six months, you'll come out stronger than ever."

Palak, still fuming, said, “And what about the legal case? That’s the root of all this.”

Mr. Lonawala nodded. “I’ll have my best lawyers go over Rajesh’s claims. If it’s baseless, we can file a counter-case for harassment and damages. That could put pressure on them to withdraw.”

Kangna exhaled slowly, feeling her power return. The vultures had circled, but they hadn’t broken her. She was still standing.

“Alright,” she said, her voice firm. “Let’s turn this game around. They want me out? Let’s show them who they’re messing with.”

Palak’s heart swelled with pride as she watched Kangna—a woman who had risen from nothing—refusing to be broken by the system. The room, once filled with anxiety, now pulsed with energy and defiance.

As the meeting concluded, Kangna stood and looked out over the Mumbai skyline. The city had given her everything—fame, fortune, and identity. But it had also tried to break her.

Not this time.

She was ready for battle.

CHAPTER - 56

KANGNA – Killer Punch (2014)

Kangna broke for a small nap, as she was up since 3 in the morning. She'd asked Raji to arrange a meeting with Raj, her manager. She woke up after an hour's nap. Raj was already waiting in Kangna's office. She asked for a cup of coffee and went down to meet Raj, alone.

She was thankful to be associated with Raj for more than a decade now; he had always been supportive, honest, and transparent; an extremely rare breed among the agents in Bollywood. She had become really fond of him. On top of that, he was always alert, with his ear to the ground, and knew the mumblings and rumblings beneath the surface.

As expected, she did not have to brief him about the happenings of the past few days. He had caught up with what was going on. She asked him for his feedback on the situation.

Raj came straight to the point, "The situation is bleak now. Most of the companies will cancel the endorsements."

"What about the films that I have signed. How many of them will break the contracts?"

"Mam, I will be very blunt. I know you also like it that way."

"Yes, yes, of course."

"Right now, you are bad news. The bigwigs have shown their power, and nobody wants to be seen working with you or supporting you directly or indirectly. None of the bigshots were anyways directly associated with you. The smaller players, if they play ball with you, will be hit harder than ever and will be out of the industry, for keeps. Then, they have political backing, so if anyone plays too smart, they may even threaten them or their family, indirectly."

"So, out of the 10 projects that I have signed, how many do you think will see the light of the day?"

"Maybe two. There is the old Mr. Dabbawala, who does not listen to any nonsense from anyone, but then he has limited resources, and even if he releases his movie, it will not have a great impact."

Kangna thought for a moment. "This is one hell of a battle, Raj. I have my back to the wall, and they have all the resources. But I am going to go on the front foot. I will take the offensive into the enemy camp, and I will wallop them; they will not know how to deal with it. You see, Raj, look at it like a boxing match, where a boxer is so good with aggression, that he had never been hit in the underbelly, and his defence is weak. With the first killer punch in the belly, he folds up. So that's what I am going to do to them. I will hit them in the underbelly, and hit them hard."

Raj looked at her admirably. She was one gutsy girl. He had known Kangna since she was 17. She was fighting all alone then, and she was fighting alone now.

Kangna continued, "I am going to be like the Jhansi Ki Rani. We all know who Jhansi ki Rani was, don't we? She was surrounded by the British and by the traitors of her own kingdom. Yet, she fought with all of them, with her little child tied to her back; she killed them and created dread in the hearts of her enemies, although they outnumbered her more than twenty to one. That's what I am going to do to them. I will create dread in their hearts."

Suddenly Raj had a bright look in his eyes. "Mam, a friend mentioned that an industrialist is looking to make a movie on the brave Queen of Jhansi. I feel you would be perfectly suited to that role."

Kangna's eyes lit up, "See, isn't it amazing. The thoughts and vibrations in our subconscious mind help us attract similar vibrations from the consciousness."

Raj was excited, "In case we can sign such a project, which would be a historical movie in itself, the endorsements will be back in your lap, and we can get out of this mess."

"Go for it, Raj. Set up a meeting as soon as possible."

Later that night, as Kangna lay in bed trying to wind down, her phone rang unexpectedly. It was Mr. Lonawala. They had already met earlier in the day, so she wondered what could be so urgent. Answering, she said, "Hello, Mr. Lonawala, is everything alright?"

His voice was low and hesitant. "I am sorry to call this late, but I needed to tell you something important before I turn in."

Kangna was now wide awake, "I am listening, Mr. Lonawala."

"As you know, I am an advocate for many folks from the film industry, and I look after their affairs, which could be regular and sometimes, not so regular, you know what I mean?"

“Look, I don’t want to hear about any client details. I appreciate discretion; but what’s the point?” she pressed, already uneasy.

“Ms. Kangna, I’ve learned that some people are actively trying to ruin your career. I knew about the criminal case that had been set up to cancel your endorsements.” His voice wavered slightly.

Kangna was stunned. She’d trusted Mr. Lonawala completely. “How could you be involved in this conspiracy? I trusted you more than anyone else. You were recommended by Wasim Bhai. Do you realize what you’re doing? You talk about confidentiality and ethics, yet here you are.” Her tone was a mix of hurt and anger.

After a long silence, Mr. Lonawala spoke again. “You’re right. I’ve let you down. I’ve been under enormous pressure and facing threats in ways you can’t imagine. I can’t reveal names; they’re dangerous. I’ve always admired your courage, and today I felt compelled to be honest with you. I understand if you want to terminate my contract. I’ll transfer all your files immediately if that’s what you choose.” He paused. “I am truly sorry, Ms. Kangna. Good night.”

The line went dead, leaving Kangna in a heavy silence. As she lay down, her mind raced with questions: How long had this been going on? Who else was involved? And what exactly were these threats? The shock of betrayal mixed with a surge of determination.

Struggling with a rush of overwhelming emotions, she realized she needed to clear her head. Remembering a technique she’d recently learned, Kangna began taking slow, deep breaths, focusing solely on the rhythm of her breathing. Gradually, the torrent of emotions subsided.

She got up, grabbed a piece of dark chocolate, and made herself a cup of chamomile tea. The small acts of self-care helped steady her thoughts. Despite the complications with Mr. Lonawala and knowing he often juggled conflicting interests, she felt a renewed sense of resolve. His confession, though painful, had not broken her trust completely. In fact, his honesty, risky as it was, reinforced her belief in him.

Still, the threats he mentioned gnawed at her. She considered calling Wasim Bhai to fill him in but decided against it, fearing that could complicate matters even more. For now, she would handle things her way.

Kangna closed her eyes, determined to face whatever came next with the same fierce resolve that had carried her through every challenge so far.

CHAPTER - 57
SAHIL – Game Plan (2014)

Sahil was riding high on the success of his movie *Rainy Days*. When he saw an interview where, Kangna, an actress known for speaking her mind and calling out the established Bollywood families, spoke openly about industry corruption, he didn't hesitate to back her up publicly. Although Kangna's boldness earned her praise from the general public, few insiders had the guts to stand by her. Sahil, however, wasn't afraid to speak the truth when asked about his views in a media interaction.

Not everyone was happy about Sahil's rising stardom or his outspoken support. Late one night, Umesh irked by Sahil's success and his comments on Kangna, met Vikram Seth along with Kamal. Vikram was already down about half a bottle. As he came in, Kamal was sitting in the lawn in Umesh's house, sipping wine.

Vikram snapped, "You're such a wimp; sitting around with your wine while these new talents are rewriting the rules. Ever thought about acting like a man for once?"

Kamal tried to placate him, while Umesh grinned from ear to ear, "Vikram, calm down, that's what we are here for, to discuss how to handle these people."

Vikram glared at Kamal but shut up and sat down.

Umesh said, "Well, Kamal, your soft diplomacy isn't working; We cannot look like fools while the likes of Kangna openly insult us. You need to maintain your dignity, at least in the eyes of the public."

Kamal retorted, "Right now, this Kangna is like a hot charcoal. We will only burn our fingers, trying to handle her. I feel we should leave her alone for the time being."

Umesh was thoughtful. Vikram glared at Umesh, "you think of something. Your last idea was such a blunder; not only it failed, but she also took the rupees 10 crores I had invested to finance the deal of the Pali hill villa."

Umesh came up with an idea, "Kamal is right. Let the girl cool off for the time being. We will deal with her later. As of now, let us focus on this upstart, who thinks he is a superstar, just because of a few freak hits. I have a plan; Kamal, you offer him a film, drag its production for a year, and make it so badly that it cannot be released at all. Let me ask Amar Gehlot to sign him for one more such project, and I will personally offer him a project. Let these projects look great on paper. Let us take three years to complete these three mega films, and then dump them on the public. By then, he'll be so beaten down that he'll be forced to disappear from the scene."

And so, the plan was set in motion. Sahil was signed on for three big projects with major studios. The first film, Rodeo, was being produced by Kamal. They started shooting in Mumbai, then reworked the script and reshot several scenes in a small town in Bihar. Before long, the director fell ill and scheduling conflicts piled up. What was meant to be a straightforward production stretched on for over a year, and every twist was carefully engineered to derail the project. Even though Rodeo might have drawn crowds; after all, it was still Sahil's film; the powers that be leaked claims that it was so poorly made that the producer refused a theatrical release.

About a month later, Sahil and Shamita were at home. Sahil's second movie, which was to be directed by Umesh, was still not on the floor and would not be for another month or so. It was about two months behind schedule as of now. Sahil had not been doing much these last few weeks and the inactivity got to him. The burst of endorsements that come one's way after a successful movie also did not happen. Sahil was worried. His mind went around in circles, but without any result.

Shamita had been busy with her shoots and had worked continuously for the last 15 days and could not give him much time. Today, they were together after a long time. Shamita had asked Usha also to come home, as she felt it may help Sahil get over this phase and they could help him look at the situation more objectively.

As the three sat and discussed the problem on hand, Shamita asked Sahil, "But I still don't understand why Kamal did not release the movie?"

Sahil replied, "He thinks it's a bad film and not worth releasing. It will bring the Thapar production house a bad name."

"Come on, they have done much worse before; we have seen such shit come out from their studios," replied Shamita.

Sahil was thoughtful. Usha asked him, "Sahil, you know this contract was not through me. If you don't mind, can I ask you if they have paid you and all the others who were involved in the production of this movie?"

Shamita replied, "Yeah, it's bad that they did not release the film, but what's worse is, he has not been paid anything after the initial signing amount of 10%."

"Really? Why so?" Usha was equally shocked

Sahil looked sheepish, "It was Kamal Sir's production, which is one of the biggest production houses, so I was not worried about the money. Besides, he'd offered me a good deal, a 30 percent share in profits in addition to my fees, so in a way, I am a producer of the movie."

Usha was quiet. Shamita spoke up, "What do you think Usha, is that a good deal?"

Usha answered diplomatically, "If I see the contract, I may be in a better position to comment."

Shamita came back with the contract and gave it to Usha.

The shock showed on Usha's face as she read through the main conditions, "I have never seen a contract like this. They are bound to pay you, if and only if the movie gets a release. This has been justified and tied up with the clause of 30 percent profit sharing. If the release does not happen, you have to return the 10 percent signing amount as well. It's the weirdest contract I have ever seen!"

Shamita was seeing red and was losing her cool, "I think they have outright cheated you. Even a newcomer does not sign a contract like that."

Usha was justifiably alarmed. "Who is your advocate who vetted this contract for you, Sahil Sir? There is no clause to protect you if the movie does not get released."

Sahil spoke in a low, thoughtful voice, "I have always been using the advocate of Amar Gehlot productions, as I came in through them. I did not see any reason to change them."

Shamita was now almost screaming, "And Amar Gehlot is a close friend of Kamal Thapar. So, they had no intention of releasing this movie in the first place. They have cheated you and wasted one year of your career with this movie."

Sahil looked puzzled, "Why would they do that? And will they not spoil their reputation by not releasing their movie?"

Usha was curious now. This was getting more puzzling by the minute, "Did they pay the others who were involved in the production, and other artistes?"

Sahil thought carefully, "If I think back now, the characters required for the plot were very few, mostly junior artists. The heroine was new; as the idea was that the story required a new face, and the director was in-house again, one of Kamal's assistant directors."

Shamita continued in her high-pitched voice, "All in all, it means they have not paid a penny to anybody. They shot one schedule locally, which was scrapped. The other schedule was shot in a small town in Bihar, which would have not cost them too much, so they hardly spent much on the entire movie."

Usha picked up from there, "I am not sure how much of post-production work they have completed on the movie. If they were not planning a release, they would have just done a sham job and not spent too much there. Also, it is again in-house in their own labs. Tell me one thing, Sahil Sir, did they hold a trial? And if so, what was the response of the industry?"

Sahil replied, "The trial was in-house, with our team, and a few other directors like Umesh Sir, Vikram, and a few close friends of Kamal Sir."

Shamita added, "basically, all their own group and cronies, not a real trial actually."

"Actually, I liked the movie in the trial, I mean it was different, not bad at all, but the others thought it was awful and could not be released. I was voted out."

Usha said, "In that case, they could have at least released the movie in about 2000 theatres instead of the usual 6000 to 8000 that they do. By not releasing the movie, they have also completely saved the promotion budget."

Shamita, by now, was shouting at the top of her voice, "I get it now; they never had a plan to release this movie in the first place. All they wanted to do was to waste your time."

Sahil said, "But why would they do that? After all, it's their loss too."

Shamita continued, "Don't you see it, Sahil? Kamal is a good friend of Amar. First, Amar kept you trapped in his contract for three years. Then you gave two big hits. Amar wanted you to do a film with Kamal, but you turned down the movie because of the condition attached. They now want to destroy your career."

Usha was in shock. So was Sahil. He had never thought about it this way. The more he thought about it, the more he realised that Shamita, minus her histrionics, was getting quite close to where the truth lay. Was it not the reason they had scrapped the first schedule done in Bombay altogether? They had taken over a year for a project, which could have easily been completed in six months.

On top of that, they had decided not to release the movie. It probably did not come out as bad as they wanted it to be. But during the trial, they outvoted him and scrapped the release. "Oh my god, I have been taken for a ride and a long one at that. They have been playing with me for so long, and I did not even see it. I have been such an emotional fool."

Shamita added, "And the other two movies that they signed with you, one with Umesh and the other with Amar, are all again part of the same plan. They plan to stall you for at least three to four years, by which time you would be a spent and defeated resource, and then they will stomp you out like a smoked cigarette."

Sahil agreed, "Yes, you are right. And that's the reason why they are not starting the second project, just delaying and prolonging it, as that would be their plan. They want to finish me off professionally."

Usha was flabbergasted, "Oh my god, what is with this scheming and planning! If only these people used such creativity in their scripts!"

"Sahil Sir, if you need to change your lawyer, let me know. There is one Mr. Lonawala, a very reputed lawyer, and he handles the files of many top actors of Bollywood.

After a week, Sahil got to meet Umesh in his office. He had been trying to set up a meeting for the last one week, after his discussion with Shamita and Usha, but apparently, Umesh was too busy with another script. However, he reached Umesh's office and was ushered in, and was surprised to see Kamal was also there.

"Oh! my superhero, come in, come in, nice to see you, how have you been?"

"Good sir, how are you? How are you, Kamal Bhai?"

"All good, just a little down after *Rodeo* did not work out," Kamal replied, shaking his head, "how are you doing?"

"Really bad! Actually, that's why I wanted to meet you, Umesh Sir. When are we starting the movie? We are already two months behind schedule. And I have been whiling away time, doing nothing."

"We are reworking on the script. Do you want it to be a fiasco like *Rodeo,* Sahil? I want to be very careful this time."

"Umesh Sir, I appreciate it. But what happens if we are not able to start the movie for the next six months? I will be wasting my time doing nothing. I had kept myself free as was decided earlier.

Umesh's tone hardened, "This isn't a factory line, Sahil. Creativity doesn't work on a strict timeline. We, the producers, take the risk and invest in these films. You're not in charge of the deadlines."

Taking a deep breath, Sahil said, "That's exactly why I want to change the terms. I don't want any profit-sharing clause; just a fixed fee. I'm not comfortable being held hostage by these conditions."

Umesh was now shouting, "Who the hell do you think you are? This is not a pawn shop. The movies have been offered to you as a cluster and you can't at this stage say you want the contract altered for one project. I will have you thrown out of the industry."

"Look," Sahil replied calmly but firmly, "I respect you both, but I'm not intimidated. I'm going to start my own production house; one that values genuine creativity, supports fresh talent, and operates fairly. And if you try to block me, I won't hesitate to expose everything."

Umesh rose from his chair, advancing menacingly, "Get out of my office, or I'll have you kicked out."

Kamal tried to defuse the situation as Sahil seized the moment to walk out. As he opened the door, a cluster of staffers, eavesdropping on every word, nearly stumbled into the room.

The days that followed were a blur of anxiety and self-doubt. Sahil sank into a deep depression. He realized he'd made a grave mistake by trusting these big names and signing those contracts without independent legal advice. He'd declined other offers after Rainy Days, thinking he'd landed deals with Bollywood's elite. Now, he felt cornered, with his career deliberately stalled and his options dwindling.

He confided in Shamita about his desire to retreat to his hometown and reconnect with family. But both Shamita and Usha warned him against it. "You need to stay in the industry to find a way out; and to untangle these rigged agreements," they insisted.

CHAPTER - 58

KANGNA - Up For A Fight (2014)

A few days later, Sahil found himself sitting in the sleek, modern office of Mr. Lonawala, a seasoned lawyer in his sixties known for his calm demeanor and incisive advice. Usha had arranged the appointment, and from the moment Mr. Lonawala greeted him, it was clear that his soothing voice concealed a razor-sharp mind. No wonder Bollywood's top stars trusted him with their legal battles.

Mr. Lonawala carefully scanned the contracts Sahil had signed with Umesh and several others. His expression darkened as he said, "Sahil, these agreements are extremely one-sided. The lawyer who reviewed them didn't act in your best interest at all. I'm going to start the process of terminating the contracts with Umesh and Amar. As for the contract with Kamal, there isn't much I can do right now; but since *Rodeo* hasn't hit theaters yet, we can at least argue that you don't have to repay that ten percent advance."

As Sahil was leaving Mr. Lonawala's office, while waiting for the elevator in the building's modern lobby, Sahil nearly collided with a familiar face. It was Kangna; now a household name and one of the industry's biggest stars. He recalled her recent interview where she had fearlessly critiqued the dark underbelly of Bollywood.

"Hi, Kangna! How are you? It's great to finally meet you in person," Sahil said, a bit awed.

Kangna smiled warmly and replied, "Hi Sahil, I'm doing well. Nice to meet you too. I believe this is our first real conversation."

"By the way, I really enjoyed your performance in your latest film," he added.

"Thanks, Sahil. It's nice to know you appreciate films outside your own work. So, what brings you here today?"

"I just met Mr. Lonawala; he's now handling my legal issues," Sahil explained.

"That's good to hear," Kangna said. "He's been my lawyer for over a decade now. Honestly, he's incredible. But I have to run; I'm sure he won't wait long."

With a quick farewell, Kangna headed off.

As Kangna went in to meet Mr. Lonawala, he seemed sheepish after last night's conversation. "So, you have come to collect your files. I could have just sent them over to you, Ms. Kangna."

"Mr. Lonawala, I have not come to collect my files. Do you think relationships of so many years can be broken off just ike that? You are as old as my father, but that does not mean I will not admonish you. You deserved what I told you last night. Even so, you have looked after my interests for so long, Mr. Lonawala, and I still trust you."

"Even after what I told you last night? You are still going to work with me, Ms. Kangna?"

"I am not going to let you off so easily, Mr. Lonawala. I was thinking about what you told me last night. I still don't understand what exactly happened and what sort of pressure you were under, but I am sure there must be some compelling circumstances to make you do what you did. Having said that, I appreciate your courage and integrity to come out with the truth."

Touched, Mr. Lonawala's voice wavered. "Kangna, thank you for your trust. I promise I won't let you down."

Kangna's eyes softened as she recalled their long history. "I still remember when I was 17 and Wasim Bhai introduced me to you. I owe a lot to you both for helping me get to where I am today."

Clearing his throat, Mr. Lonawala's tone turned somber. "Kangna, this industry isn't what it seems. People keep up appearances even off-camera. With your fearless stance on so many issues, you're bound to ruffle some very dangerous feathers. All I'm asking is, be careful.

Kangna's eyes narrowed slightly. "Who exactly is threatening you, Mr. Lonawala?"

He shook his head. "I can't disclose names; it would violate my professional ethics, and frankly, it wouldn't serve you well. These are powerful people, and knowing them might put you at risk. Please, just be cautious."

Kangna wasn't easily intimidated, though his warning didn't leave her unaffected. "I ran into Sahil outside, earlier. He seemed really down about his situation. Is he okay?"

"He's in deep trouble, cornered by the industry's heavyweights with these exploitative contracts," Mr. Lonawala explained. "Both of you are up against the same rigged system. Trust me, taking on Bollywood's top dogs on your own is like fighting a mafia."

Kangna's gaze hardened. "If this industry is so corrupt that newcomers have to sacrifice their freedom, endure exploitation, or even risk their lives, then what are we really dealing with? Is this a space for creative souls, or has it become a criminal enterprise?"

Mr. Lonawala sighed. "Kangna, it's become a mafia. It's enormous and deeply entrenched."

"Then I'm not going to cower," she declared. "I respect those who earn it, not those who instill fear. I'm not leaving this industry. If these influential families and power brokers think they can break my spirit, they've got another thing coming. I'm willing to risk everything, if that is what is required for cleaning up this mess."

Mr. Lonawala reached out and gently held her hand. "I admire your passion, Kangna. Truly, bless you."

As Kangna turned to leave, Mr. Lonawala called out, "One more thing; I'm switching our communication to Skype from now on."

Kangna looked puzzled. "Skype? Who still uses that?"

He offered a wry smile. "My phone might be tapped, and Skype's end-to-end encryption is the best defense I've got right now. Plus, it has a secure call-recording feature."

Kangna chuckled softly. "Fair enough. Stay safe, Mr. Lonawala."

With that, they parted ways; both acutely aware that the battle against an industry run like a modern-day mafia was only just beginning.

CHAPTER - 59
SAHIL - Fiasco (2014)

A few weeks later, Sahil's phone buzzed with a call from Usha. "Hey Sahil, are you free this evening?" she asked.

"Yeah, I've got some time. What's up?" he replied, curious.

"Not exactly the news you were expecting. A girl named Kimi reached out to me. She wants me to be her manager; and I think you should meet her, since she's also had a rough time with Umesh."

"Really? That sounds interesting."

"I'm meeting her tonight at 8 at the Novotel in Juhu. You in?"

"Absolutely. Shamita will be home soon; we'll drop by together."

At 8:30 pm, Sahil and Shamita arrived at a modern beachside bar in the Novotel. Usha was already seated with a pretty girl whose animated chatter almost drowned out the ambient music. Shamita leaned in, listening intently as Usha introduced them.

"Hey, meet Kimi. Kimi, this is Sahil and Shamita."

Kimi got up and shook hands with them, and continued her narration, "So, as I was telling you, he offered me this film, and he wanted me to accompany him on a recce to Nepal before he actually signed me for the film. So, I asked him, who works like that. How can I go for a recce with you, even before you sign me up? And anyway, what work does an actress have on a recce? It is the job of a director, DOP, and the producer. So why should I go on a recce at all? But Umesh was insistent; you want to sign a film with me, then you have to go on a recce. No recce, no film. I said, Umesh, you think I am a fool to fall into your trap. I may be only 24, but I have seen the world and seen enough guys like you to know the score by now."

Usha interrupted her, "Sahil Sir also had an awful experience with Umesh Sir."

Kimi said, "Really? I didn't know he was into boys too! Hahaha...," she laughed at her own joke.

Usha was embarrassed, "No, no, it's not about that. And then she told Kimi about the way these guys had planned his contracts."

Kimi agreed, "Real set of bastards these guys are. All they do is copy these foreign flicks, put in copied music, get new heroines whom they don't want to pay, and then they want pussy on top of that."

Everyone laughed at the way she had put it. To the point!

Nothing much came of the meeting. But at least Sahil felt better, knowing that he was not alone.

He had liked Kimi's confidence too. There was something about her devil may care attitude towards life; she was so full of energy that life bowed at her behest, that made troubles disappear, and gave hope. She had the verve to take life by the horns. Although, she had only two movies so far, and that too B-grade ones, she carried the aura of a superstar.

Sahil had enjoyed the evening. They had decided to keep in touch as both were in the same quest; looking for movies to act in.

Later, as they made their way home, Sahil couldn't stop talking about Kimi's fearless handling of Umesh and her vibrant energy. Shamita, though less impressed by what she considered endless chatter, was glad to see him in high spirits.

About two weeks later, Usha had invited them to her birthday party at her house in Malad. She stayed on the top floor of a bungalow in a one-bedroom apartment. She had access to the rooftop of the three-floor bungalow for the party. They reached around 9.30 pm, and there were about 20 guests, some of whom they knew, but casually. Everyone knew Sahil, and most of them knew Shamita from the TV series as well. There were four round tables with four to six plastic chairs around each. There were large potted plants decorated with lights, and there was a music system playing Hindi songs, placed on a low table, at one end of the terrace. A barbecue pit was installed in a corner with some chairs around it, and a few people were grilling meat and some cottage cheese cuts on them while they drank and talked.

Sahil and Shamita joined Usha and some others who were sitting at one of the tables. A houseboy and a maid were helping the guests with the drinks and the food. Usha asked them what they would like to drink, and Sahil chose a Budweiser while Shamita went for a vodka with orange juice. As they chatted, enjoying the wonderful and soothing evening sea breeze, the guys around the barbeque seemed to be having the most fun. Kimi was the one who was bossing the table. She regaled the group with her endless anecdotes that she brought back from the shooting stints of the two films she had done so far. She had everyone captivated, and the boys and girls could not stop guffawing at her comments. After finishing his beer, Sahil said, "Let me join the barbeque gang. I want to try the chicken."

As he approached them, Kimi said, "Come sit next to me; I will feed you chicken if you promise to tell us all about your experience on the sets of *Shikara*."

Sahil sat next to her, "Kimi, I want to hear your stories; chicken is only an excuse." Everyone laughed aloud.

Someone said, "He is interested in the chick, not the chicken." There was a wild roar.

Kimi, continued unabated, narrating the weird incidents which she had encountered in her life. If someone did not know her background, they would think that Kimi was a veteran of the film industry and not just a two-film old babe in the woods, as far as films were concerned. She had the audacity to address even the seniors with their first name. While even Sahil would address them as Umesh Sir or Kamal Sir, it was Umesh or Kamal for Kimi. She loved to be the centre of attention. Even though she had met most of Usha's friends for the first time, but they were like old buddies by now.

Everyone was having a good time. Liquor was flowing, and inhibitions were ebbing away.

Suddenly, one of the guys, Rajbir, a director of photography, asked, "Sahil Bhai, if you have the chance, would you like to take Kimi as the heroine in your next film?"

Sahil was a little high but not really drunk. He tactfully said, "Arre, I still have not signed any new film. We will cross the bridge when we come to it."

"Sahil Bhai, that's a very diplomatic answer. Kimi, it means he won't take you as his heroine!"

Kimi took on the challenge, "Really, Sahil, am I not good enough to be your heroine?"

Sahil said, "Come on Kimi, did I say no? After all, you are as beautiful as anyone in the industry. And bolder than most. I am sure you will be a great star one day."

Kimi said, "Why one day, Sahil? I am already a star in my mind. You guys better take my autograph before it is too late." Everyone clapped and laughed loudly.

Sahil said, "Well, I can say one thing for sure, Kimi has the chutzpah required to be a star."

"What the hell is chutzpah?" Kimi asked, coming closer to him.

"Chutzpah is a quality a star must possess. The talent is secondary. Chutzpah is self-obsession resulting in extreme self-confidence," Sahil told them.

"Well, sometimes chutzpah, without enough talent, gets you into trouble, more than anything else." Shamita said loudly as she also joined the barbeque group. She had been quietly drinking her vodka and had downed a few by now.

Everyone looked up at Shamita and stopped talking. She had spoiled their party.

Shamita had been listening to Kimi's nonsense for some time. Kimi had been gradually getting on her nerves. Shamita could see right through her put-on behaviour. And most of her so-called anecdotes were pure lies, Shamita knew. She had encountered many such shallow personalities in her career and could see right through them.

Kimi was not going to take this lying down, "Shamita, you will not get it. We are talking about movies here. It's a very different platform from the soaps that you do." And she mimicked Shamita from an act in her popular daily soap, like how they would repeat some dramatic sentences thrice, for effect, "Stop it, stop it, stop it, Shamita." Everyone doubled up with laughter.

Shamita's eyes were blazing at the insult. She wanted to wring Kimi's neck, but she controlled herself. "How many films have you done, Kimi? Just two, and they were C grade films, which only you watched along with your director. I have been doing soaps for eight years now, and the whole nation knows me. Nobody even recognises you. Guys, did you know who she was until she told you about those two silly films she acted in?" There was a stunned silence.

Usha was getting very uncomfortable with the direction this encounter was taking. After all, she had become quite close to Shamita and liked her a lot. She'd met Kimi only recently, but she was still a client. Usha tried to hold Kimi by the arm and take her away, but Kimi was not the one to give up without a retort, "The very fact that you have been at it for eight years and you have still not got anywhere, speaks volumes for your talent, Shamita. You have only another year or two left. Your expiry date as an actress is pretty near, darling!"

Shamita, who had been simmering near boiling point for a long time, tipped over. She was standing right behind Kimi. She caught hold of her hair from behind and yanked her head around. Kimi fell backward and on the floor near Shamita's feet. Shamita, in her rage, wanted to crush her face beneath her heels. Fortunately, in the melee, her heel had fallen off. Her right foot was on Kimi's face. "You two-bit actress, having acted in those stupid films, you act like you are a superstar! And I know how you would have gotten those roles, you bitch," she yelled as she ground her bare foot into Kimi's face and mouth, "lick my foot, you bitch, I will teach you your worth…"

Sahil had jumped up from his perch and held Shamita by her shoulders while putting his other hand on her mouth to stop her obscenities. Usha was also tugging at Shamita, but quite ineffectively. Ultimately Sahil carried Shamita off. Usha picked up the fallen and sobbing Kimi.

As Usha was consoling Kimi, she signalled to Sahil to take Shamita away, who, like a raging tigress, wanted to tear Kimi apart at the other end of the terrace. Sahil quickly took her down, and the party was over.

CHAPTER - 60

SAHIL - Hijacked (2014)

The next afternoon, Sahil woke to a blurry light filtering through the curtains. He'd spent a restless night haunted by strange dreams and an overwhelming sense of regret over what had happened the previous evening. His thoughts kept returning to Shamita; her behavior was completely out of character, and he couldn't understand what had driven her to act that way. Meanwhile, Shamita still slept peacefully, unaware of the storm she'd stirred up. With Kimi on his mind, Sahil picked up his phone and dialed Usha.

"Did I disturb you? Were you sleeping?"

"Not really. Have not slept much, managing the mess from last night."Usha replied softly.

"Really sorry about what happened."

"No, no, it's not your fault…"

"I know, but Shamita behaved very uncharacteristically."

"Yes, even I was surprised. What got into her? Usually, she is so docile and sweet. I know Kimi is boisterous and unbearable at times. But she is a party animal and loves to be the centre of attention."

"I know. I think I will call Kimi and get Shamita to apologise. I think she was too drunk to realise what she was doing."

"Sahil, you men are so stupid sometimes. She was drunk, so she was able to express her bottled up feelings. Maybe she reacted to Kimi's behaviour, as perhaps, you were giving Kimi too much attention; maybe she was jealous."

"No, not at all. I was just going along with the fun."

"I hope so. But sometimes women can feel what the men don't even know about themselves."

"What time did Kimi leave? Was she okay?"

"Yeah, she is actually quite a girl. Got over it soon enough."

"Great, however, I will get her over and let the girls sort it out between themselves."

"Thanks, Sahil, take care."

By 2:00p.m., Shamita had woken. “Good morning,” Sahil greeted as she shuffled into the room.

“Morning. My head’s killing me,” she muttered.

“Let me get you some aspirin and coffee.:”

Within minutes, the maid appeared with the medication and a cup of coffee. After a quick sip and a few moments to steady herself, Shamita said, “I have to get ready; I’ve got a four-hour shoot today.”

Sahil offered a tentative smile. “I talked to Usha. She thinks we should invite Kimi over so everyone can talk it out. Last night was rough for her.”

Shamita was still angry, “Did you see how boisterous her behavior was? Insulting me in front of everyone?”

“Even so, what you did was a bit much. You really lost it.”

“Are you taking her side?” she snapped.

“No, I’m not. We were all just having good fun; until things got out of hand.”

"Fun, really! She was feeding you with her own hand, and you were eating it like a baby. How stupid can you get?"

"I am sorry. I did not see it that way. Anyways, I am calling her in the evening, and we can just say sorry, as you really beat her badly."

Shamita crossed her arms. “I’m not apologizing to her. I’m not the one who made a mistake.”

“Alright, I will apologize. I’ll give her a call this evening. When do you get back?”

“By 9. My schedule ends at 8.”

“Okay. I’ll set things up for after that.”

By 9:20, Kimi arrived; a quiet, understated presence carrying a bottle of wine.

“What are we celebrating?” Sahil joked, trying to ease the tension.

“Last night,” Kimi replied with a wry smile. Her calm demeanor surprised Sahil; he’d expected anger and a storm of apologies.

Sahil tried calling Shamita again, but her phone remained off; habit she reserved for shoots, but this time the silence felt odd. After about half an hour of waiting, Kimi broke the tension.

"Let's open the wine," she suggested. "Maybe Shamita's caught up with work and will call when she can."

"Sounds good," Sahil agreed, pouring two glasses. "Cheers."

"Cheers to unpredictable nights," Kimi toasted.

As they sipped their wine, the conversation flowed easily. Sahil, who usually carried an aura of reserved celebrity charm in public, was animated in private. He talked about everything; from ancient philosophy and history to modern science and even light-hearted debates about whether the chicken or the egg came first. Kimi listened with an amused sparkle in her eyes, her mind more interested in the immediate pleasures of life; good food, travel, and enjoying the moment, than in abstract theory.

Before they knew, it was past 11. Sahil's initial calm was giving way to frustration. Shamita still hadn't called or shown up, and he suspected she was too stubborn to apologize or face Kimi's anger. In his mind, it was all a messy issue to move past and best be forgotten.

"Shamita's busy on set," he said. "Her schedule's overrun."

Kimi shrugged. "That's fine."

Feeling the need to make amends in his own way, Sahil suggested, "How about we grab dinner? I know you can't resist a good chicken dish."

Kimi's eyes lit up. "Sure! Any place in particular?"

"An evening on the beach, maybe. There's this spot at Novotel called Gadda da Vida."

At the restaurant, with a view of the sea and a cool breeze blowing through, they settled into a comfortable booth. They ordered a bottle of champagne and a dinner featuring Punjabi murg tikka and chicken kalami. The meal was hearty and satisfying, and Kimi devoured the chicken with gusto, least bothered what came first-the chicken or the egg.

After dinner, they decided to take a walk along the beach. Kimi pulled a cigarette from her purse, lit it, and held it out. "Want one?" she asked.

"Sure, let me try," Sahil replied, accepting the cigarette. He coughed after his first drag, "Hey, it's loaded!

"Not bad, right? Sometimes I need this to unwind," she said, smiling.

"This is what gives you the energy!"

"Haha, you like my energy?" She stopped and turned around to look at him.

As they strolled along the moonlit beach, the conversation eventually gave way to a charged silence. In a spontaneous moment, Kimi reached for his hand and pulled him close. Their kiss started gently but quickly deepened, fueled by pent-up emotion and the intimacy of the night. In no time, they found themselves back at Sahil's place; a decision made on impulse. The love-making was so intense that Sahil was surprised by his response to Kimi's advances. He was literally blown off his feet and their naked bodies entwined seeking complete union for better part of the night.

The next morning, Shamita called. Sahil was in no position to answer, with their bodies still intertwined. As reality began to settle in, he realized with growing alarm that he'd never been unfaithful before. He told himself he'd get up, leave Kimi's side, and later meet Shamita to smooth things over. No more apologies were required.

But as the morning unfolded, Kimi stirred again. Sitting up in bed, she lit another cigarette and, catching Sahil's hesitant gaze, leaned in for another kiss. Despite his internal turmoil, he found himself pulled back into her orbit. Their morning intimacy resumed, raw and urgent. Her tongue was in his mouth in a deep kiss, dissolving his earlier resolve. As she rode him in a frenzy, they both exploded in another mind- blowing orgasm and she said in a quiet, almost desperate whisper, "You're mine, Sahil. You belong with me."

At that exact moment, the sound of a key in the door shattered the fragile calm. Shamita had arrived. Expecting to find Sahil alone, she instead discovered him in the throes of a scene that confirmed all her worst fears. For a heartbeat, the three of them froze; Kimi's defiant stare meeting Shamita's eyes filled with a mix of shock and hurt disbelief. Kimi's eyes said it all, "Yes, you bitch, I have got your man, and look what I have done to you. You wanted to enslave me, now he is my slave," and simultaneously the middle finger of her left hand, which held on to Sahil, went up involuntarily. All this happened in a fraction of a second, and Shamita ran out of the room, with a subdued shriek. Shamita was out of the house, defeated and humiliated, never to come back again, into Sahil's home or his life.

In that instant, as Sahil looked on, everything had irrevocably changed. The night's choices had unraveled into a new reality; one marked by betrayal, shattered trust, and consequences that none of them had anticipated.

CHAPTER – 61
SAHIL - Party Time (2015)

It had been three months since Sahil moved in with Kimi, and life had taken on a new vibrancy. No longer was every day about work; Kimi had a way of making even the mundane feel like an adventure. In that short span, they'd managed two holidays: a quick getaway to Ooty and a weekend in Mauritius. Kimi's outgoing nature meant she was always in the middle of new friend circles, hosting impromptu gatherings at Sahil's apartment. With parties spilling over into every corner; from casual dinners to late-night soirees; their home had slowly transformed into a social hub. Despite their current creative lull, thanks to the fallout from Umesh's orders, money wasn't an issue for Sahil, whose savings gave him the freedom to live simply yet luxuriously.

One lazy afternoon, the couple met with Usha for lunch at the JW Marriott's cafe to talk about their next steps. Usha, who still managed Sahil's work, couldn't help but think how upset she was about how quickly Kimi had stepped in to replace Shamita. Kimi, with a glib tongue managed to talk Usha out of her blues. By the time dessert arrived, Usha's mood had lightened considerably.

They gathered around the dessert counter. Sahil's plate was a decadent mix; plate of jalebi, a serving of ras malai, and a generous scoop of vanilla ice cream. Kimi had opted for a warm slice of apple pie, while Usha chose a mango tart. As Sahil alternated between bites of jalebi and spoonfuls of ice cream, both women exchanged amused glances.

"Look at you," Usha teased. "You really enjoy your sweets, don't you?"

Sahil grinned. "I am a true country boy at heart. I grew up with this stuff."

Kimi rolled her eyes. "Maybe, but if you want to fit in with the city crowd, you need to upgrade your style a bit. Look at your clothes; you're too much of a rustic."

"Sure," Sahil said, half laughing. "But I'm proud of where I come from."

"That's sweet, but imagine a makeover; designer clothes from 'Sarah and Sandeep' in Khar, and then a session at Rashid Siddique's salon at the Taj. You'd be unrecognizable when you step into our new pad."

"New pad?" Usha echoed.

"Yeah! We just bought a duplex penthouse in Juhu," Kimi announced with a flourish. "Four bedrooms, plus a separate apartment for the staff. And guess what? You're invited to the housewarming next week."

Usha smiled, a little reservedly. "Wow, that's impressive. But why a separate space for the servants?"

Kimi shrugged. "Privacy, Usha. With our current setup, it's hard to have a party without the prying eyes of the help."

Weeks later, Usha found herself at yet another party at Sahil and Kimi's place. Although she wasn't part of their usual crew, she came once a month to stay connected with Sahil and to keep an eye on business. Their duplex four bedrooms, a small living room and kitchen on the ground floor, and a sprawling living area with French doors leading to a terrace with a dip pool on the upper level, had become a mini-club by night. The French doors were often folded into the wall to create one massive open space perfect for hosting.

That night, there were about thirty guests, mostly new faces from Kimi's circles. Sahil, whose true friends had always been fewer and quieter, sat with Usha at a quiet table, observing the revelry. As the night wore on, one of Kimi's friends, Vicky, sidled over and gave Usha a quick peck on the cheek.

"Dance with me?" he asked, grinning.

Usha laughed off his invitation. "I think I'm good. Last time my legs barely recovered!"

As the music pulsed, Sahil suddenly asked, "So, have you heard from Shamita? How is she doing?"

Usha smirked. "Oh, you still remember her?"

"Of course," Sahil replied. "Things happened so fast; I still wonder what went wrong."

"She's fine. Actually, we still talk about you," Usha teased.

"What about me?" Sahil prodded.

"Your whole new lifestyle: the fancy cars, the swanky house, the designer clothes and the new, upgraded version of you."

Sahil's cheeks warmed. "And the new cook, maid, and driver."

Kimi interjected with a playful tone as she rejoined them, "Hey, come on. Try this!" She thrust a joint into Sahil's hand.

Usha raised an eyebrow. “Since when did you start smoking joints? You never did before.”

“Since when did you become so nosy?” Kimi laughed and gave Usha a light tap on the arm. “Relax, it’s good for him. Doesn’t he seem more at ease?”

Before Usha could respond, Kimi grabbed Sahil and led him to the dance floor.

The next day, over brunch at Fifty-Five East in the Grand Hyatt, the tension from the previous evening still lingered for Sahil. He nibbled at his meal, lost in thought, while Kimi animatedly recounted the highlights of the party. Frustrated by his silence, she finally snapped, “Why are you just nodding along? Tell me what’s really going on in your mind.”

Sahil sighed. “We have a cook, a helper, and a maid at home. So why do we keep eating out?”

Kimi waved a hand dismissively. “They’re not just cooks; they’re a full-service team. After last night’s party, we needed extra hands to manage all the guests. This is exactly why we upgraded to a bigger place.”

“But why are we spending so much on salaries, food, and luxuries? I haven’t signed any new contracts, and our expenses are piling up,” Sahil countered.

"Hello! Where is all this coming from? I saw you and Usha talking very closely for quite some time at the party yesterday. Did she feed you all this shit?"

"Of course not," answered Sahil defensively.

Kimi’s tone hardened slightly. “Are you implying that my way of entertaining isn’t working? If we don’t host events, people will forget who we are. It’s all part of building your brand.”

Sahil frowned. “I was a star even before all this. Fans don’t just come from throwing parties.”

"And where will the money come from? I spoke to Mr. Parikh, our accountant, and you know what, he was alarmed at the rate the money is flowing out. He even informed my father about it."

“Look, you can buy followers and likes if you have to,” Kimi retorted sharply. “It’s not only about acting; it’s about creating a legacy. And besides, if we invest our money right, we won’t run out of cash. I’ve been reading ‘Rich Dad Poor Dad’ by Robert Kiyosaki. The idea is simple: let your money work for you. Imagine if our 40 crores doubled every three years; where’s the shortage?”

"Then why don't we do it?" Sahil asked quietly.

"Because your old accountant's ideas are outdated. We need someone modern; someone like Mr. George Fancy."

Sahil's eyes widened. "George Fancy?"

Kimi explained, "My father swears by him. He's been advising our family for years. I trust him."

A week later, Sahil's phone rang. It was his father.

"Hello, son!" his father's warm voice filled the line.

Sahil's demeanor changed instantly. "Hi, Papa."

After a brief exchange, his father's tone grew serious. "I heard you replaced Mr. Parikh. Why would you do that?"

"Papa, Parikh wasn't offering any new ideas. Our money was just sitting there at a nominal interest rate; barely beating inflation."

His father sighed. "He's been with the family for 20 years. If you want investment advice, hire an investment banker alongside him."

"But Papa, we've already brought in Mr. George Fancy. He's an expert."

"Has he come with references, son? In this business, trust and reputation are everything."

"Papa, Kimi's family recommended him," Sahil tried to reassure.

After a long pause, his father said, "I urge you to reconsider this decision."

Before Sahil could respond, the call ended abruptly.

For the next week, a heavy silence and gloom settled over Sahil. Even his daily workouts, something he never missed earlier, fell by the wayside. The terse call from his father stung deeply; family had always meant the world to him.

That evening, sensing his melancholy, Kimi sat beside him. "It's our tenth monthly anniversary today, you know," she said softly.

Sahil managed a half-hearted smile. "That's nice."

"Really? That's all you've got?" Kimi chided gently, then brightened her tone. "Come on, let's go out for dinner. I've got a surprise."

Sahil's eyes lit up as she pulled out a bottle of Reveillo wine; the one she'd given him when they first got together. He chuckled as he took it, the familiar bottle easing his mood. Later that night, they returned to Gadda da Vida at Novotel Juhu; the very place they'd first met. They ordered the same dishes, popped the same champagne, and ended up on the beach, laughing and dancing away the night. By the time they got home, the intimacy and ease between them had restored a bit of Sahil's spark.

Sometimes, a little good wine, some bubbly champagne, a relaxed smoke, and a lot of sex are all it takes to get the life force flowing. With a tentative smile, he finally agreed to plan their future. Kimi had already set up a meeting with Mr. George Fancy for the next day; a promise of change that, despite everything, still felt full of hope.

CHAPTER - 62

SAHIL - Big Game (2015)

Mr. George Fancy's office was the kind you'd expect in today's corporate world; a sleek space in Mumbai's Bandra Kurla Complex (BKC), a hub known for hosting top multinational firms and high-end companies. The fact that his firm occupied a large, well-appointed office and employed over 25 people was a clear signal that they were on top of their game. Sahil couldn't help but feel impressed; and Kimi's confidence in leaving behind their old, clumsy advisor, Mr. Parikh, was proving well founded.

Inside one of the many minimalist meeting rooms, a long rectangular table with eight modern leather chairs dominated the space. The decor was clean and contemporary: off-white walls, a plush white carpet, and floor-to-ceiling windows dressed in neat Venetian blinds. The room was a study in modern design; everything was pristine and deliberate, except for the two people who didn't quite match the color scheme. Mr. Fancy cut a striking figure in his tailored black suit and polished shoes, while Sahil and Kimi, dressed more casually, stood out in contrast.

Without wasting time, Mr. Fancy initiated the meeting by starting a timer on the table's built-in display. "Mr. Sahil, we've reviewed your files. I understand you're interested in hiring us as your financial consultants and money managers." His voice was measured and precise. As he spoke, Sahil found himself distracted by the gleam of Mr. Fancy's black cufflinks against his crisp white shirt; a small detail that somehow embodied the meticulous nature of this operation. His secretary, equally poised in her white skirt and matching coat, kept pace with his every word, her fingers flying over her tablet to take notes.

While Sahil was lost in thought by the clipped tone and the immaculate sorroundings, he didn't realise the meeting was at it's end when Mr George Fancy's words brought him back to the present. Mr. Fancy paused, glanced at the timer, and said, "57 minutes and 32 seconds. Let's call that 57 minutes; our clients aren't billed by the second." The precision wasn't just for show; at Rs. 300 per minute for his time and Rs. 120 for the secretary's, this meeting was set to cost around Rs. 24,000. Including the charges for the back-office team, their monthly expenses could easily run into several lakhs. Sahil couldn't help but wonder if the back-office staff were as exacting with their own timekeeping. In that moment, he was flooded with fond memories of Mr. Parikh; with his worn-out shoes and disorganized approach.'

Later, as Sahil and Kimi drove back from the meeting, Kimi was practically buzzing with excitement. "See? I told you, Mr. Fancy is brilliant. He's laid out a fantastic plan for us," she said. "We can set up three private companies to handle our film projects. By inter-company billing, we can boost the turnover on our main company and make it look robust enough to go public in two years. Then we can use that public listing to secure funding for our films, while all our expenses get tax benefits."

"But how are we going to form three companies?" Sahil asked, still processing the details. "He mentioned that each company needs at least two partners."

"That's why we hired him," Kimi replied confidently. "Mr. Fancy will take care of all the legal and financial structuring. You just focus on the creative side." With that, she leaned over and kissed him; a small, affectionate seal on a big, risky plan.

In that moment, amidst the hum of the city and the promise of a bold new venture, the future seemed both uncertain and thrillingly within reach.

CHAPTER - 63

USHA - A Friend In Need (2016)

It had been a couple of months since Usha last saw Sahil. She'd been calling his number over and over, but it always went straight to voicemail. Even when she texted Kimi, there was no reply. Worried, she reached out to Shamita; but Shamita had been off the grid for ages.

Finally, one afternoon, Usha decided to drop by Sahil's apartment without an appointment. The new staff didn't recognize her at first, but eventually someone led her into the living room. After waiting about ten minutes, Kimi appeared.

"Hey Usha, how have you been?" Kimi said, pulling her into a quick hug.

"I'm fine, thanks. But I've been trying to reach Sahil; his number isn't working," Usha replied.

"Yeah, he had lost his mobile and has a new number."

"Oh, I see," answered Usha, wondering why someone would get a new number as they could just replace it with a duplicate sim card.

Kimi, as if reading her mind, said, "You know, the sim got into the hands of some shady guys, and we got it disabled, and he had to get a new number."

"Oh, okay, can I have his new number? I have a project for him and would like to set up a meeting."

"Great, Usha! But please, just give him some time. He has not been keeping well of late."

"No worries, I can ask the producer to hold on. They are quite keen to work with him on this project. Can I see him, if that's okay?"

"He is actually resting now. He didn't sleep the whole night."

"Really, what's wrong? Is he seeing a doctor?" Usha was now worried.

"Of course, I have consulted a doctor. They have put him on some anti-depressant pills.

Actually, you know the problem started a couple of months ago. He had started smoking a lot of these joints and had gotten into cocaine too. I wanted him to drop these habits, but he was finding it hard. Also, he has not been getting any movies, so all this led to a major depression."

"Really, that's so strange. As I always knew Sahil to be a very balanced person, who would get up early in the morning and be in the gym and train for two hours every day. How did he give up all that and get into drugs? In fact, if I remember right, he was not even smoking when I first met him."

Usha was anxious about Sahil now. He had been such a happy-go-lucky person in life. Usha could not believe that the same Sahil could be lying in a helpless and depressed state due to overuse of drugs. Tears came to her eyes, "Kimi, please give me Sahil's number. I would like to speak with him. He has always been so positive. It's only in the last year he has got into all this trouble."

"Are you trying to blame me, Usha?"

"No, no. I don't mean that. I am just worried about Sahil. Please give me his number. I will speak to him once he is awake." Usha was insistent.

"Usha, I don't want you to disturb him now. I will tell him that you came by. And he will call you if he wants." Kimi dismissed her.

A couple of months had gone by since Usha had met Kimi. She remembered, last time she had almost been shown out, rather unceremoniously by Kimi. Usha gathered her courage and landed at Sahil's house to meet him. This time, she found both Sahil and Kimi sitting on the balcony. After a warm greeting and a quick hug from Sahil, Usha said, “I dropped by a couple of months ago, but you were asleep.”

Sahil looked momentarily blank. Usha turned to Kimi. “I thought you’d tell him I was here?”

Kimi gave a small shrug. “I did, but he’s been really forgetful lately.”

“But you promised you’d have him call me,” Usha pressed.

Kimi’s tone became defensive. “I said he’s forgetful, not that he’s always on schedule.”

Right then, Kimi called out to the maid, “Hey, can you get me a glass of water?” Returning with a glass, Kimi pulled out a small bottle and handed two tablets to Sahil. “Take your pills, please.”

Sahil frowned, “Kimi, these aren’t really helping. I’ve been on them forever, and I don’t feel any better.”

Kimi’s reply was firm, “The doctor said it’ll take six months for the meds to work. Just take them.

Usha was shocked by Sahil's appearance as he seemed to be completely dazed. This was not the Sahil she knew at all. Usha picked up the bottle of pills and looked at the label. Kimi quickly snatched it out of her hand, but Usha had been able to catch the word 'Amphetamines' in the subtext.

Kimi was angry. "Usha, don't be nosey. This is very personal. You can't intrude into our privacy like this."

Usha was going to get to the bottom of this. Something was fishy here. Why the antidepressant pills now? And what was so personal about these pills that Kimi did not want her to know. She was angry too, "Kimi, if you are forgetting, let me remind you, I was the one to introduce you to Sahil in the first place. In no time, you displaced Shamita out of his life, then you changed his house, his maid, his cook, and then you kicked his family out of his life, and now you don't even want me to see him, what's wrong with you? I don't even see his close friends around here anymore. And last time I came here two months ago, asking Sahil to call me, as a producer wanted to make a new film with him, and you didn't even call me back!"

Suddenly Kimi burst into tears. She sat on the sofa and sobbed uncontrollably. Usha moved to her side and started comforting her, "I am sorry, Kimi, I did not mean to hurt you. I really don't mean what I said; it just came out the wrong way. But I am worried, seeing Sahil like this."

Kimi sobbed some more, "You know Usha, you are right. I am so worried about Sahil. He seems to be getting worse by the day. I don't know what to do. And I am so alone; there is no one to support me. I am afraid that if anything goes wrong, everyone will blame me."

Usha's anger had melted, and she wanted to console Kimi. "Don't worry, Kimi, don't worry dear, you are not alone. We will find a solution to this. Let us consult some other doctors. You give me his medical file; I have a good friend who is a doctor, let him check it and refer us to a specialist. Now go and wash your face, dear. You will feel better."

Kimi went in. Usha sat by Sahil gently holding his hand and gradually Sahil relaxed and was more energetic. Usha was thankful. The medicenes seemed to be working. She gave a missed call to her phone from his number and saved it under 'Sahil last.' When Kimi returned a few minutes later, looking calmer, their mutual friend Vicky unexpectedly showed up.

“Hey Usha, long time no see!” Vicky greeted, his tone casual.

“Vicky, you’re rubbing elbows with the big leagues now,” Usha joked, recalling all the buzz about his connections in politics and Bollywood.

Vicky laughed. “Why don’t you come to my birthday party tomorrow? It’ll be a great chance to catch up.”

Usha hesitated for a moment. “I’m not sure; I don’t really fit that scene.”

Kimi chimed in, “Come on, Usha. Sahil and I are going too. It’s been ages since we all hung out. Let’s have some fun.”

“Alright, send me the details,” Usha said. Deep down, she knew this might be her chance to speak with Sahil privately; to warn him about what she suspected and to get to the bottom of things.

Usha forgot to collect the medical file she had asked Kimi for. She decided she’d pick it up at the party the next day. Her worry about Sahil deepened; if he didn’t get better, his career could be over, and no one would be willing to work with him. Then she recalled the ‘Amphetamines’ label. A quick Google search confirmed her fears: while amphetamines can treat certain conditions, they’re notorious for their side effects, potential for dependence, and a dangerous cycle of highs and crashes. In street slang, they were often called ‘Speed’ and were known for inducing a temporary euphoria and increased libido; followed by deep depression. Prolonged abuse could even lead to lasting brain damage and symptoms that resembled bipolar disorder.

After confirming her suspicions with her doctor friend, Usha’s concerns about Kimi’s handling of Sahil’s treatment, and the sudden appearance of Vicky, grew even stronger. That night, Usha resolved to find a quiet moment with Sahil. She planned to warn him about what she suspected was going on, and she’d also contact Shamita, who knew Sahil’s family well. Usha wasn’t going to let things spiral any further without uncovering the truth.

CHAPTER - 64

USHA - Final Destination (2016)

Usha preferred not to drive to today's party, to avoid drinking and driving. The Mumbai police had been doing an excellent job of punishing drivers who were behind the wheel under influence, and the patrolling was very strict during the night. Usha took a cab to Vicky's house.

She arrived at 9 PM and could already hear music pulsing from the lobby. Vicky greeted her warmly at the door and introduced her to a small group gathered there. There was Dinesh Pathak, a once-popular actor, now mostly seen on the party circuit, in his forties; Ravi Shreshta, a younger actor whose reputation was tainted by his drug habits and questionable associations. Raj and Praveen, both in their early thirties and looking like they came from powerful families, rounded out the group. They were all casually dressed, gathered around a barbecue fire on a spacious balcony, casually roasting meat. The atmosphere was less like a birthday bash and more like an informal friends' get-together.

Usha noticed something off right away. There were no other women in sight, and she felt uneasy. “Vicky, where are the other girls? I don't see Kimi or Sahil anywhere. I'm not comfortable here,” she said.

Vicky held her hand, sat her on a couch, and switched on the TV, as he sat down beside her, he said, "You are early, Usha, the others should be reaching shortly. Dinesh's wife is reaching any moment. I spoke to Kimi. They have just left and will be reaching in half an hour. The other girls should be here soon."

He poured red wine into a glass and handed it to her, "Relax, let's watch some television," and he started surfing channels.

Kimi sipped her wine tentatively, hoping the others would be there soon.

They chatted while watching some music videos, just to pass the time.

Vicky played a song on youtube. Usha was easing up a little now. Suddenly one of the boys called him from outside, "Vicky, where is Lakshman? We need more coal for the fire."

Vicky said, "Lakshman is off today. I will get you the coal,” and he went into the kitchen.

Vicky's phone buzzed with a notification; he had forgotten it on the couch. Usha looked at it. It was a message from Kimi- 'KIMI- Sahil is…'. Usha wanted to see if they were reaching now. She pressed the key, and luckily the phone was not locked.

Kimi had typed, 'Sahil is sleeping now. Who all are there?'

Usha panicked. *Why did Vicky tell her that they had left?* She scrolled up and started going through the messages between the two of them, right from yesterday.

K: Usha is here now and she is getting really nosey.

V: I am coming, will take care of her.

Messages from later that night:

K: I spoke to Bhai. She has to go, she is getting too nosey, maybe in touch with the family again. She can spoil the whole plan.

V: Okay, will take care of it.

K: Don't be so casual about it, stupid. It has to be done correctly. Who all will be there?

V: Chill Kimi, only the five of us.

K: Don't play around with her. Stick to the plan. Don't want you junkies to go overboard. Let it look like a suicide.

Usha's hands were trembling. Obviously, they were talking about her. She turned to see if anyone was looking. Vicky was still in the kitchen, arranging the coal. She scrolled further up, a few days earlier.

The conversation continued with chilling details: talk of eliminating Sahil by overdosing him on a drug called dexie, and instructions to stage it as a suicide. Vicky's casual language and references to 'Bhai's orders' and 'George cleaning up the money' made it clear that a high-stakes conspiracy was unfolding behind the facade of a simple party.

Usha's hands trembled as she scrolled through more messages. She realized with horror that the people she trusted were plotting not only against Sahil, but also against her. Panic surged through her as she heard footsteps. Vicky, returning from the kitchen with the coal, stopped short when he saw her on the phone. His eyes, red with anger, locked onto hers.

She had been caught. Dropping his phone, she ran to the toilet and locked herself in. She was trembling with fear. She had stumbled upon a deep conspiracy to eliminate Sahil and now her too.

In a desperate bid for help, she dialed Sahil's number. When he didn't answer, she called Shamita instead.

"Usha? What's going on?" Shamita's voice crackled through the phone as she heard the chaotic sounds in the background.

In a hushed whisper, Usha tried to explain, "Shamita, listen. They're planning to kill Sahil. Vicky and Kimi; they've been setting everything up. They've drugged him for months so they can steal his money. I just stumbled onto their plan."

The sound of heavy banging on the bathroom door made her freeze. "Open up, Usha! I'll break this door down if you don't come out!" Vicky's voice thundered.

Desperate, Usha turned on the tap, hoping that the sound of running water might mask her voice. But it was too late. The door was forced open. In a moment of frantic fear, Usha dropped her phone into the toilet and flushed.

Shamita could barely make out a muffled sound that resembled a strangled 'shhh…' over the phone. Meanwhile, Vicky's rage escalated. He slapped Usha across her face, sending her reeling. As she crumpled to the floor, Ravi grabbed Vicky's arm. "Calm down, man. Remember the deal; we need to subdue her before we move on," he hissed. Without warning, Ravi scooped Usha off the ground and dragged her into a bedroom.

Usha's protests were drowned out by the chaos.

In the meantime, Vicky called Kimi, "What is it, you duffer? I told you not to call me. We can't leave a trail…"

Vicky was high on cocaine and had lost his nerves with the unexpected turn of events, "Shut up, you bitch. Always using me! What do you think I am, your slave?"

Kimi was quiet at the uncharacteristic outburst. This was no time to panic.

Vicky told her what had happened. Kimi still kept her nerves. "Okay, wind up your party soon, and don't use the girl. I will handle Sahil. And don't call me anymore. Just text me."

Kimi went to Sahil's room. He seemed to be sleeping, and she checked his phone. Yes, there had been a call from Usha. Stupid Vicky, she thought. She made the biggest mistake to rely on him, always cocky and overconfident. She vowed that she would cut him out of her life after this incident; good for nothing idiot.

Back in the bedroom, Usha fought to resist Ravi while Dinesh too closed in. In a burst of adrenaline, she kicked Dinesh hard. He stumbled, his head colliding with the wall, but quickly recovered to grab her hair. Usha clawed at his face, leaving streaks of blood. The other two men watched, paralyzed by fear. Then Vicky returned, his voice dripping with contempt: "You're going to learn a lesson." He tore at her clothes, stripping away her defenses piece by piece. In the ensuing struggle, Ravi jabbed a syringe into her arm. The drug hit her almost immediately; a surge of energy and detachment washed over Usha, as the body betrayed her, and she could no longer fight back.

They ravished her the whole night. Hours later, Usha found herself being carried out. A fleeting moment of clarity came as fresh air hit her, but only before an impact sent her crashing to the ground, pain and numbness mingling in her fading consciousness.

The next morning, headlines splashed across every channel:

"Sahil's Manager, Usha, Commits Suicide."

In the ensuing media frenzy, stories spun wildly: Sahil was depicted as a drug addict with a violent temper, suffering from bipolar disorder and a history of sexual misconduct on set. The narrative even claimed that Usha was pregnant with Sahil's child and had been driven to desperation. Simultaneously, back-channel reports painted a picture of a tangled conspiracy led by Kimi; a scheme designed to ruin Sahil and seize his fortune.

Shamita, stunned by the portrayal of Sahil, knew the truth. In an exclusive television interview days later, she revealed her suspicions: "Kimi orchestrated Usha's murder. They set her up to look like a suicide, all part of a plan to destroy Sahil's reputation and steal his money. Usha uncovered their plot, and they silenced her."

Despite her impassioned claims, the police refused to reopen the case, citing insufficient evidence. Meanwhile, Shamita's own life was now under threat from unknown sources. When she pleaded for protection, the authorities dismissed her concerns as the over-reactions of a heartbroken ex-girlfriend.

In a city where power and money often ruled over truth, Usha's final night had become yet another carefully staged tragedy; one that the media and influential figures seemed all too willing to exploit.

CHAPTER - 65

KANGNA - Taking Them On (2016)

One morning, Raj arrived at Kangna's office for a project meeting. While scrolling through his phone, he noticed a flurry of notifications. "Mam, can we switch on the TV? There's breaking news; Sahil's assistant has been found dead," he said, his voice tinged with disbelief.

News channels and social media feeds were awash with similar headlines: "Tragic Loss: Sahil's Assistant Dies by Apparent Suicide," "Inside Scoop: Pregnant Assistant Forced to End Her Life?" and even salacious allegations like "Sahil's Dark Side: Bipolar Disorder, Drug Abuse, and Sexual Assault Claims." Frustrated by the sensationalism, Kangna quickly muted the television.

"What do you know about her?" Kangna asked.

Raj replied, "She was talented, educated, and had a good reputation. I've never heard any troubling rumors about her; it's hard to believe something like this could happen."

Kangna frowned, deep in thought. "I met Sahil a while back when he visited Mr. Lonawala. He seemed down-to-earth and genuine. I can't imagine him being capable of such acts."

Raj hesitated. "He's been in a steady relationship for over a year now, and apart from whispers about his drug use; meth, apparently, there hasn't been any real talk of infidelity or abuse. Yet, there are those who claim he exploited a co-star on set."

Kangna's eyes narrowed. "The film industry is rife with rumors and power plays. These so-called 'scripts' off-camera can be even more damaging. I'm convinced that this whole situation is a setup; a deliberate attempt to sabotage Sahil's career. They even tried to ruin me once for not playing along with their games."

The conversation left both of them uneasy, and they postponed the project discussion for later. Raj left, and Kangna couldn't shake the feeling that something far more sinister was unfolding.

Later that day, Kangna tuned into an interview featuring Shamita on a major streaming platform. Intrigued and desperate for the truth amid the chaos, she arranged to meet Shamita privately. To protect her identity, Kangna instructed that Shamita wear a burqa to avoid recognition in public.

When they finally met in a discreet, low-lit café, Kangna was taken aback by Shamita's plain appearance; nothing like the glamorous image circulated in tabloids. More striking was the evident grief etched on Shamita's face; she looked utterly broken. Rumors had suggested that Kimi had swooped in to steal Sahil away from Shamita, which could be a possibility. But, more than anything else, the raw pain in her eyes told her story.

As they spoke, Shamita recounted the fateful phone call from Usha, even showing Kangna the call log on her smartphone. Kangna found herself believing every word of Shamita.

Almost a month after Usha's death, the police had conveniently closed the case, chalking it up as suicide. That didn't sit right with Kangna. Determined to expose the truth, she instructed her assistant, Raji, to contact Umang Chaturvedi from National TV and set up an exclusive interview.

During the one-hour live interview, Kangna spared no detail. She questioned the police's investigation and hinted at possible collusion. Revealing that she had insider knowledge about exploitative, one-sided contracts used by big producers; contracts designed to ruin Sahil's rising career; she painted a grim picture of an industry steeped in corruption. Kangna also denounced the rampant drug culture and the predatory practices that coerced new talent into illicit behaviors.

"I've seen how deep this rot goes," she declared. "They targeted me too, but I'm still here. I have evidence linking these practices to powerful names in Bollywood, and I'm willing to hand it over to the authorities. Usha's case must be reopened, and those involved need to be held accountable."

The fallout was swift. Under mounting public pressure and with fresh forensic evidence, the police reopened Usha's case. As more witnesses came forward and additional arrests were made, the scandal that had long been simmering beneath the surface of the film industry began to unravel, exposing the dark nexus of power, drugs, and exploitation.

CHAPTER - 66

KANGNA - It's All Happening (2016)

Kangna had recently gone public with allegations against several prominent industry figures. Instead of confronting her directly, the power brokers in the film world activated a carefully orchestrated campaign. A network of actors, directors, and influencers; long groomed for just such a moment, suddenly sprang into action. Their task was simple: flood social media with glowing praise for their benefactors while launching subtle, disparaging remarks aimed at Kangna and her supporter, Sahil.

That afternoon, Amelia woke up around 12:30 PM and instinctively grabbed her phone. Twelve missed calls flashed on the screen, from someone saved as "Bhai." Alarmed, she recalled that Bhai hadn't called in over six months; not since the Monte Carlo awards when she'd landed two film deals. With a sinking heart, she called back.

"Amu, you really forgot about me? Your films aren't finished yet," Bhai said, his tone carrying a mix of mockery and command.

"I'm so sorry, Bhai; I overslept," Amelia stammered.

"Overslept? You know how important it is to stay alert for your roles. Where are your tweets?" he pressed.

"I'll post immediately; I promise," she replied, anxiety lacing her words.

"Good. I expect a steady stream; morning and evening. Let the little bird lead the flock," Bhai instructed, his voice firm.

"Understood," she managed before the call ended abruptly.

Moments later, another directive came through:

"Also, Amu, expect a visitor tonight. Make sure he's treated exceptionally well. He won't be in uniform, but he runs the show; and you'd be better off not knowing his name."

The order left Amelia numb. She could only murmur a hesitant "Yes, Bhai" before the line went dead. Collapsing onto her pillow, she fought back tears. In that quiet moment, she recalled her late father's warnings. Once adored by millions, she now felt nothing more than a puppet dancing to the whims of powerful people. The loss of her free will stung deeply; she envied even those on the street, who could make their own choices. Every achievement now felt like a hollow victory paid for by her soul."

Desperation pushed her toward a familiar escape. Needing a serious boost to face the day; and not the mild high from marijuana, she reached for her phone. With trembling fingers, she dialed her secret contact, saved as '#1.' As usual, there was no answer, and moments later a call from an unknown number appeared.

"What do you need; coke or something stronger?" the husky voice asked.

"Send both. I'll need two doses each," Amelia replied curtly, already anticipating the needs of the mysterious visitor later that night.

Within thirty minutes, a courier arrived at her door with what looked like a bouquet. After collecting the package and paying a steep fee, Amelia discarded the superficial floral wrapping to reveal a concealed sachet. Modern drug traffickers had perfected disguising their shipments via everyday online delivery channels.

She spread the white powder onto a small piece of aluminum foil, inhaling deeply as it heated. The rush was immediate, clearing her mind of doubt. Energized, she logged onto Twitter and posted confidently:

"The film industry is one big family; don't let Kangna sully the legacy built by those who came before."

She planned to add more later.

Not long after, Amelia called Rajshree; a former leading actress who now catered to high-end clients at luxury hotels under Bhai's orders. "Hey Rajshree, you've been off the grid on social media for the past month. Everything alright?" she inquired.

"Not really, Amelia. I haven't been feeling well," came the subdued reply.

"Listen, you need to bounce back or you risk fading away completely. Get online and start posting against Kangna; and in favor of, well, you know who. Consider it a direct order," Amelia insisted, the lingering effects of her high making her tone sharper.

"Understood, Amu. I'll get on it right away," Rajshree replied, though the words carried the weight of resignation.

"Just be subtle this time; don't let your desperation show," Amelia advised.

As Rajshree ended the call, she couldn't help but reflect bitterly on her own decline. Once the toast of the industry, her early career had been launched by a director boyfriend who had made her a star. But as newer, younger talent emerged, she'd been cast aside; both on screen and out of his life. Now, her survival depended on entertaining wealthy businessmen through arranged meetings, a lifeline that came with its own dark strings. In order to keep this precarious setup afloat, she was forced to comply with demands from dangerous figures; even if it meant orchestrating online attacks against Kangna. Shaking off the sinking feeling, Rajshree waited for her next dose to clear her mind and help her play the part once more.

In the days that followed, criticism of Kangna exploded across every platform; Facebook rants, Twitter threads, and explosive media interviews. The barrage of conflicting opinions left the public unsure of what to believe. This was precisely the point; by flooding the discourse with doubt and dissent, the orchestrators hoped to erode her confidence. But Kangna wasn't one to back down. She saw through the calculated ploys and resolved to confront her detractors head-on.

Unexpectedly, support for Kangna began to build. Tina, the wife of megastar Ramesh Bajaj, stepped forward to back her, accusing the industry's elite of using their clout for personal gain, at the expense of true art. Even Ahana, a former co-star with lingering ties to Ramesh, lent her voice in support. Actress Sripriya, once linked to influential actor Vikram Seth and now married to Sudhanshu Banerjee, joined the chorus. A young singer named Kirti bravely shared her personal ordeal of abuse at the hands of a well-known music director, Rahi, and credited Kangna for exposing the rot festering behind the scenes. For many, these revelations were a catalyst for demanding long-overdue reform. Kangna's fight had become a stand for a more transparent, respectful industry; a return to values once taken for granted.

Meanwhile, law enforcement had stepped up its investigation. Under intense questioning, minor figures like Kimi and Vicky quickly cracked and began naming key personalities. Soon, more than fifteen individuals; including actors and drug suppliers, found themselves under the scanner. Unlike hardened criminals, many in the film world buckled under police pressure, and whispers began to circulate that even the industry's heavyweights were next. Names such as Kamal and Umesh emerged, sending tremors through their circles.

A few days later, Kamal received an official summons from the CBI, which had taken over the probe. Kamal's anxiety spiked. Unaccustomed to dealing with the authorities, the very idea of appearing before the CBI filled him with dread. He tried calling Umesh, but his phone went straight to voicemail.

On dialing the family landline, the maid informed him that Umesh and his family had left the country the previous night.

Panicked, Kamal phoned Vikram, who answered while at the gym.

“Why the early call, Kamal?” Vikram asked.

“Kamal, I need to see you urgently; I just got a CBI summons,” Kamal blurted.

“Can’t talk now. Meet me at my place at 4,” Vikram replied curtly.

At 4 PM, Kamal arrived at Vikram’s house and sat in the quiet living room. Twenty minutes later, Vikram finally emerged. Kamal rushed forward and embraced him.

“Man, you look terrible. What happened?” Vikram asked.

“I’m in deep trouble,” Kamal confessed. “The CBI has summoned me; I have no idea what to do.”

Vikram shook his head. “You should have called Umesh. You two were in this mess together. And be careful; if the CBI is calling you, they’re probably monitoring your communication.”

“I tried, but Umesh is unreachable. The maid said he’s out of the country, on a holiday,” Kamal replied, voice trembling.

“Not on holiday, Kamal; he fled as soon as the heat turned up,” Vikram said with a sigh. “When things go south, everyone looks out for themselves.”

“Please, Vikram, I really need your support. I have no one left. Even my mother is alone,” Kamal pleaded.

“Look, you’re close with Bhai. You’ve shared more than a few wild nights. Why not call him?” Vikram suggested.

“Vikram, you know Bhai only reaches out when he needs something. I’m counting on you,” Kamal insisted.

Vikram’s tone hardened. “I’m sorry, Kamal. The CBI doesn’t take personal favors. You need to consult a lawyer and handle this yourself.”

Defeated, Kamal returned home. After dismissing the maid for the day, he locked himself in his room, and with no one to support him, Kamal his despair consume him.

The next day, the maid discovered Kamal’s body. His skin was discolored; blue around his nails and lips; and a half-empty can of insecticide lay spilled on the floor. There was no suicide note. Within days, rumors were rife; some whispered that Kamal had been silenced for knowing too much; others claimed he was entangled in a sordid network that linked drugs, exploitation, and even a pedophilia ring. The conspiracy, it was said, was vast; with Kamal at its center; while Umesh remained a ghost.

Amidst the fallout, Shamita had moved in with Sahil to care for him. With Kangna's assistance, they secured appointments with leading psychiatrists and neuroscientists. Following their advice, Sahil was admitted to a drug rehabilitation center overseas. Determined to help him recover, Shamita accompanied him, fully aware that his therapy would be a long, challenging journey.

CHAPTER - 67

KANGNA - Shocker (2016)

Kangna was cruising through Bandra in her sleek Mercedes, en route to a live breakfast interview at National TV, when her secondary phone, her go-to for social media, buzzed with an incoming video call. Smiling at the familiar face on screen, she answered and casually hit the record button to test its new feature.

"Kangna? Kangna? Where are you?" Mr. Lonawala's usually composed voice now carried a trace of panic.

"Mr. Lonawala, are you alright?" she asked, a note of concern creeping into her tone.

"I'm fine, but where exactly are you right now?" he pressed.

"I'm heading to the National TV studio for an 8 AM live interview," she replied.

"Bandra?" he confirmed.

"Yeah."

"Listen, I need you to come by my office immediately."

Kangna frowned slightly. "I'm almost at the studio, and your office is only ten minutes away. What's going on that it can't wait until after the interview?"

"No, Kangna. This is urgent; I need you here first. In fact, cancel the interview," he insisted.

"But this interview has been in the works for weeks. How am I supposed to cancel at the last minute?" she protested.

"There's a serious threat to your life," he said, his voice lowering. "Did you catch today's headlines? Kamal's been taken out, and Umesh has already fled the country. You're next. You're stirring up too much trouble; digging into matters that certain dangerous people would kill to keep hidden."

Kangna's pulse quickened. "How can you be so sure? And who exactly are these people?"

"Remember our last conversation? I mentioned I had insider information. Everything's connected; murders, drug trafficking, a pedophilic ring, and an underground porn production that's raking in millions. With everything you're trying to expose, they can't let you live." His tone was grim. "I can't give you names over the phone, but trust me, these are people you don't want to cross."

"But I need to know who they are," she pressed, determination mixing with apprehension.

"Come to my office," he said firmly, "and I'll tell you everything."

Kangna exhaled slowly. "Alright, Mr. Lonawala; Umang will get a heart-attack when he gets to know I am not making it on time, but I'm on my way."

After ending the call, she turned to her driver and directed him to head for Mr. Lonawala's office instead of the studio. She quickly texted Umang, letting him know she'd be about thirty minutes late. Despite his inevitable protests, Kangna knew he'd scramble to adjust the schedule; after all, there wasn't much choice when the stakes were this high.

CHAPTER - 68
KANGNA - Climax (2016)

As Kangna entered the building, she found the elevators were not yet operational. Since Mr. Lonawala's office was only on the mezzanine floor, she took the stairs and walked right in.

She called softly, "Mr. Lonawala?" as she walked into his chamber.

Her heart froze. There he was, slumped in his chair, eyes wide open, staring at her, with a knife plunged into his chest. She moved towards him and checked his pulse…nothing. She tried to recollect the conversation they were having and realised they had been speaking only 10 minutes ago. Who would kill him and why? Where did the killer disappear or would he still be around? She looked around the room frantically but didn't see anything. His computer was still on, with the skype window he had forgotten to close. Or maybe he was murdered as soon as he had finished his conversation. She did not want to touch anything, as she might complicate things by leaving her fingerprints around. Suddenly she was worried; what if she got falsely implicated?

Just as she was about to run out, Wasim entered the office, as usual in his all-white attire. He saw Kangna and waved to her, "What are you….?" He froze in mid-sentence as he saw Mr. Lonawala's body slumped in the chair.

Wasim Bhai was shocked, too, "What the hell happened? Who killed him? And what are you doing here, Kangna? And that too at 8 in the morning!"

"Mr. Lonawala was alive ten minutes ago. In fact, he called me to his office. He said my life was in danger and that he would give me the name of the person who planned to kill me," blurted Kangna and started crying.

Wasim Bhai embraced Kangna, "Kangna, calm down. We need to find the culprit. He must not have gone far. And I think we should inform the police."

It suddenly struck Kangna, "Wasim Bhai, why are you here?"

"He called me too. He told me the same thing that my life was in danger, and he would tell me about the conspiracy; but only in person, as the phone lines were tapped."

"Yes, he told me the same thing."

The police had reached the spot shortly and took their statements briefly. They sealed the office for inspection by the forensics team. They told Kangna and Wasim Bhai that they would be required to give detailed statements later in the day and would be called for the same.

As they went down to their cars, Kangna was still in shock and started crying again. Wasim Bhai hugged her, "Relax, Kangna, your angel is still alive to take care of you."

"Come, Kangna, you are coming with me to my house. I will not leave you like this."

"Wasim Bhai, I have an important meeting, let me attend that, and then I will come to your house."

"Okay, but you come in my car; ask your driver to follow. I will drop you wherever you want."

Kangna sat in the car with Wasim Bhai as his chauffer drove them. His arm was still around Kangna and her eyes wandered to a red spot, just on the tip of the sleeve of his pure white shirt. She stared at it, and realised it was blood. She would have missed it had Wasim Bhai's arm not been around her.

But how come? Wasim Bhai had not gone near Mr. Lonawala's body after he entered. And he had told her that he had just come in. Kangna's mind searched frantically for the missing link in this jigsaw puzzle. And then, it hit her. He was the killer. That is the reason he was at Mr. Lonawal's office; to finish him off and not because he had been called there. Wasim Bhai, her angel, was the kingpin of this racket of sex, drugs, and murders. She bit her lips to stop the trembling, as his arm was still around her. She was the next victim. He wanted to take her to his house and finish her too, just like what he had done to the others. Kangna recollected the words of Mr. Lonawala- 'Angels are not a reality. Angels exist only in heaven.' He had been trying to give her hints for some time now. But she had never imagined Wasim Bhai could do this to anyone.

Kangna had to get out of his clutches. But if she gave him a hint, he would not let her go, and it would be her last ride ever. She racked her brain. She did not have much time and had to think of a solution quickly. In the nick of time, an idea struck her. She said, "Wasim Bhai, I left my other phone in my car. Can you ask the driver to stop for a minute? I will get that and join you."

Wasim had no idea of what was coming. He asked the driver to pull to the kerb. Kangna's driver, who was following, also stopped. Kangna hopped out. She sat in her car and animatedly gave her driver instructions to make a U-turn and speed away, not to stop at any signals, and go straight to the National TV studio.

The unsuspecting Wasim was caught off guard, and Kangna's driver got a head start. The National TV studio was only a five-minute drive from here. Kangna recollected that the Skype window on Mr. Lonawala's desktop had still been running. She checked the phone to see if it was still recording; she was shocked to see that the recording was still going on. Kangna called Umang and told him she had big breaking news and wanted to go live on television, so he should keep the set up ready. She informed him briefly that there was a threat to her life. They reached in five minutes, but that drive was the longest in Kangna's life. She kept looking back; at times they heard tyres screeching, as other cars braked to allow Wasim's wayward car to pass.

Just as her car slowed to a halt in front of the National TV studio, Kangna jumped out and ran into the building; she ran up the stairs to the second-floor office without waiting for the lift and went into the newsroom. Umang was good as his word; the countdown to go live was underway. Since the National TV studio had been under threat for some time now, four police personnel were armed and ready and were brought inside the newsroom.

Facing the camera, tears glistening in her eyes but her tone resolute, Kangna began, "I grew up in a small town near Delhi, with big dreams in my eyes. I was captivated by the magic of cinema, the allure of the stars, and I believed in a world full of hope. I was in awe of the stars who acted in these films. I admired them; I copied their mannerisms, spoke like them, and loved them, as I watched their beautiful movies and worshipped their larger-than-life image. I am sure most of you would have had similar experiences. I was so enamored by my heroes and heroines of the celluloid world that I ran away from home at the age of 16, because I wanted to be a part of this magnificent world of cinema, of beautiful people, loving relationships."

She continued, barely able to hold back the tears, "With not one soul known to me in Bombay, I came here with nothing but passion and determination, only to discover a darker side; an industry where power and money silence the truth."

She paused, gathering her strength. "When I began to question these injustices, I knew I was making enemies. Is this how, my dear stars, you treat the the fans and their families? By trying to nip them in the bud? As long as the fans are down there, looking upto you, they are dear to you! The moment they reach up and try to be your equals, you cannot tolerate them? Hundreds of young boys and girls flock to the doors of the film industry, with dreams in their eyes and love in their hearts for their favorite stars; to emulate them and their fairytale stories, to make it big in Bollywood, only to be exploited and destroyed by this ruthless system. Isn't that what you tried to do to Sahil? He was from a regular middle-class background. Is it not why there is a mad rush to decimate Kangna and silence her? As she refused to toe the line and follow your diktat. As she refused to be silenced when all of you ganged up to bully one of your own."

"This is the precise reason why some prominent personalities have been trying to eliminate me. This morning, I received a call from Mr. Lonawala; a respected advocate; warning me that my life was in danger. I rushed to his office, only to find him murdered. And now, I have uncovered something even more horrifying."

"I have tears in my eyes as I reveal that the person who planned to kill me was none other than my own messiah. This was the person, whom I always believed to be my angel, and who was responsible for bringing me to Bombay and to Bollywood. But today, he broke my illusion, and I realised that angels really do not exist. I am talking about Wasim Bhai, who planned to send me away from this world by taking my life. It saddens me to expose Wasim bhai as the murderer of advocate Lonawala, his longtime friend. Wasim Bhai may also be the kingpin behind the drug and paedophile scandals plaguing the industry and the string of murders we have seen in recent weeks. Of course, the police and the authorities will let us know after due investigation.

And with this, Kangna played the video recording of the Skype call Mr. Lonawala had forgotten to disconnect as he was talking to Kangna, and the device had clearly recorded the murder and relayed the same to Kangna's phone.

No sooner had she finished, the newsroom doors burst open. An enraged Wasim stormed in, shouting, "Kangna, you're under arrest! I saw it all!" His voice was drowned out by the gasps of the gathered crew. Moments later, looking at the live evidence of his misdeed, his defiance faltered; he collapsed to the floor, the weight of his guilt undeniable.

In that charged moment, as the recording continued to play and the police secured the area, Kangna realized that truth, no matter how hard-fought, always finds a way to prevail. The man she once trusted was now unmasked, and with every eye on her, she had turned the tables. The era of hidden corruption was over; today, the truth was live for all to see.

Epilogue (2019)

On a chilly winter evening in Delhi, Vigyan Bhavan was buzzing with anticipation. The Directorate of Film Festivals had organized the annual National Film Awards. Only a fraction of the seats had been occupied by the film fraternity. Country's top buereucrats and powerful politicians vied for the passes to attend this prestigious event, as this was a unique opportunity to hob nob with the glamorous stars and the creative fraternity.

The nominees had been informed well in advance, and they arrived accompanied by their partners, family, or close friends, each waiting anxiously for their moment in the spotlight. With every category announced, the crowd celebrated as winners made their way to the stage to accept their awards and offer brief words of gratitude.

When the category for Best Actor in Hindi cinema was announced, every nominee sat up a little straighter; some even breaking out in a nervous sweat despite the cold weather. The Minister of Culture opened the envelope and declared, "The award for Best Actor in Hindi cinema goes to: Sahil Deb."

Sahil accepted the award with grace. As he stepped up to the microphone for his brief thank-you speech, emotion overwhelmed him. Tears streamed down his face, and his heartfelt words struck a deep chord with everyone in the room; many remembered the struggles he'd overcome to make his comeback.

"I want to thank my parents and family for supporting my decision to pursue films," Sahil began. "I also want to thank my wife, Shamita, for standing by me no matter what. I'm grateful to my co-stars, producers, directors, and everyone who played a part in my journey. I dedicate this award to my brave manager, Usha, who lost her life trying to warn me about a conspiracy meant to silence me. Her sacrifice will never be forgotten. And above all, I owe everything to Kangna; without her, I wouldn't be here today."

He paused, his voice thick with emotion. "This award is as much for Kangna, as it is for me. Often called the Queen of Bollywood, she has transformed this industry into a space where talent thrives regardless of background, caste, creed, or religion. Kangna, please join me on stage and accept this award on my behalf."

As Kangna stepped onto the stage, the entire audience erupted in applause and cheers, heralding what many felt was the beginning of a new era in Bollywood.